Four Score

Nicole Dixon

Copyright © 2023 Nicole Dixon

Lucky Thirteen Publishing, LLC

All rights reserved.

ISBN: 9798852067425

ACKNOWLEDGMENTS

Every book that I write has a special place in my heart. They are bits and pieces of me mixed with a story that is only mine to tell.

J. My heart. My inspiration. The man who welcomes countless people that only exist in my brain into our family without question. I love you big. I will always be down for testing out scenes with you as I write them. *wink*

Mom. My biggest fan. I will never get tired of hearing you brag about how cool your kids are to total strangers. We're only cool because we have cool parents.

Beth. My sounding board. To the woman who calls me on all of my bullshit and does it nicely with a smile. I love you.

Kyndall. To the woman who selflessly destroys my books with a red ink pen and does it all in the name of love and family. You will never know how much your help means to me.

Rhonda, Julia, my beta readers, and ARC team – you're my found family. Kind of like the characters in these books. I appreciate you more than words can express. And that's saying a lot.

My children. You have no idea the "scary books" Mommy writes on her computer aren't really scary at all. Not really. One day you will be scandalized by your mother and I'm not even sorry. Not even a little. Love you, babies.

My readers. Wow. Book nine. I can't believe how far we've come together in such a short period of time. Thanks for hanging with me from the very beginning, when I was winging it and praying that I didn't fall flat on my face. Who am I kidding? I'm still winging it. You guys are awesome. Let's keep doing this together. It's fun.

XOXO, Nicole

Four Score

FOUR SCORE

Four Score

Never ever, ever kiss your big brother's best friend.

This is your warning. Proceed with caution.

XOXO, Nicole

PROLOGUE
DAMIEN

We won.

I can't believe we actually won.

In the beginning, there was a year or so that was complete hell, but this one's making up for it tenfold.

"The Comeback Kid"

I chuckle to myself under my breath. That damn headline has been following me on every newspaper print and television station I've seen for the last eight weeks. The constant ache in my muscles from years of abuse on the ice definitely doesn't leave me feeling like a *kid* anymore. But, I'm here. I'm alive when everyone thought I was dead. I guess that's what matters.

Early morning rehab sessions. Late-night practices and conditioning. Weekends on the road. Years of fighting to succeed.

I defied the odds.

It was all worth it, and tonight we finally get to

celebrate a hard-earned victory.

The higher-ups had this bar shut down to the public for us tonight, but that doesn't mean it's empty. Far from it actually.

The whole team's celebrating tonight, which is a party in and of itself. Some of their spouses are here, the ones that are tied down anyway. And, for those that aren't? There's an all-you-can-eat buffet of puck bunnies that managed to sweet talk their way past the bouncer.

I sit at the bar alone and slowly sip on the same beer I've had since we arrived about an hour ago. It's warm now, but it doesn't matter. Not even room temp beer can dampen the high I'm riding tonight. Highlights from the game play on every screen in this place. A not-so-subtle reminder of just how far we've come - of how far I've come.

The atmosphere shifts. Awareness puts my senses on high-alert. I'm captivated by her presence the moment she walks in.

Dark brown hair frames her face in wild tresses of untamed curls that bounce with each step she takes. Her eyes are the color of rich milk chocolate as she searches through the sea of people that separate us. Skin-tight denim covers her toned legs from hip to toe. Her top is made of delicate white lace, a contrast to her dark almond skin. She's *not* delicate.

My eyes are quickly drawn up from the exposed skin that teases me between the waistline of her pants and the hem of her top, to the smirk on her red-painted lips the second her eyes lock in on mine. With a target in mind, she slowly begins her saunter of seduction in black stilettos that should be illegal.

I hold her gaze, refusing to be the one to look away first. I need her to see me. I've been waiting, not so patiently, for her arrival.

She doesn't stop until she reaches the barstool next to mine, sitting without further invitation. She doesn't need one. Her scent invades my space, stealing all intelligent thoughts from my mind and rendering my words useless.

She taps on the worn wooden bar top. She garners the attention of the bartender and easily every man *and* woman within a six-foot vicinity. She sits perched on the barstool like a queen on her throne.

"Whiskey, sprite, two fresh lime wedges. Make it a double." She orders without thought. It's a ballsy choice, whiskey and Sprite, but I wouldn't expect anything less from her.

The bartender moves into action quickly. He concocts her drink, sliding it across the bar without spilling a single drop. His eyes study her. He's just as entranced by her exotic beauty as I am. She's unimpressed.

Every set of eyes surrounding us watches her, but she doesn't take notice. Or, if she does, she remains completely unphased by the attention.

She delicately squeezes the fresh slices of lime into her drink, unceremoniously drops them into the glass, and stirs, before lifting the neat elixir to her lips and gulping down two man-sized swallows.

My eyes widen at the contradiction she presents. She sets her glass down, and only then does she turn her attention to me.

She props her elbow up onto the bar, leaning into it,

cradling her chin in her open palm. Her long eyelashes tease me as she looks up into my green eyes before finally speaking. "Anybody ever tell you, you're the sexiest man in the entire country?" She asks lazily. As if, merely stating a fact, not offering up a compliment.

"Only every woman I've ever met." I find my words again before I make a fool of myself.

I allow myself a moment to lean into her space, breathing her in. She doesn't wear perfume; she doesn't need it. She smells naturally of something floral with a hint of masculinity that sends a pulsing need through each and every nerve ending in my body.

"Anybody ever tell you, you're an arrogant son of a bitch?" She laughs, and the sound is raspy, yet sweet. Ever the paradox. She lifts her glass again and takes down another large gulp, leaving less than half of her tall order remaining.

Her eyes swim, but she's not drunk. She toes the line of tipsy with the precision of a tight-rope walker. A woman like this one doesn't lose control. She fucking *owns* it.

"Anybody ever tell you that you have a filthy mouth when you drink whiskey?" I nod toward where her drink is magically disappearing.

I love it when a woman doesn't try to filter herself around me.

I hate fake. Fake hair. Fake eyelashes. It's just not for me. But the one trait I hate the absolute most? Fake-ass personalities.

There's nothing sexier to me than a woman who's comfortable with being completely herself, and there's no filter on the woman who sits adjacent to me.

"Mmmm…it's a curse I am forced to bear. So, tell me, why is it that you're so damn good-looking?" She presses. The smile that tilts her lips is pure sin and seduction. Her white teeth sparkle against her bright lips, begging me to run my tongue across them. *Not yet*.

"I don't know. Ask the people over at Sports National who made the decision to put me on the cover of their magazine in a towel. Some of us are just blessed by Jesus. What did you call it? I guess it's just a curse that I'm forced to bear."

That damn cover. Talk about a curse. That photo was never supposed to see the light of day, let alone the cover of the biggest sports magazine in the nation. I catch hell in the locker room and panties at the grocery market. But it's so much worse than that. My mama framed the damn thing and hung it in her living room.

"Do not use the name of the Lord's child in vain, Damien Henderson. It's fucking photoshop, obviously." She rolls her eyes, clearly amused by my obvious discomfort with knowing half the country has seen me in nothing but a washcloth identifying as a towel.

"In vain? You're cute. I see what you did there. What makes you think it's photoshop?" She and I both know that's the furthest thing from the truth.

"You're telling me that your abs really look like…" She motions between us, and I wish she would slide her hand beneath my shirt and confirm for herself, "*That*, underneath this overpriced cotton blend?"

Instead, she touches my shoulder gently, running her fingernails from one shoulder blade to the other. A shiver races up my spine and catches the attention of the hair on my neck as I feel the tiny hairs prickle to life beneath her touch.

"Want me to prove it to you?" I take the bait she's tossing around so generously. I bite back, gently. I'm saving the best for later. She's teasing anyway.

Her shoulder brushes mine as she leans in even closer. Her breasts threaten the thin lace straps of her tank top. I don't dare divert my eyes from hers and give myself away. No matter how badly my need for this woman wants to deceive me.

"I'm sorry, Mr. Henderson. Are you hitting on me?" She wiggles her perfect ass on the stool next to mine coyly. Her breath fans my face, and the sweet scent of whiskey washes over me.

She's intoxicating.

"So, what if I am, Mrs. Henderson?" I seal my fate. I no longer care about the celebration of the night or the notoriety that comes with it. I want one thing and one thing only. *I want her.*

"My husband might have something to say about it." She answers, unashamed, tugging her lip between her teeth.

My blood heats in my veins at her insinuation. This is my favorite game.

"He doesn't have to find out. Come back to my room with me. Let me show you what being with a real man is like. I'll be your secret." I make her an offer that I know she won't refuse. The fire in her eyes makes promises that I know her body is fully prepared to keep.

"A real man, you say? I've never been with one of

those." She gently taps her chin with her delicately manicured fingernails, and I growl in response before she continues. "Tell me, what exactly are you planning to do with me?"

Not here. My cock throbs with need against the zipper of my pressed slacks.

"We're leaving. Since you love games so much, it's time for a little game of show and tell."

The frayed thread of control I had remaining snaps. This is far from over. It's only just beginning. I toss a fifty down on the bar. We stand in unison. I see Coach watching me with a shit-eating grin on his face. We're not fooling anyone; not trying to. I nod goodbye and turn toward the exit. She follows willingly. It's going to be a long night, just *not here*. We need privacy, and a key card in my pocket to a penthouse suite at a hotel two blocks from here offers me all the assurance I need.

Never in my wildest dreams could I imagine the culmination of events that led us to this night.

The perfect team.

The perfect win.

The perfect woman. *My wife.*

Sounds like I'm living a dream life, doesn't it?

It hasn't always been this way. Why, you ask?

Because the woman from the bar, the woman I sold my soul to – my wife, is my best friend's little sister, and I literally had to *die* to get here. This is the story of how I cheated death and lived to tell about it.

And, boy, am I *living*.

CHAPTER ONE
GIA
Fifteen years old
Many years earlier

"Begin again."

My head automatically falls onto the kitchen countertop, my forehead landing with an audible thud against the cold tile. I'm going to kill T for putting Damien up to this.

"Gia." He says my name, but I pretend like I don't hear it. The lights are on, but nobody's home, sucker.

Damien sits across the kitchen from me at our four-seater breakfast table. I don't know why everybody in this house insists on calling it a *breakfast* table when we eat all of our meals there. It's not logical.

The eraser of what I am certain is a deliberately targeted flying number two pencil smacks me square in the temple. Freaking Damien. It doesn't hurt, but it prompts me to move my lips - a little. I'm ready for this to be over with. I have photos I need to go upstairs and edit. I need to clean the lens of my camera. Maybe I could vacuum out my camera bag. Anything but reciting the words of a dead man for the ten millionth time. This is torture of absolutely epic proportions.

"Four score and blah blah blah…is this really necessary, Damien?" My head remains firmly attached to the countertop. My butt rests on an old wooden barstool. I don't look up. My braids hide my face away from my big brother Tyler's best friend, also known as my own personal pain in the rear end.

Mrs. Hightower, my history teacher and current archnemesis, made a call to my mama two weeks ago about my less-than-exemplary mid-semester test scores and now Mama is on a war path to make me bring my grades up. She tried to recruit Tyler to tutor me, but he refused, citing irreconcilable differences. The joker thinks he can take one high school law class and, all of a sudden, he's an attorney. Yeah, right.

He knows I won't listen to him anyway. So, I guess, he's not wrong.

"If you don't learn this stuff, you're going to fail history, and your mama will never cook chicken and waffles for me again." Damien huffs, finally bringing the truth to light…at least part of the truth. I knew he was being bribed to tutor me.

I've known Damien all my life. He's an only child by birth, but sometime back before I have any solid core memories, Tyler claimed him as his brother by another mother, and he's been a part of our family ever since. This is his senior year, same with Tyler.

The two of them are the definition of high school royalty. They're star hockey players, and when they're not on the ice being cheered on by hundreds of their already adoring fans, they're being worshipped by *the pineapples*. You know the type. They look cute and sweet and oh-so-fun on the outside; but in reality, they're pokey, and if you eat too much the acid in them will burn the inside of your mouth. They're always too much if you ask me.

Good thing they don't know I exist. Nobody does. Well, except for Mrs. Hightower. Crotchety old woman.

There is no way Damien Henderson was volunteering to tutor me without some sort of compensation. Family or not.

Scratch that. Especially family.

"So, this is about you. Typical. Self-absorbed, much?" I roll my eyes at the pale blue tile.

It's a lie. Damien isn't self-absorbed. If anything, he's the opposite. I'm not necessarily mad at him – per se. I'm mad that I can think of at least fifteen things I'd rather be doing than sitting here right now. He gets the brunt of my anger by proximity.

"You're smart, Gia. I know you know this stuff. Why are you failing?"

Now, he's getting frustrated with me; I can hear it in his voice. Good. Maybe he'll give up and just let me be.

Besides, why does it matter? If I fail, it's on me. My actions, my consequences. Nobody around here gets me, I swear.

"I understand history, Damien. I understand the significance. I get it. I get how our past affects our future." My voice begins to rise with every sentence.

"What I don't understand is why I need to memorize the entirety of the Gettysburg Address. It's just that, memorization. I want living history. I want to see life in motion as it's happening. I want change and deliverance. You wouldn't understand." I finish on a deep exhale of breath that rushes out with the remainder of my words.

I attempt to explain to him the unexplainable. These are the things that keep me awake at night developing film in my closet instead of sleeping. They're also why I don't have much of a social life to speak of. I don't fit in…anywhere.

Damien sighs loudly, and I feel it as if it came from me instead.

Me too, brother, me too.

"I see you, Gia. You want to live history. You want to be the change. I will never fully understand, but I will listen. I will learn. I will educate myself. And right now, I'm trying to help educate you. I'm trying to help you not fail your history class."

I register a hint of passion in his voice that I don't think I've heard before. Silence isn't always understanding, just like it's not always ignorance. Maybe he understands more than I'm giving him credit for. His words make sense. Well, up until the part about his need to educate me, or whatever that nonsense was. I tuned him out after that.

"Ugh, you're the worst," I growl, and drool drips from my lip onto the counter. Stupid gravity. Stupid Mrs. Hightower. And stupid Damien for following through with this charade when he knows I know this stuff.

"You lie." He laughs, and it's a deep sound for his

young age. Damien laughs with his whole body. Even about the smallest things. I feel the vibrations coming from him from across the room.

He's not wrong. He's not the absolute worst. I could be dealing with Tyler right now. I shudder at the thought of being stuck studying for hours with my big brother. He's so serious about literally everything. Tyler is the complete opposite of his best friend. Well, other than the whole being good at hockey part. I guess it's true what they say about opposites attracting.

A book slams closed behind me, and I sit straight up with the abrupt noise. Blood rushes to my face, and I know for a fact before I even turn around to face him, I have grout lines on my forehead. It's whatever, Damien doesn't care what I look like.

"Why did you volunteer to tutor me anyway?" I spin around on my barstool and eye him curiously as he slides a textbook into his backpack. I guess he's done, score one for Team Gia.

"Huh?" He finishes zipping his bag and stops to look at me. His lips tip up into a grin that makes me feel warm and cozy inside. He silently studies the ridiculous lines on my face without daring to say a word about them.

His shaggy, long hair is tied into a ponytail at the base of his neck. It's a dirty blonde color; strands of yellow and blonde mixed with light brown. The colors remind me of an unplowed field of wheat just before the sun sets. The texture is different from mine. His are soft, loose curls whereas mine are a thick, coarse mess. That's why I keep my hair braided most of the time. It's less of a hassle to deal with.

"Why did you volunteer to tutor me?" I repeat the question. I track his green eyes with my curiously narrowed brown ones.

"Your mama asked me to?" His words hang on a question. He shrugs, and his eyes dart to the hallway, where I know no one stands because we're the only one's home. Tyler is getting in extra hours at the rink and Mama is working late. It's something else. But what?

"Try again." I roll my shoulders and twist my neck to the side trying and failing to make my joints crack and release a little bit of the tension I feel in my shoulders.

The only place I truly can relax is behind my camera. The rest of the time I walk on eggshells trying not to make trouble. There's enough stress around here as it is. I don't want to add to it. Add that to the list of reasons I can't stand Mrs. Hightower. She made trouble for me the moment she picked up that telephone.

"You and I both know why I'm here. Your brother will make both of our lives hell if you fail this class, and then I will never hear the end of it." Damien lifts his backpack onto his shoulder, bumping up against the back of the wooden oak chair he sits in. The straps dangle beside him, they're worn and frayed along the seams.

Damien doesn't live far from here. His house is just down the street, actually. Our neighborhood is nice, but we're not the rich kids. The streetlights don't work half the time, and we have carports instead of fancy garages, but the boys play street hockey in the summer in the cul-de-sac without fear. And we live close enough to school that I can walk instead of riding the bus. It's safe, and it feels like home. That's all that matters.

"Closer." I edge, pushing him to tell me the truth when I know he's holding something back.

He stands from the table, but I stay where I am. The toes of my sneakers brush the linoleum flooring beneath my feet.

Damien takes a step toward the back door before looking over his shoulder at me. There's a seriousness in the golden flecks of his eyes that I want to study. My fingers itch to capture his features in time so that I can dissect them later.

It's how I learn. I study the world through moments trapped in time. It's amazing what you can learn in those brief seconds when our minds react instead of responding.

"I don't know. I see the potential you have inside of you, and I don't want to sit back and watch you waste it. You need to graduate, Gia. Your education is important. Nobody can take that away from you. I guess I care about your future." He looks from me to the floor at his feet and then back to the door.

The boys go directly to hockey practice after school. Damien came straight here from the rink. He wears a pair of faded blue jeans and a grey hooded sweatshirt with our high school mascot on the front.

"You care?" I ask surprised by his answer.

I know Tyler cares. Dare I say, he cares too much. He never misses an opportunity to remind me that my education is the only thing I have in life that will allow me to secure a future outside of these walls. The way Damien says it though, it feels different. Less like some box that needs to be checked off of a to-do list, and more like hope and confidence in *me*. Just me. Not some idealized version of who I'm supposed to be when I grow up.

"Yeah, we're family. You're my best friend's little sister. Of course, I care." He clears his throat, and I try not to laugh at his sudden awkwardness. The air shifts, the seriousness between us dissipating as quickly as it arrived.

"I'm not little." I cross my arms in front of my body ready for a fight.

It always comes back to this. I get so sick and tired of the both of them telling me how young I am. News flash, I know for a fact Tyler's prom date is in the same grade as I am. Two years is nothing, and yet they treat me like they're my self-appointed babysitters and not one hall over for locker assignments at the high school.

"You can't even drive yet, Click." He says my nickname with a smile as he grabs the brass doorknob to leave.

Click.

Damien's been calling me Click since I was eight. My mama bought me my first camera that year for my birthday. I remember being so excited about that camera. It was a Polaroid. I'd been asking for a camera for months. That thing was glued to my face from that instant forward. I'd do any side job, take any dare, anything to scrape together enough money to buy film. I once licked the bottom of T's shoe for a dollar. I'd do it again.

Damien's the only one who calls me Click, and it doesn't bother me as much as it probably should when he says it. It started as a joke, but now it's kind of nice.

Four Score

Nobody's ever given me a nickname. It feels special.

"Two more months, and I'll be free." I let out a monster of a sigh, tossing my head back to stare at the off-white ceiling tiles. A couple of them have yellow spots from roof leaks long since patched.

In two months, I turn sixteen. I don't have enough money for a car, but my curfew will get bumped to midnight on the weekend. Mama says nothing good happens after midnight, but I beg to differ.

I'm not looking for trouble. I just want to stay out long enough to capture the stars twinkling in the sky at night. Or the way the streets look after most people are asleep and the only lights on are those on the marquee of the old movie theater in town.

"Don't grow up too fast, Click. I've heard it's a trap." Damien walks through the door and closes it behind him.

I quietly whisper the words to myself that I know by heart…

"Four score and seven years ago our fathers brought forth, upon this continent, a new nation, conceived in liberty…"

CHAPTER TWO
DAMIEN
Twenty Years Old

It's just after midnight. I had a text message waiting on my phone when we hit the locker room after our game tonight. Gia needed me.

Her text said to meet her here, in her dorm room, when we finished up. *No rush*. She added the last two words like I didn't realize they meant the complete opposite. Something in my gut twisted. The moment I read the text I knew something wasn't right. Her tone was all wrong. She was too direct. There was a level of professionalism there that worried me. Her words lacked her usual joking sarcasm.

Lucky for me, and the highway patrol, we played at home tonight. I didn't waste time in the shower, I didn't speak to anyone at all; our win completely forgotten in my haste to get to her. I came straight here. I *rushed*, because I knew good and damn well that something was up.

Now I sit silently on the small twin-sized bed in Gia's room, and I wait.

I watch her carefully as she paces back and forth in front of the sink, the door to the bathroom stands ajar between us. She and her roommate share a bathroom with an adjoining room next door. Her roommate went back home for the weekend. It's just the two of us tonight, and I've never been more thankful for the privacy.

A bead of sweat rolls down my spine, but my face doesn't show the fear that churns in my stomach.

I fucked up.

"It's positive." Her words are clear. There is no question, merely facts that changed our lives weeks before we knew the repercussions of our actions.

My spine snaps straight. My mind instantly begins creating solutions to problems that aren't even problems yet. More adrenaline races through my veins than during any game of hockey I've ever played.

Gia snatches the test from where it sits on the edge of the porcelain sink as if it has personally offended her. She storms into the dorm room and slams the bathroom door at her back, turning the lock behind her before leaning back against it in a flourish.

"Shit." It's all I manage to say as I stand up from where I've been waiting. I stare at the woman in front of me, gauging her reaction to one of the most pivotal moments in our lives. She's like a ticking time bomb, ready to explode at any second.

We're not kids anymore. We haven't been for some

time. I can't pinpoint when exactly it happened. I just know that, somewhere along the way, Gia became less of a little sister to me and more…well, *not* a sister.

Tyler and I made plans years ago. Plans of fame and fortune. Plans for hockey and law degrees. Plans that I was never able to fulfill like we imagined because I couldn't afford Chambliss.

I didn't get the hockey scholarship I applied for and couldn't qualify for grants. We were too rich for assistance but too poor to pay the tuition. I didn't want to be a walk-on; I couldn't gamble my future on a *maybe*. I definitely couldn't gamble my mama's money on it. She worked too damn hard to give me every opportunity growing up. Being a single mom wasn't easy. I watched her struggle every day, and she never complained about it.

Rafferton is a good college. It's close to home and I was offered a full scholarship. There was no choice in my mind, I did what I had to do. Sure, Rafferton's hockey program is still new. We're gaining momentum, but it's slow. We're finally starting to get attention from league scouts. My dream isn't over, I just took a different path to get there. Unfortunately, my decision to stay created a crack in what I always thought was an unbreakable bond of friendship.

Tyler was my best friend; he was my brother. Time and distance change things whether we want them to or not.

Some changes we can plan for, others we never see coming - like this one.

"Double shit." She laughs, but it's not filled with the

joy that should come at a moment like this. It's heart-wrenching and laced with fear. She's in shock.

She tosses me the test, and I catch it without hesitation. My reflexes are fast. Not much different than the decision that's already been made in my mind in the minutes we've been standing here looking at each other.

The truth? I made this decision in my heart long before those lines turned pink.

"I'm in." I clutch the test in the palm of my hand without looking at it. I trust Gia. She's family. Anybody else, and I'd assume this was about some puck bunny shit, but not Gia.

"What?" Her breath catches on a single word. She looks at me, her eyes brimming with questions that I'm already prepared to answer.

My dad left before I was born. I never knew him. I have vague memories of Gia and Tyler's dad before he died tragically in a car accident, back when we still thought we were Power Rangers – we thought we were invincible. We were barely in elementary school. Gia was even younger - too young. She doesn't remember, but I still hear his laugh sometimes. I remember playing hockey in the street with him when Tyler and I could barely grip the stick.

I'm sure he had his flaws. Hell, don't we all? I know I probably placed that man on a pedestal all those years ago that maybe he deserved, maybe he didn't. But, in my mind, he was a real man. A man that I've strived to be like for years. He gave me something to work toward when the only man I never knew left.

Tyler and Gia's dad, though? He didn't run away from

his responsibilities. He ran toward them. Ultimately, it cost him his life.

I won't run away from my responsibilities. No matter what the sacrifices might be.

"I said I'm in, Click." I take a step toward her. I don't touch. Our relationship isn't like that. We're friends. Friends that made a choice one night, and now we're friends that need to make another choice. A big one. Her cheetah-print-covered bedroom slippers brush up against the toes of my sneakers.

"How can you be in? I don't even know if I'm in yet. This test might not even be right. It could be faulty." The pupils in her eyes are so dilated that her usual midnight brown color looks almost solid black. She stares at me in disbelief. Fear marks her every feature.

I glance down from her eyes to where the black cotton robe she wears is tied around her slender waistline. Her stomach is flat, but it won't be for much longer.

"Let me get this straight. You called me over here in the middle of the night because you don't think you're pregnant?" She knows it's not a false positive.

She bites down on her bottom lip.

"No." She admits reluctantly.

"Exactly. You didn't do this by yourself. Don't steal this opportunity from me, Click. I know this is your body. Ultimately the decision rests in your hands. But, please, let me be a part of the verdict." My fingers wrap around the test that I still hold in my hand, gripping it with a possessive force that surprises even me. I struggle internally with the need to reach out and brush the palm of my free hand over her abdomen.

Mine.

"How is this an opportunity? It was one night, Damien. We slipped up one single night. I don't understand how this could have happened. It's not supposed to happen like this. None of this was supposed to happen. We're so young." Her voice cracks.

My eyes dart back up to where her's pool with unshed tears. She's breaking. The shock is wearing off, and the realization of what we've done is crashing down around her. It's like watching a movie unfold in slow motion, but you already know how it ends.

This is her first year of college. She hasn't even been here a full semester yet. I'm still working on my general studies. We've only just begun.

"We did not slip up, Gia. Say it for what it is. We ended up at the same party, which you had no business being at, might I add. I drug you back to my place kicking and screaming about your rights and freedoms. It was late. One thing led to another. You kissed me, and now my baby is in your belly." My words are harsher than I intend them, but I can't help it. We're family, and this is how family communicates. I won't sugarcoat it.

Her mouth pops open and, as I stand there, watching her, I'm briefly taken back to the night that would forever change our relationship. I don't go out. Ever. Despite what Tyler probably thinks about me, my future does matter to me – and not just playing professional hockey.

Hockey has always been one of the biggest parts of my life, if not the biggest. I'm good at it. Damn good at it. But apparently not good enough to get a full ride to a fancy-ass Ivy League college like Chambliss. I'm a goalie.

There are only so many goalie spots, and I needed the scholarship money. I should have told Tyler the truth, but I didn't - I couldn't. My pride wouldn't allow it. So, I told him I didn't get in at all. It was easier than admitting we couldn't afford for me to walk on when I had a full scholarship to play in Rafferton's new program.

Truth or not – it wouldn't have mattered anyway. Tyler can't see beyond the plan he's had set in his mind since we were kids. He wouldn't have understood. He walks around with blinders on, too driven by his own childhood trauma to recognize that I have challenges of my own. We're all human. Now he's there, and I'm here. And what's worse? So is *his* Gia.

Rafferton has an excellent fine arts program. Gia's the most creatively talented person I've ever met. She was an artist from the moment she picked up her first camera. She lives her life behind a lens.

Tyler has blinders. Gia has a lens.

They're more similar than they'll ever admit. This is why it was so easy when Gia moved here for our relationship to grow into a different type of friendship.

"So, that's how you're choosing to remember the night we slept together?" She chokes out a laugh, and a lone tear streaks down the smooth skin on her cheek.

I can't help myself; I reach out and swipe it away with my thumb.

There's nothing funny about this moment. Our lives hang in the balance of one single decision. A decision that I have to convince her to make *with* me. We have to do this together. We need to be on the same team. Right now, I feel like it's the third period and I'm down with only seconds to go.

"You were flirting with fire, and I wasn't going to stand there and watch you burn." The words come out a growl.

Gia doesn't go out either, she's not a partier. I got a text that night. It was late. I was already in bed. It was from one of my teammates. They knew Gia's connection to me. They saw her at a party and suspected something wasn't right. They were right, but it wasn't in the way I suspected.

"Well, don't treat me like I'm a damn child. I'm sick of it. You sure as hell didn't treat me like a child that night. I can handle myself, Damien. I make my own choices. I didn't need you that night and I don't need you now. I can do this myself. Maybe if you'd minded your own damn business that night, we wouldn't be in this situation right now." Her words hit me in the chest like bullets, one right after the other.

She pushes off of the bathroom door, and her chest brushes mine when I don't budge.

Evidently, we've moved from shock directly to the anger stage. My proximity and involvement in the situation make me the bullseye and, apparently, we're having target practice.

I inhale deeply. I try not to move when all I want to do is grab her and pull her to me.

I want to make her understand that she doesn't have to do this alone. I'll take the blame. I'll take every hit she throws at me. I need her to understand that this isn't the mistake it feels like it is. We can do this together. Something beautiful can come of this, if only we can find a way to work together.

"Sure, you can do this by yourself. I know you can. I never doubted you could. I'm trying to tell you that I don't want you to. I want you to let me help raise this child." My lips are a breath away from her forehead.

She tilts her head back and stares up wildly into my eyes. She doesn't speak, so I take that as my opportunity to continue.

"I'm ruining your future. This is my fault. I didn't…I messed up. You know I never meant for any of this to happen, Click. I would never purposely put either one of us in this situation. We've already gone over this a million times since that night."

Gia wasn't drunk that night. She wasn't out partying it up for the hell of it like my teammate assumed she was when he sent me that text, like I assumed she was before I knew better.

I should have known better. You know what they say about assumptions.

"It was perfect though, wasn't it?" Her words are a hushed confession. She reaches out and brushes my hand with her fingertips. The hand that still grips the test that's irrevocably altered our future.

"What?" I can feel my brows pull together in confusion. My heart beats erratically in my chest at the implications of her words. I'm getting whiplash from the rollercoaster of emotions we're riding.

Every conversation we've had in the weeks since that night has been about how what happened between us that night can't happen again. How it was one time and one time only. Our secret.

"That night was perfect, wasn't it, Damien? Despite all of this." A small smile ghosts her lips, and my stomach plummets to my feet. If we're going to do this, I can't afford to let myself think that way. I can't allow myself to focus on the past.

Gia was working on an article for her photojournalism class. It was her first big assignment. She was documenting micro-movements of the body. Specifically, how hormones related to male and female social interactions cause minute changes in our body's natural reflexes.

That night. That party. She was flirting…with fire. Quite literally.

It was my fault. I didn't give her time to explain. But she was using herself as a test subject. She was her own fucking decoy in a dangerous game with real people. Gia never saw the danger in what she was doing. In her mind, it was a controlled experiment in an environment that was anything but controlled.

When I walked into that party and saw her all over a guy that I know for a damn fact is bad news, I drug her out of there and back to my place without a single word…from me. She threw plenty of words in my direction.

The bigger problem? I was blind to the danger too. Even when it was staring me right in the face like a giant neon warning sign.

When we got back to my place and I finally let her explain, well, she still needed to finish her experiment. It was just the two of us. I agreed because every fucking time I thought about her back at that party my blood boiled. It was late. I've never been very good at telling her no. It had to be me.

That's the thing about art. The beauty is in the abstract – the unexpected.

I don't think either of us expected what happened next.

"More than that. I lost it. I lost my control." I admit as I exhale weeks of conflicting feelings in one confession. I shouldn't be saying any of this. We should be focusing on the issue at hand.

I've replayed that night in my mind so many times. I've never been reckless. I've never broken my own damn rules. I've never been weak. Until that night. I was lost to her. And every night since then I've tried and failed to wrap my mind around the why and the how when it comes to my relationship with Gia.

How did we go from homework after hockey practice to making the biggest decision of our lives standing in the middle of a dorm room?

How did she go from the young girl with braces and braids to the woman I see standing in front of me today with her wild dark hair combed out, framing the sleek cheekbones of her beautiful face?

She rocked my world that night and turned everything I thought I knew to be true upside down. I haven't recovered.

Her hand tightens around mine.

"I'm in too." Three words. She utters three single words that crack the façade of my carefully constructed fortress of strength.

I've tried so hard to remain strong in the midst of the

chaos unfolding around us.

I need to be strong for Gia. I need to remain strong for our baby. But those three words nearly bring me to my knees at her feet.

"Are you saying what I think you're saying?" I dare ask the question that beats like a drum in my head relentlessly. The answer to everything that happens from this point in our lives forward hangs in the balance between us.

"I'm saying that…I don't know. I don't know what the future holds for us, but I know that I want to do this, even if it's hard. Because it will be hard. I…I guess I'm saying that I want to raise this baby." My heart stalls with the conflicting emotions I feel in her words.

"That's my baby in there. My future." What's left of my control snaps. I try and fail to choke down the emotions that crash over me in waves.

Another tear falls from her cheek onto the exposed skin of her chest where her robe crosses and forms a deep V.

"Your future is hockey. That's your dream. It's not fair. None of this is fair. You said it yourself. I won't let you throw away your future. I can do this, Damien. I can do this by myself." Her words are final, but this discussion is not over yet.

She's giving me an out.

I don't want it.

There's another way. There has to be. I need more time to think. I need a plan.

"Let me ask you something, Gia. What do you want most in life? More than anything on this entire planet." I drop my free hand to her hip. I need to ground my thoughts somehow so that I can think this through. Get it together, Henderson.

"And all the galaxies of the universe?" She asks as she smiles through the pain that's etched on her face. Her playful words offer a levity that feels like a breath of fresh air that I think we both desperately need.

"To infinity and beyond, yes." I smile at her briefly before continuing because I already know what the answer is, and I need her to remember too. "What do you want?" I repeat the question quietly. She's told me this before. Maybe not the answer to this exact question, but I know her.

Her eyes search mine, and I recognize the instant she begins tracking with me.

"Legacy." She answers confidently.

My memories of Gia date back further than she herself might remember. You learn a lot about a person over a lifetime of memories.

"To leave your own personal mark on this planet," I suggest because I know what's most important to her. I know what drives her. It's one of the things that makes her so special.

She's not driven by personal gain. Not in the way that most successful people are. Gia is one of the most selfless people I've ever met. I'd also bet my entire future career on her becoming one of the most successful. Just not from the standard societal viewpoint.

Not just in her career, but in the game of life. Gia will be a phenomenal mother to this child.

"Exactly. I want to make an impact. I want to be a

ripple in the sea of change and growth." I hear the strength in her voice rise as she slowly comes back to me.

This is our moment.

"You hold our legacy inside of you. That baby is our legacy, Click. He or she is our future." My voice trembles. I pour my heart and soul into every word that leaves my lips.

"Our future?" She tilts her head to the side as she looks up at me. As if just now considering the fact that she's bound to me for life. I can't figure out if she likes the idea of that or not.

I suck in a breath and prepare myself to present her with the plan that's quickly been coming together in my mind the longer we've stood here.

Another way. Another option. A future for us. Together.

Everything falls into place. Now if I can just get it out without her falling apart before I can get her to understand how this can work.

"Hear me out. We don't have to make this weird, Click. We're already family. Now our family is growing by one more. We're both admitted students on scholarship here at Rafferton. We both already live on campus. Separately, but we don't have to. We'll get married before the baby comes. They have housing specifically for married couples. It will be affordable, and we'll both still be able to attend college. We can adjust our schedules to accommodate the baby's schedule. I saw a posting just the other day for a maintenance position at the rink. It's part-time. I'll get a job. We'll get extra help if we need it. Some of the older guys on the team have kids already. I'm sure they'd be more than happy to share what they know about raising a baby on campus." The words rush from my mouth. I try to get it all out in the open before she can cut me off. Even as I say it, I know how absurd it all sounds, but it's all I've got.

Yesterday I was worried about midterms. Today I'm proposing marriage to my best friend's little sister.

"Hell no," she reels, her voice louder than it's been all night. "Nobody said anything about marriage, Damien. This is the twenty-first century. I am not marrying you just because we've decided to have this child together." She pulls her hand from mine, but I won't give up. I see our future. I see us as a family. Not in the traditional sense, but nothing about this is traditional.

"Temporarily. It doesn't have to be forever, Click. It's not a bad idea if you'll just consider it. It's a way for us to do this affordably and still be able to accomplish our goals. We won't have to switch off weekdays and weekends. We already know we're good together as friends. Neither of us is in a relationship. We can have it all. Do you want to raise this baby with me? As equals?" I reach for what feels like the unreachable.

Two parents. One home. For now, anyway. We can give this baby everything we never had. We can co-parent together. We're already family. This can work. Even if something about calling it co-parenting feels weird. For some reason, the term doesn't feel like enough. Regardless, it is going to have to be. I'm hanging on by a single thread of hope here.

"You're asking me two very different questions and expecting a single answer. Yes, I will agree to co-parent with you as equals. My dad died when I was still in preschool, you know this about me. My memories of him come from photo albums. Until Jeff came along, T was my dad, or he thought he was. Still does. I want this baby to know their daddy." My heart stutters with one word...*daddy*. A smile stretches my lips, and my eyes fill with tears that I don't try to hide from her.

"Daddy," I whisper the word. "Say that again, Click." I've never been in love, but my heart is so full at this moment that it feels like it might burst from my chest. I already love this baby so damn much.

"You're going to be a daddy, Damien. It's weird, huh?" Slowly, Gia brings her hand to her belly.

She gives me permission with a single nod of her head, and I don't hesitate to place my hand over hers.

Two hearts will become a third. The miracle of life is an amazing thing to behold. We did this. We created this child together. Planned or not, there is a living, growing baby in there, and part of it belongs to me.

"My dad bailed before I was born," I confess, but she already knows. It's hard to keep secrets when you've known someone your entire life.

My hand remains firmly planted over hers on her stomach.

"I know, I'm sorry." Her apology is so genuine. It is not without thought or consideration. She's truly sorry my father left before I was born. He abandoned us. Gia never knew her dad, much like I never knew mine. The circumstances were different, but the brokenness of our families was much the same. She'll see my loss over hers, though; she'll recognize my pain before admitting her own.

"Don't be. He did me a favor. He showed me the man that I didn't want to become one day. He had a choice, and he chose to leave. Your dad didn't get to choose. I'm not going to be like the man whose blood runs through my veins. Never. I get to choose, and I choose you and this baby. I'm going to be present. I'm going to be involved. All hands on deck. Let me be your partner in this, Click. Let's do this together. Partners?" I restructure the arrangement. Less *marriage* words and more *partner* words. Because legal marriage is just a piece of paper, it means nothing in the big scheme of things except convenience. Once she's able to take a step out of the emotion of this decision, she'll realize that.

"I don't understand what you're saying." She shakes her head back and forth.

That makes two of us. But I've never been more sure of something in my life.

"Think of it like a pact. The family piece, that's easy. We've been doing this for years already. We can raise this baby together. That part will be hard, but I've never been afraid to do the hard things, and I know you haven't either. We'll be united. Two people committed to giving this child the best life possible. We can hammer out the details later. What do you say?"

I hold my breath waiting for her response. She studies me for what feels like an eternity before slowly nodding.

"T is going to kill me." She groans and her head lands with a thump against the bathroom door.

"Correction. He's going to kill me." I remove my hand from hers and pull her to me, having already been granted permission to touch, and way past caring what is and is not acceptable for our newly-formed arrangement.

A brief feeling of relief replaces the nervous flutters that have been overwhelming me the entirety of our conversation. This is only the first of many obstacles we'll face, but now we will face them together. She folds into my arms without hesitation, burying her face in my chest.

It's at that moment that I remember I left the game tonight without a shower.

"I'm scared, Damien. This wasn't supposed to happen." She mumbles against my chest.

The wild strands of her dark hair tickle my chin, and I smile. Her hair has always been a gorgeous dark black, but when she allows it to just be in its natural state – I'm sure she would argue that her process to fix it is anything but natural – but I love it. It matches her personality. *Wild and free*. I hope that if we have a girl she looks just like her mama, wild hair and all.

I'm going to be a daddy.

"It will be okay. I promise. I will make sure of it." I run the palms of my hands up and down her back. I try to relieve some of the tension and fear that I imagine she's feeling. She weaves her arms around my back. She doesn't realize it, but she's holding me just as much as I'm holding her.

"We will tell Tyler together. He'll understand. We're brothers. This is his niece or nephew. Sure, he might get mad, but he'll come around." Even as I say the words, I'm not sure that they're true. I'd like to think they are, but my relationship with Tyler has been strained since we graduated high school and went our separate ways. I'm not entirely sure Gia realizes to what extent.

"We can do this?" She props her chin up on my chest and slowly batts her long dark eyelashes up at me.

"I believe in you. I believe in this baby. I believe in our future." I answer resolutely. I'm determined that this will work and, when I set my mind to something, I don't quit. You don't have to be the best. You don't have to be the smartest or the fastest. There will always be someone better than you.

You have to be the hungriest. And I'm fucking starving for the family that I never had.

Gia's lips twist to the side and her nose suddenly scrunches up adorably. "Okay, enough about our future for tonight. Present you is in serious need of a shower. Damn, boy, you stink."

CHAPTER THREE
DAMIEN
Two-ish months later

"I can't do this. I can't do this, Damien. We don't have to do this today. We can turn back now, and he'll never know. I'm hardly even showing. We'll say I ate a cheeseburger. A really big cheeseburger. Maybe that's my new thing, I'm a food blogger. Oh, that's it! I'm putting on weight because I've decided to turn my photography career into a career about blogging food. Specifically, cheeseburgers. It's the perfect plan. We can wait…forever." Gia wears a path on the navy-blue shag carpet of her childhood bedroom.

She knows forever isn't an option, just like I know my friendship with Tyler will never be the same again after today.

Gia is sixteen weeks along. Ten whole weeks since I found out I was going to be a daddy. We saw our baby on an ultrasound at her doctor's appointment just last week. We're having a little girl. Ten tiny little fingers and ten tiny little toes. I'm going to have a daughter. I'm not sure who cried more when we found out. That little girl might not be here yet, but she's already got me wrapped.

I wasted no time buying a pink Rafferton onesie with my number, lucky number thirteen, on the back. I'm going to wrap it up and surprise Gia with it on Christmas morning.

Gia and I will be married by the end of this month. After we took a step back, we were able to truly look at our options and make a decision that will work best for the three of us. Does it make the most sense?

Logically? Probably not.

Financially? Maybe.

Will I be able to sleep at night without breathing the same air as they are? Absolutely not.

Is that selfish of me? Hell yes. You know, I never considered myself a selfish man. Add that to the list of new things I find out about myself daily since those pink lines showed up on that cheap plastic drugstore test.

We're currently referring to this as our five-year plan. It's a working plan - fluid, if you will. We can call it whatever she wants to call it, as long as it means I get to keep my family.

We will file the paperwork in private, but we both agreed we needed to talk to our moms first…and Tyler. We were both raised to know that a certain level of respect must be maintained for family dynamics to work without creating animosity. Respect is important to us. We've put this off long enough, it's time.

Hell, I'm ready to scream it from the rooftops. Sure, I

was scared at first, fucking terrified. But now that I've had time to process, I want everyone to know that that's my baby in there. Beneath the tiny little baby bump that's just recently started showing on Gia's slender frame is our daughter. Her little heart beats to a rhythm all its own. One that Gia and I created together. *Ours.*

The how's and why's of it don't matter anymore. That's what I tell myself every night anyway when my mind starts to wonder about things it shouldn't. All that matters is that our baby is growing in there, and she is so loved already. Safe and loved. That's what I'm choosing to focus on.

We arrived back in our hometown this morning. It's Christmas break, but we only have a couple of days before I'm needed back at the rink for practice. Our parents were expecting us, just not together. Gia took two steps into the foyer of her childhood home and Mama Patterson started crying. I was still carrying her bag in from the car, I hadn't even made it into the house.

Somehow, she already knew. Seeing Gia only confirmed it. Maybe it was mother's intuition? Maybe it was our joint arrival throwing up red flags all over the front lawn. All I know is that by the time we got all the words out everyone in the room was crying, most especially Gia. But, Gia cries at everything lately.

They were shocked, at first. I can't say that I blame them. If anything, their reactions were full of love and understanding that I'd hoped for but hadn't let myself anticipate.

Jeff didn't hit me. Mama Patterson didn't hit me either, which was a relief because I was sure she'd throw

Four Score

me right out of the house for touching her daughter.

We explained everything. Well, not exactly everything, but enough. They know they're having a granddaughter and that we're getting married. They also know that we're planning to finish our degrees and raise this child while we do it. They don't know the specifics of our nonexistent romantic relationship.

Our moms were raised in a different time. I guess you could say that they're *old school*. Giving them a grandchild is a blessing. Doing it out of wedlock is walking a fine line. Admitting the details of how we ended up in this situation and how we plan to parent, well…let's just say it wouldn't be kosher.

Then we went over to my mama's house down the street and did it all over again. Unfortunately for me, my mama did hit me, but it didn't hurt. I'm two for three so far.

We still have to tell Tyler. That punch might land a little harder. I'm just hoping he aims his anger at me and not Gia. I can handle the brunt of it, but if he tries to tear her down, I'm not sure I'll be able to control my temper.

Tyler's flight in from Chambliss arrived about thirty minutes ago. Mama Patterson and Jeff went to pick him up at the airport, but they agreed to let us be the ones to tell him the news. I want to face him in person. I'm a lot of things, but a coward isn't one of them. Gia might be scared, but I've been ready and waiting for this moment.

"Wait for what exactly, Click? The longer we wait, the worse this is going to be. Not to mention, how exactly will you explain your newly acquired baby? Or our marriage?"

Gia wrings her hands together nervously. I approach her slowly, taking her hands in mine to calm her nerves.

"You're right. We have to tell him. He's going to hate me." Her bottom lip trembles, and I hate that she's so scared of the one person she should be able to count on in this situation more than anyone.

Tyler spent so much time trying to protect Gia, but, in the end, his need to guard her so vigilantly stole the relationship they should have had. The loss of their father was so much more than the loss of one single man. That's the way death goes though, I guess.

Tyler lost his childhood, Gia lost her brother, and it's nobody's fault.

Life is hard, but so is death. Resilience from death for those left behind us is seemingly unattainable. It's a fleeting hope. What is resilience if not survival? We live to die and then leave those behind us to survive. It's depressing.

But, with death comes new life. It's a cycle. Life continues onward with or without us.

I choose life.

-o-
GIA

I bite the inside of my cheek to keep from crying – or screaming. My hormones rock back and forth between the two, unsure of which emotion we're feeling at the moment. Spoiler alert, the answer is probably all of the above. Mama and Jeff left to grab dinner, leaving Damien and me alone with Tyler.

I've barely spoken a word to him since they all arrived back from the airport. A thick layer of impending doom hangs in the air as I finally utter words to my brother that I never thought I would have to say. An admission. A confession.

Mama and Jeff agreed to let us tell him in private. Now I'm starting to think we should have kept them here for backup.

As I stand in front of Tyler and wait for his reaction, I feel like I die a thousand times. It feels like I'm on trial, awaiting sentencing for a crime I am so totally guilty of. The evidence hides beneath the flowing grey tunic I wore today.

"How could you do this?" Tyler seethes from the couch that's been in our mama's living room since before I can even remember. We've got so many memories here. The worn threads of that old sofa have seen so much of our lives.

Looking around the room, it's hard not to become overwhelmed. We have so many reminders that we're family surrounding us. Mismatched frames filled with photos of our childhood line the walls. Tyler's hockey trophies sit up on the fireplace mantle beneath a framed photo I took my senior year for my art final.

Damien is an optimist.

I knew better. I knew he wouldn't see it that way. Not Tyler. Family or not, this is betrayal. We've committed high treason and, as the king of his proverbial castle, he's preparing to exile us from his life. I feel it down deep in my bones.

What he fails to realize? We have the princess.

Damien doesn't swoop in to save me. He lets me handle this, and for that I'm appreciative. I take a deep breath and debate my approach to his obvious anger. His response upsets me, but it's not unexpected. The fact that he's confirmed what I knew all along only makes me that much angrier with him. I try to channel that anger into an intelligent response before I allow the words to leave my lips, but, unfortunately, my sass wins out over logic.

"Well, they taught us in sixth grade that when semen penetrates…"

I let my voice trail off as I throw fuel on an already roaring flame. I end up with sarcasm and a side of salt. I'm sure there's a better way to go about this, but I seem to be completely out of good ideas right now, so this will have to do. I can't allow myself to break in front of Tyler. I can't show weakness. If he thinks I'm weak it will only further support his theory that we're not ready to be parents. He doesn't have to say it. I know that's how he feels.

And, fine, I can admit to myself that we aren't ready, but we're going to do everything in our power to make sure this little girl doesn't realize we're totally winging this parenting thing. I'd bet money that's what most parents do anyway. *"I was totally prepared for rocking parenthood."* Said no parent in the thick of parenting ever.

And maybe Damien is so sure of us that he's almost got me convinced. *Almost*. Doubt still creeps into my thoughts when I'm alone at night. We won't move in together until the start of the new semester. I've been living in the dorm, per our agreed-upon arrangement. There's no reason for us to move in together until we have to. We're just two friends that happened to conceive a baby together. One night. One slip-up. Nothing more.

When Damien's not in class, he's at the rink. He picked up a job there just like he said he would. He's already saving for our expenses, he's already preparing. I've had a hard time adjusting to the idea of us sharing everything. Responsibility. Finances. For most of my life, my mama did everything on her own. Up until Jeff came into our lives, but we've had more years without him than we've had with him. Same as the few years we had with my daddy. I don't remember those.

My mama didn't have help. Sometimes I feel guilty knowing that I will. It doesn't seem fair, to anyone, but none of this does.

I've started singing to our baby when the doubt creeps in. When I'm scared for what our future will look like, I sing to her.

This little light of mine,
I'm gonna let it shine,
This little light of mine,
I'm gonna let it shine, all the time, let it shine.

Our baby girl is going to shine bright. Like all the stars in the night sky. I like to think my daddy is up there watching me. I bet he's the brightest star of them all. He'll watch over her too, I know he will.

Not going to lie, I'm still waiting on him to send a hurling meteor to Earth and take out Damien. Damien is a good man, but I don't think anything would excuse what's transpired between us in a father's eyes. Just like I don't expect it from Tyler. The difference? I know in my heart that my daddy would forgive, just like my mama did.

Tyler? He won't forget so easily.

"Oh, my God. I think I'm going to be sick." Tyler pushes back from the couch and stands. He covers his hand with his mouth and begins pacing in front of where I stand next to Damien.

I step toward him, but he takes a step away. His eyes widen wildly. He's big mad, just like I knew he would be. I might have mentioned to Damien that we didn't have to tell him, a time or ten. But the truth is, Damien's right, he needed to know. We couldn't continue to hide. As much as I wanted to put off this confrontation, it was happening now or six months from now. May as well rip off the Band-Aid.

However, I still think at the very least waiting until the baby was born had some solid pros. I mean, Tyler's pissed now but he's also a big mush. He's a protector by nature. He'd have taken one look at his niece and this would have all been a formality. Instead, we're here, and a war is brewing in our midst.

Tyler looks from Damien back to me, passing judgment when he has no business doing so. He's not perfect. None of us are, and to hold me to some unattainable standard of perfection he has in his mind is wrong. I just need him to tell me it's going to be okay.

That's not what he does, though.

"Look, Tyler, it's not what you think." Damien steps between us when he senses the tension rising to dangerous levels. We all feel it.

The big bang is inevitable. It's coming. Tyler's jaw ticks. Damien grunts. I mentally countdown in my head, taking small steps away from the two of them as I do.

Three, two…

"It's not what I think? It's not what I fucking think? How is this not what I think, Damien? Huh? Tell me. Because my baby sister is growing a baby in her stomach, and your semen is the reason it's in there." The way Tyler says the word *semen* to Damien sends my stomach swirling.

"Now I'm going to be sick, seriously, T, it makes me nauseous when you say semen." I try to take a deep breath and pray the fresh oxygen keeps my lunch where it belongs.

I was sick for about a month and a half at the very beginning of my pregnancy, but luckily, I think I'm mostly over the 24/7 stomach bug. Or I thought I was until Tyler decided to say the word *semen*. Needless to say, it didn't have the same effect as it did when I said it.

"But you can say it, Gia? You're not even supposed to know that word. This is your fault, Damien; I can't believe you'd do this to us. You're supposed to be my best friend. We were supposed to be brothers." Tyler brushes his chest against Damien, effectively pushing him.

I watch the way Damien's fists flex at his sides, but he doesn't push back. Not yet.

Tyler's a hot head, always has been. He's fierce when it comes to guarding those he loves. Damien might be his best friend, but I'm his baby.

Where Tyler is loud and demanding, Damien is quiet and comforting. Damien has a silent strength, and I know he's harnessing every ounce of it as Tyler tries to push him to react. When Damien doesn't take the bait, Tyler shifts his focus to me.

I'm as ready for this as I'm going to get.

"I'm so disappointed in you, Gia." Tyler shakes his head back and forth.

Or I thought I was ready, but his words of disappointment take me by surprise. I've worked so hard my entire life to live up to his standards. To not disappoint my mama. No ripples in the sea. His disappointment is a punch to the gut, and I can't stop the tears as they come.

I should have known better. My hormones are unpredictable. My tears betray me as I begin to ugly cry in the doorway that connects the living room to the kitchen. I've almost fully retreated from the room, and now I want to turn and run. I want to run far away from here.

"You don't get to say that to her." Damien growls and the hair on my arms stand at attention.

His blatant defense on my behalf rekindles the fleeting strength inside of me. I know this is only because I'm carrying his child, but it gives me strength all the same, and I'm taking all of that I can get.

"Don't you tell me what I can fucking say. You're a traitor. The enemy. Why are you still here, anyway? Leave." Spit flies from Tyler's mouth as he yells at Damien, and my blood begins to boil. He has no right to speak to him that way.

"No." I step back into the room.

"What? Gia?" Tyler turns his anger from Damien to me, momentarily surprised by my outburst.

Sure, I've sassed him before, but I've never stood up

to him like this. I've never had a reason to. But I refuse to stand back and let him treat either one of us like this for a second longer. We're a family, we always have been, but this is not how a family reacts to adversity. Instead of picking us up, he's chosen to tear us down, and there's only so much of that I'm willing to tolerate.

"I said no! You can back the fuck off right now. I'm legally an adult, Tyler. I can make my own decisions. If I am old enough to go to war and fight for this country, I can sure as hell make a decision about my own fucking body. I'm keeping this baby." I hurl words at my brother I would never dare say before, unable to contain my anger at Tyler's reaction to this entire situation any longer. He's not the only one allowed to be mad.

I see Damien's small smile from the corner of my eye, but it's short-lived.

"Of course you're keeping the baby. You can move home with Mom and Jeff. You'll be able to finish your degree and credentials online." Tyler suggests an alternative that completely cuts Damien out of our lives. The brief smile on Damien's lips is gone, replaced with a sadness that breaks my heart.

"You don't understand, Tyler. You aren't listening!" I scream to be heard in a room where the emotions are deafening.

"Oh, I think I understand clearly. I think it's you that isn't thinking this through." Tyler fires words back at me. He swings his wild eyes to Damien, pointing toward the front door. "And you, Damien, leave. If I have to tell you again, I'll remove you myself."

Damien takes a step toward Tyler, and I see the fire

light in his eyes.

"Damien and I are getting married." The words burst from my lips.

"The fuck you are." Tyler booms.

There it is - the explosion.

I knew it was coming, but I won't stop now. I couldn't if I wanted to.

"We're getting married, and we're raising this baby together. I know it doesn't fit into your great big plan, but it's our plan and it's happening whether you like it or not." I stand my ground. I won't allow Damien to shoulder this alone; we're a team.

"I refuse to stand by and watch the two of you make one of the biggest mistakes of your lives, because that's what this is. You're making a huge fucking mistake." Tyler enunciates every word. He puts a voice to some of my biggest fears, but I won't allow his negativity to deter me.

I will not allow him to change my mind about decisions I've already made. This isn't about what's best for me anymore. I can't afford to only think about myself, that thought process went out the window the minute that test turned positive.

This isn't about Damien. This isn't about me. This is about this baby. *Our daughter.*

Damien and I have an opportunity to give this baby something neither one of us ever had. That can't be a mistake. It just can't.

"I think *you* need to leave, Tyler," I say already knowing I have no authority in this house to kick him out. My words are a wasted threat.

"This is my house, he can leave." Tyler snaps back as if he has any more authority here than I do.

His words are bull, and he knows it. I won't allow Tyler's toxic attitude to tear down a man that has done nothing but help me stand when I've felt like crumbling over the past few months. A man who has shown me that I'm braver than I ever imagined I was.

I can do hard things. I'm about to do one of the hardest things I've ever had to do. I close my eyes slowly, breathing deeply through the words I know I have to say.

I open my eyes again, and I break my own heart to give life to the tiny one that beats beneath the fabric of my shirt.

"That's how you want this to be, fine. But hear my words right now, Tyler Eugene Patterson. I will never speak to you again, and you will never know the beautiful human this baby will be. You've lost so much today, and you don't even realize it yet. Your sister. Your best friend. But most of all, you've lost a lifetime of knowing the joy that this sweet baby will bring into the world. I will call Mama and Jeff later. Damien, we're leaving." The words burn my throat like acid as I say them, but this is what has to happen. I won't allow him to poison this baby. I won't allow his negativity to infiltrate my mind. I have to protect my own mental health.

"Are you sure about this, Gia?" Damien walks to where I'm standing and takes my hand in his. A silent show of support. I thread my fingers with his. I need him. I need him so much more than he knows.

"Yeah, Gia, you sure you want to do this?" Tyler sneers as he watches us with a look of pure disgust on his face. It only confirms the decision I've made in my heart already.

I need to say goodbye. Sometimes relationships have to die so that others can thrive.

This baby is my priority. Damien is the father of my child. I choose them. I choose this life. And I choose to say goodbye for now. Maybe even forever.

My heart breaks a little bit more, but he did this. Tyler did this.

"Goodbye, Tyler. I hope you never forget that this was your fault. You chose." My voice cracks, but I force the words out. "You broke our family." Damien squeezes my hand.

Tears streak down my face. My throat burns. I can't breathe. It's time to go.

When I turn to leave, Damien follows me. I leave my suitcase. I leave my childhood home. I leave it all behind. I choose this baby. I choose Damien. I choose my family.

I cry as we slowly drive away, and I silently mourn my childhood.

CHAPTER FOUR
GIA
May of the following year

"**B**reathe through the pain, Click. In and out, just like they taught us in that class."

I shoot shards of broken glass at Damien with my eyes. As far as I'm concerned, this is all his fault.

Also, the crunchy moms. This is their fault too. Fuck them and their steel-cut oats.

This is what happens when you wind up on the granola side of TikTok. Dammit, I should have known better. My own mama tried to tell me to take the drugs, but no, I was convinced that I was totally prepared to push a basketball out of my vagina unmedicated.

Alert the media.

I. Was. Not. Prepared.

"Damien, I swear to God, I will cut your dick off." The threat is a battle cry that I fully intend to follow through on. *If* I survive this. Death feels imminent.

Oh, God.

"You heard that, right? That's a premeditated threat. I might need a witness after this is over. Would you be willing to testify in court, if needed?" Damien has the nerve to joke with the nurse that currently has her entire hand inside of my body.

The man has a death wish.

"I heard nothing." She looks up at me with a small smile teasing her lips.

I like her, but the audacity of her to smile at a time like this is beyond me.

I can't smile. I can't do anything but grimace and hold my breath as another wave of white-hot pain burns through every square inch of my body. It's excruciating. This pain is like nothing I've ever felt before. I'm living for the brief seconds of reprieve I get in between the waves of hell that continue to move closer and closer together in a relentless tsunami of torture.

"Gia, you are at a plus one. I'm going to get the doctor in here. Then you can start pushing. Okay?" No, ma'am, the fuck it is not okay.

I completely ignore the nurse that, by all apparent observations, is just doing her job. I hate her on principle. It's not her fault.

It's Damien's fault. Damn you, Damien, and your handsome face that shouldn't be handsome, and your long blonde hair that's prettier than mine and your willingness to drop everything to be here.

By everything, I mean the Rafferton spring prospect game. Our little girl has impeccable timing. She has since the day she was conceived.

I look back at the man that impregnated me. Another wave of agony hits me. I don't know how much longer I can do this. I hold my breath and pray for mercy until it passes, and I can direct my rage back at the responsible party.

He's a vampire. Damien is a vampire. That's the only explanation I have for what's happening to my body right now. This baby is half vampire and she's clawing her way out of my uterus with her vampire fangs leading the charge.

1...2...3...I can breathe again.

"Get this baby out of me, Damien. Get her out. Oh God, my vagina is never going to be the same. Fuck!" I scream every obscenity that I can think of as another wave of pain washes over me.

I must look as feral as I feel because Damien's eyes widen in fear as he turns back to the nurse.

"She's fine. We're totally fine. Please get the doctor. *Fast.*" He begs.

The nurse strips off her gloves and nods as she heads toward the door. A fucking snail moves faster than this woman.

"I am not fine!" I yell at no one in particular or everyone within a ten-mile radius that can probably hear me. I lost my give-a-damn somewhere around the time they broke my water with an oversized crochet hook.

"Squeeze my hand, Click. Squeeze it as hard as you need to."

I whimper and Damien slips his hand into mine.

Why is he so nice? Is it out of responsibility? Obligation?

The last five months have been…surprising.

Damien and I moved into a small two-bedroom apartment in a housing unit on campus designated for married students. I didn't realize that was an option, but I guess Damien knew what he was talking about. A few of the other players on Rafferton's team live in the same complex. We're still able to walk to our classes, and Damien can get to the rink by bus.

I built and designed a website myself and have been selling some of my photography online to earn extra income while also attending my classes. Damien works at the rink and is picking up any extra hours he can between school and his regular practices.

He never complains. He does what needs to be done without me asking. Dishes, laundry, taking the trash out – it doesn't matter. We're a team. I can admit that I've fallen short a few times over the last few months. This pregnancy has been exhausting physically and emotionally. He picks up my slack without question.

But, why?

A cold sweat breaks out over my skin. I think I might be sick.

I squeeze Damien's fingers with every ounce of strength left in my body, which isn't much. Okay, judging by the poorly hidden grimace on his face, maybe there was more left than I thought.

I try to hold it in. Really, I do. My body heaves, and I hurl the remnants of last night's double cheeseburger all over the floor. Well, that's karma. I knew I shouldn't have eaten that damn cheeseburger on the way to the hospital.

I will reiterate. Childbirth is not nearly as glamorous

as I was led to believe by social media.

"Let's have this baby!" The door swings open and my overzealous, completely bald, middle-aged, Indian OB walks in with a wide grin.

Like I didn't just hurl all over the floor.

I normally really like this man, love him actually. He's been wonderful throughout my entire pregnancy, but I can't handle his sunny-side-up bedside manner right now.

Doesn't he see that I'm dying?

How have women been doing this for centuries? The fuck if we don't get enough credit for populating the world.

The next thirty minutes pass in a blur of blood-curdling screams – mine and Damien's – and then a new scream, one that changes my life forever.

"Congratulations, mama, she's beautiful." The nurse places my daughter gently onto my chest and tears cascade down my cheeks.

The pain from moments ago is replaced with an indescribable euphoria.

Dark black hair and pink skin covered in a thick white film. She's part Damien, all right. I look up, just in time to see his reaction. His eyes are filled with wonder and adoration as he watches me hold our baby for the first time.

Somewhere off in the distance, I think I can hear the doctor trying to get his attention to cut the umbilical cord, but his eyes don't stray from mine.

Love. Unconditional love.

I feel it infiltrating every nook and cranny of my heart and body. I'm wrapped up in it like a cocoon. Love that's no doubt meant for our daughter. His love consumes every ounce of fear and worry that I've had over the previous nine months and replaces it with a contentment that I never expected. My heart is so full as this tiny new life squirms on my chest.

She's really here. I did it. *We* did it. Partners.

Damien kneels next to the hospital bed and meets me at eye level.

"I'm so proud of you, Click." The words are a hushed confession as he reaches out and runs his large hand over our baby's exposed skin.

He watches her and not me. I understand, I get it, and it's okay. I just need him to love her. If our plans fail and none of this works out the way we've hoped, if he'll always love her like he loves her right in this moment, that's all I can wish for.

Chaos ensues around us as the hospital staff continues to work. It doesn't matter, it all falls away into the background as we watch each other. We remain frozen in what feels like the most perfect moment in time. I want to live in this happiness for the rest of my life.

I choke down the tears that continue to overwhelm me. I look back at our daughter, and I see my future. I see her future. Damien was right. He was so right.

I softly hum the song that's been in my heart this entire pregnancy.

This little light of mine,
I'm gonna let it shine,
This little light of mine,
I'm gonna let it shine, all the time, let it shine.

"Astria," I say her name aloud as I hear it in my mind.

Damien and I never decided on a name. We wanted it to happen naturally, no matter how long that took. But at this moment, I know. I hear her name as clearly as if it's belonged to her since the beginning of time.

"What?" Damien asks, and I glance back up into his watery green eyes.

"Her name. Her name is Astria. It means star. She's going to shine so bright, Damien." My voice shakes. His hand brushes mine as we hold our daughter against my chest.

"Astria." He whispers her name and tears track down the chiseled line of his cheekbone, landing on the white cotton sheets of the hospital bed.

CHAPTER FIVE
DAMIEN

She's perfect.

I rock slowly back and forth in the faux leather recliner of Gia's hospital room. There's a bassinet beside the bed that they prepared especially for her arrival. She hasn't been in it once. If I were a betting man, I'd bet she won't touch it before we're discharged. Not if I have anything to do with it.

Gia finally fell asleep about an hour ago. She's exhausted. I've never been more in awe of another human than I was today.

I snuck into the hall just after Gia fell asleep and asked the nurses not to bother us if they didn't have to. She needs the rest. I'm running on adrenaline that just won't release me. I don't think I could sleep if I wanted to. My eyes have finally adjusted to the darkness of the room.

Our little girl lays flush against my skin. *Skin-to-skin* is what Gia called it. She said that it would stimulate bonding between the two of us. I don't need any help bonding with the little girl that already holds the key to my heart. But I didn't hesitate to lose my t-shirt the moment our very hungry daughter finally decided to unlatch from her mama's breasts and allow me a chance to snuggle her. She gets her appetite from her daddy.

I never thought being a dad would feel like this. I don't guess I knew what to expect. This overwhelming love for another person is like nothing I could have ever imagined.

Her hands form tiny fists that she perches up near her cute little chin. Her hair is dark just like Gia's. She feels so fragile in my arms. So precious and innocent.

"Astria. Baby girl," I whisper to her softly. "She did good, didn't she?" I smile down at her.

Gia might have been scared in the beginning, but she didn't let that stop her. She's read every book. She's researched every article and published study she could get her hands on. Not that any of that prepares you for the moment they hand over a living breathing human to you and expect you to know how to keep it alive. But she prepared for this baby in the best way she knew how. All the while taking classes for her degree and starting her own business. I'm not even sure she knows that I know about her photography business, but I've been paying attention. I've always paid attention to her. I'm so damn proud of her.

"I never doubted she would. Your mama is so strong, and you will be too because she's going to raise you. We're both going to raise you." I run my fingers over her soft hair. She's so tiny compared to my big hand.

"I need to make you a promise, Astria. My daddy left before I was born. He left before he ever saw me." My eyes fill with tears as I finally get to tell my daughter the words I've held in my heart for the last nine months. Words that she doesn't understand…but she will. I will show her.

"I promise that I will never leave you, baby girl. I promise that I will always be there for you. I will be your biggest fan in life. I will help you face every trial. Sure, I might let you fail a time or two. But I'll be there waiting for you at the end when you finally figure it out, and you will figure it out. I don't have all the answers, but I promise to try so damn hard for you." I rock back and forth rhythmically.

"Your mama, Gia, she's amazing. She's stubborn as hell, but she's…she's so good. The two of us go way back. We've been friends since, I guess, forever. This situation we've gotten ourselves into is kind of a weird one. Just issuing a fair warning. It might be chaotic, but I promise your mama and I are in this for the long haul." Gia murmurs something in her sleep and I hold my breath. I hope I haven't woken her. She rolls over with her eyes closed and her breathing evens out, and I'm finally able to relax back into my one-sided conversation again. I allow my heart rate to return to normal. I have to get this off my chest. I need her to know.

"I promise, Astria. You will remember me. I promise to be here with you until the day I die." A lone tear falls from my cheek and lands on her tiny fingers.

There was a saying my mama used to tell me growing

up – *don't put all your eggs in one basket*. That saying seems kind of silly in the wake of something this monumental. All my hopes and dreams are wrapped up in this tiny pink blanket. The moment that sweet baby whose been your every fear and every hope is thrust into your arms – every egg I ever had is here. My life is changed forever.

"I'm betting my future on you, Astria. I'm betting on a future with you…and with Gia. I'm all in. I promise to love you forever, sweet girl."

-o-
GIA

"Gia, baby, your brother's been sitting in the parking lot for hours." Mama paces the hardwood floor next to my hospital bed.

Astria and I should be discharged this afternoon, and then I can go home. I've never been so ready to be home. We've only had a handful of visitors, but even that feels like too much. I just want to be in my own space with Damien and our baby; just the three of us.

It's so strange to think that we're truly a family now.

I tuck Astria against my chest as she suckles on my sore breasts. My boobs hurt like a bitch. My poor vagina is never going to recover, I'm certain of it. Everything aches and hurts in places that no human should ever have to ache and hurt.

Ya know, it's amazing how quickly you forget all of those things the instant your baby looks up into your eyes, and you realize you did this - you created life. It's all worth it.

Or at least that's what I repeat over and over again every time she latches and unlatches. Dammit, man, boob pain was not in the owner's manual.

"No," I answer resolutely, looking up from Astria's sixth breakfast – or is it still dinner -to meet my mama's eyes.

This was his choice. I could be the bigger person. But I won't, I can't. I don't have it in me.

"No? You're serious? You won't at least let him…" Her voice trails off, but my resolve only strengthens.

I see the sadness building in her eyes, but it doesn't compare to the heartbreak I felt that day. Or the heartbreak I continue to feel every time I replay the events of that afternoon as if they were just last night.

Tyler is my big brother; I idolized him. He was the one person who was always supposed to have my back. And he didn't. I'm not ready to forgive him for that. He doesn't get a free pass because we share blood.

"Mama, I said no. Please respect my decision about this." I don't falter in my words. I don't hesitate. I knew this moment would come, and this decision is one that I'm certain of.

I'm responsible for the tiny human in my arms, and I won't allow a toxic environment to invade her peace.

"It's his niece, Gia. The two of you haven't spoken in months. Don't you think it's time you put this behind you and move on? For all of us? I can't stand this." She continues, and it bothers me that she won't let this go. This isn't her decision to make.

This is my baby. This is my family. This is my choice. I love my mama. I respect her opinion, but my family and my mental health come first.

"You weren't there, Mama. You weren't in that room. I'm sorry, but you can't understand where I'm coming from. And that's okay, but I need you to support my decision. This is my family, and if he can't support that, he's not welcome here. I will not have that kind of negativity around Astria." I try to maintain an even tone even though I can feel myself getting upset. I've read enough to know that Astria can feel my distress. I need to calm down.

"You know he meant no harm. This is my fault. Your brother was just trying to protect you. I should have never let him take on so much responsibility so young."

My heart sinks. This isn't her fault at all. She has to know that.

"What? No. Daddy died and we all had to pull together in our own way to get through it. We survived. Not to sound brash, but people die every day. That's no excuse for the hateful things Tyler said to me that day, or to Damien." I don't want to sound hateful, but it's not fair to use the death of our father as an excuse for Tyler's barbaric behavior.

I watch as Mama turns her attention from me to where Damien sits quietly in the rocking chair next to the bed. He hasn't left my side. A nurse came in to perform her checks just after sunrise, and Damien was asleep with Astria on his bare chest.

Something in my heart tightened at that moment. I don't know how to explain it, but the sight was so beautiful, so reassuring and calming that my chest physically ached with a feeling I'd never felt before.

His wide, rough hands held her against his chest with a gentle, yet secure touch. She looked so tiny but slept so peacefully.

My mama, bless her, she means well. She used to tell me that we get small glimpses into heaven throughout our lives. Tiny peeks. Reminders of the good in the world.

If I never get another moment like that, I'll know that was one of them.

"And you're okay with this, Damien? You're my son too, and Tyler is your brother. Is this what you want?"

My heart stalls as Damien's green eyes lock on mine. He leans forward, placing his elbows on his knees. I see the wheels turning. He's thinking, debating what to say. I hate that I've put him in this position. I never wanted him to have to choose between his best friend and this situation we've found ourselves in.

"Mama Patterson, you know I love you fiercely." He sighs, and I hold my breath, unsure of what he might say next. I hate that he's in a position to choose, but I'm selfish. I want him to choose us.

"You're right, Tyler is my brother. But this little girl means more to me than anything else in the entire world. I support Gia's decision. I will always back up my wife. I'm sorry, but that's just the way it is." He clasps his hands together with a finality that rocks me to my core. His words of support are surprising. They shouldn't be, this isn't the first time I've heard something similar. He's reassured me time after time over the past few months during my moments of weakness and doubt. But that's when we're alone, not to my mama's face.

Tears fill my eyes, and I try to blink them away quickly

before someone in the room notices. I swear, my hormones are still a jumbled mess.

"You know, Damien, you're a good man. Despite the fact that I disagree with the decision the two of you have made." She pauses before continuing. "Fine. You've said your piece. I'll send Jeff down to talk to him, but I want it known that I am not happy about any of this."

"Other than my grandbaby. I'm plum smitten with those sweet little cheeks. Give me that baby and let me get some sugar. She'll heal my broken heart. Won't you, Astria?" I kiss the top of Astria's head before lifting her gently and placing her in my mama's waiting arms.

"Don't be dramatic, Mama." I roll my eyes. I relax back into the most uncomfortable bed known to man, grateful to rest my aching body, if only for a second.

She ignores me completely; I knew she would. I know that she wants to make us hug it out and say we're sorry and move on, just like we did when we fought as kids. But this is so much bigger than *whose turn it is to sit in the front seat on a long car ride*.

I can't forget the things he said to me that day. I can't forget the horrible things he said to Damien. I'm not ready to forgive him, and I won't allow that type of toxic relationship into my life. Our lives are too fragile right now as it is.

I grab my camera from the wooden table next to my hospital bed as I hear my Mama begin speaking softly to Astria.

"Do you hear this nonsense, Astria? These kids think they know everything, I'm telling you. Don't you worry, baby. Don't fret your pretty little mind. You just wait and see. One day this family will heal, and it wouldn't surprise me one bit if it's you that brings them all back together." Damien stands and she eases into the rocking chair next to the bassinet we've yet to use. "You've got your Grandpapa's nose, you know that? And your mama's lips. But those eyes, your Daddy marked you good. Your Grandpapa is smiling down on you so big."

My chest tightens, and I grip my camera harder in my hands. Yes, he is, baby girl.

Click. Click Click. The only sound in the room is the echo of my camera lens. I snap photo after photo of my mama rocking my daughter, her granddaughter. Three generations together. That's the beautiful thing about art in print. I'll capture these images for a lifetime, and every time I look back at them, I will remember the love I feel in my heart. This is my peace.

I'll remember how hard I had to fight my own demons to get here, and every single reason why I will continue to fight against anything or anyone that might tarnish it.

CHAPTER SIX
GIA
Six months later

Sweat rolls down the crevice between the two giant milk jugs formerly known as my breasts, as I simultaneously bounce Astria on my hip and attempt to pull laundry out of the dryer. I've already restarted this thing on three separate occasions to shake the wrinkles out.

I'm thankful that we have a washer and dryer inside our apartment. I am thankful that we have a washer and dryer inside our apartment.

I repeat the words again. And I am truly thankful that I don't have to haul our laundry to and from the shared laundry space in the basement of our complex with a baby in tow. I'm just hot. And tired. And overwhelmed.

"Gia?" Damien chuckles as he says my name again, and I realize I haven't responded to him. I was lost in the sea of thoughts that run through my mind in a constant state of disarray. People always talk about *pregnancy* brain, but *mom* brain fog is a whole other level.

Astria coos and Damien scoops her into his arms. My hip continues to bounce on its own accord.

"How was practice?" I ask.

I finally look up at him. Mistake. Abort mission. My heart stutters. I think I have a heart murmur. I should really get that looked at. It's the strangest thing, though, because it only seems to happen when Damien's near me. Or in the other room in the shower. Or singing ridiculously off-key as he is giving Astria her bottle before laying her down at night.

His hair is still damp from his after-practice shower. It's knotted in a low ponytail at his neck, and his dirty blond curls look even more golden with the moisture that clings to them.

Astria's tiny hands grip at the v-neckline of his white t-shirt, but it doesn't appear to bother him in the least. His broad shoulders and chest stretch the thin cotton material, and I know what's underneath. And not just from the memory of our one night together. God, that seems like a lifetime ago. No, I know what's underneath because his favorite pastime is walking around our apartment without a shirt on.

It's torture.

Chiseled. Tan. Muscular.

Torture.

I know one thing with absolute certainty. I took our one night for granted. Because every single night we have lived together since, I've thought of all the things I wish I'd done – touched, explored, licked.

I shouldn't allow myself to even consider those things because I am fully aware of our agreement. I realize our relationship works so well *because* it's platonic. I'm cognizant enough to realize that I am having these weird thoughts and feelings because I desperately need to get laid. That's got to be it, I took a psychology class last semester for my general studies.

I'd say there are cobwebs down there at this point, but I know that's not true.

Stitches? Maybe. Scars? Sure. Loneliness? Definitely. But no cobwebs.

The weirdest part about that? I'm not lonely. Not at all. Actually, my life is the complete opposite of lonely; I'm never alone. My life is full; I have Astria and I have Damien. Not to mention the other wives that live in this building that have quickly become my friends, spouses of Damien's teammates, and their children. I didn't realize how many college athletes have wives and children until I became one of them. It's like we're our own little community. It's a community I've easily become a part of over the last several months.

Not to mention, I still have my camera, and I've never been lonely behind a lens.

Despite all of that, something is still missing. I'm just not sure what it is.

Damien drops his bag on top of the countertop and begins pulling out more dirty laundry with his free hand. When will it ever stop? How did adding a baby quadruple our laundry? It doesn't add up. Math has never been my strong suit, but I swear this defies all logic.

"Practice was good. I still have a few things I need to

work on, but Coach says we're ready."

He leans in and blows raspberries onto Astria's neck and the action elicits my favorite smile. It's the one she reserves only for her daddy. You carry a child for nine months, and you get no credit. She always saves the best smiles for Damien. *That smile.* I'm not even a little bitter about it. He makes me smile like that too, baby girl.

You read things about the bond between a daughter and her father, but this is different. It's sacred. I wonder if I had this kind of bond with my dad. I'm sure I did, but I can't remember, and that breaks my heart a little. I hope Astria always knows how much she's loved.

"It's a good thing, season starts next week," I smirk as I fold Damien's briefs into the basket on the floor.

It should seem weird, folding a man's underwear right next to my black lace panties, but it doesn't faze me anymore. We're a team. We wash our laundry together. Our dishes go into the same dishwasher. We share meals. The only thing we don't share is a bed.

My bed is set up in Astria's nursery. It makes the most sense. I'm still breastfeeding. I've got that part of motherhood down to a science. Things are so much smoother now that my nipples have basically gone numb. Doctor Google says that the sensation will return eventually. I have my doubts.

When Astria wakes up hungry in the middle of the night, I roll over, pick her up and she latches. Half the time I'm not sure I ever fully wake up. We're a well-oiled milk production machine, and it works. Everyone sleeps-*ish*.

"Are you coming?" Damien smiles at Astria as he asks

me a question I've been avoiding for weeks.

I miss photographing hockey. I miss getting shots for the love of it. I took the summer off from taking classes after Astria was born, but now that we're both back into the swing of things, I've barely found any time to get out and behind the camera for me. And I love photographing sports, even though I'm not a huge fan of the actual sports themselves. I love the details. I love the spray of the ice. The droplets of sweat. The look of drive and intensity in the eyes of an athlete just before they make the game-winning shot.

Astria is still so young. I've left her at the childcare center on campus while I attend classes a few times, but for the most part Damien and I have adjusted our schedules this semester so that one of us is with her at all times. I'm not sure I'm ready to leave her with anyone else yet. Just the thought makes my stomach roll uneasily.

"I don't know, Damien. She's still so small, and her little immune system isn't fully built up yet. I mean, I know she goes to the childcare center some, but if she gets sick, I'll miss class because you can't miss a game. Who would we leave her with? Would it cost money? I just…"

I stumble as I try to put what I'm feeling into words until Damien interrupts me with his calm reassuring voice.

"It's okay, I promise. I understand." He stares into my eyes, and I know he gets it. Without another word from me, he knows. "If you change your mind, you promise you'll let me know?" His smile doesn't falter.

"I promise." I close the dryer and stare over his

shoulder at the dishes in the sink that sit taunting me. At least Damien's here now. Help is here, and suddenly everything seems less daunting. His presence is comforting. He's so much more than I could have ever anticipated.

I take a step toward the sink, but Damien maneuvers his large frame into my path.

"No." He stops me in my tracks with a single word.

"What?" I ask, now irritated that he's impeding my progress.

"Don't even look at those dishes." He shakes his head back and forth as he begins bouncing Astria on his hip mimicking my movements from earlier.

My eyes dart around the apartment we share. It's not dirty or disorganized, it's lived in. This is our home base, and the dishes in the sink and the toys on the floor just mean that we're doing life here together. I'm fine with the daily chaos, but I need to reset before I can rest at night. I won't sleep knowing I've left things undone.

"Damien, you know I can't go to bed with a mess. You know this about me. I just need to wash the dishes and pick up the playmat, and then…" I count off my mental list of things that still need to be done before I can blissfully collapse into bed but am interrupted before I can finish.

"Nope." His large hand lands on my shoulder and he turns my body in the opposite direction with an easy movement that makes my skin tingle beneath his touch. "You are going to waltz right on into that bathroom and run a tub full of steaming hot water. You're going to sprinkle those delicious smelling salts that you love so much in there, and then you're going to stay until your toes wrinkle."

A hot bath does sound so glorious when he says it that way, but my brief fantasy is quickly interrupted by my to-do list. Sleep is at the top of my priority list and those things all stand between me and my bed.

"What about everything else that needs to be done?" I huff, mad that I almost got my hopes up about a hot bath.

"Astria and I have it covered." I glance back at him over my shoulder, and my heart melts. "We're going to do the dishes. I'll give her a quick bath in the sink and get her all ready for bed. I'll get her things picked up out here."

"But…" I start.

"The only butt I'm interested in is your naked one in that bathtub." I feel my face flush, and I hope he doesn't notice. I know he's kidding.

He pushes my shoulder gently until I take a step toward our shared bathroom.

"Well, when you say it like that. How can I argue?" I try not to think too much about his comment as I smile over my shoulder and I walk away, snatching a clean folded towel from the laundry basket on my way out. I put a little extra sway in my hips because this is what my life has come to. Flirting with a man that I can't ever have.

If this man thinks for one second, I won't use the image of his chiseled jawline and the heat in his gaze the moment I sink into that hot water, he's dead wrong. I'm shameless. This Mama's got needs too.

CHAPTER SEVEN
DAMIEN

"Don't look at me like that."

Astria smiles her gummy little grin up at me, and I know it's a match to the goofy grin on my face.

I'm an idiot. I know it. Astria knows it; that's why she's silently judging me in a way only a six-month-old baby can. And Gia knows it.

"You think the comment about her butt was too much? Crap, her booty. Don't say butt, Astria, it's a bad word. Shit. Don't say crap either. Okay, let's stop now and pretend this conversation never happened. We'll let this be our little secret." I take a deep breath and turn to the sink full of dishes with our daughter seated solidly on my hip. I send up a silent prayer that *shit* is not the first word out of our daughter's mouth.

I work through the motions of cleaning the kitchen and picking up Astria's toys, and I use every tactic of distraction I can think of to not imagine Gia's naked body soaking in a hot bathtub just a few feet away.

One wall. That's all that separates us. That damn wall. It's the story of my life. There's always something standing between us. Age. Tyler. A mutual agreement, also referred to as our signed marriage certificate, to remain platonic and co-parent our daughter. And that wall. I guess, in a way, it's symbolic of our relationship.

Don't get me wrong, I love having them here. I love sharing our space. The transition to co-parenting was so much easier than even I thought it would be. It feels less like the formal obligation that it sounds like, and kind of like a real family.

Gia and I work together seamlessly. We laugh over dinner. We work as a team to get the housework done, both realizing when the other person needs a break. We respect each other and communicate openly.

About everything except the one thing I can't tell her. Because if I tell her that she's the first person I see in my mind when I wake up in the mornings and the last person I imagine before falling asleep in an empty bed every night I'll ruin everything.

I can't tell her that I wish it was my bed that she lays her head down in each night.

I can't tell her how fucking adorable she looks in the silk hat she lovingly refers to as her bedtime bonnet.

I can't tell her that every fucking time I hear her in the shower my dick gets hard.

I definitely can't tell her that I love the sound of her voice when she calls me just to check in or that I wish more than anything she'd come watch one of my games.

Not just be there to take photographs, but be there for me, wearing my number on her back.

It's never been my number. Even when we were kids, she always wore T's number.

Astria babbles and I'm pulled from my thoughts. An abrupt reminder of why I have to keep my feelings on lock. It's normal. What I'm feeling is normal. Any man in my position would feel this way about the mother of his child. Right? I'm biologically programmed to want her. It doesn't mean I can have her.

Actually, it means the opposite.

I can't have her.

I smile to myself knowing that as long as I get to keep them both in my life one way or another that's all that matters. I can live with that. The alternative is something I don't want to ever have to be faced with considering.

I take Astria to the room she shares with Gia and begin her bedtime routine. She's getting restless, and I move faster, grabbing up a diaper and a package of wipes, realizing I'm holding a ticking time bomb. We're seconds away from the world imploding. There's nothing like trying to put to bed a baby that's already crossed the line into being over-tired.

I lay her down on the changing table and proceed to change her diaper and get her into the sleeper Gia's already laid out for her for the night.

When she starts to cry, I sing a Rolling Stones song to her that my mama used to sing to me. The lyrics seem relevant. It's a good reminder for me that I need to focus my priorities on the things that I do have. I have a good life, a nearly perfect life. I have everything that I need regardless of the things that my heart wants.

Astria's cries slow to a soft whimper by the time I'm finished dressing her for bed. I pull her up to my chest, softly bouncing her, but stop abruptly when I notice Gia leaning against the doorframe of the bedroom with nothing but a small white towel wrapped around her lean frame.

She may as well be naked. She's so beautiful it hurts, and now I'm contemplating the true definition of need versus want.

"Please, don't stop on my account." She smiles broadly, her words just above a whisper so as to not get Astria worked up again.

"I...um...I think she's ready to eat and then go to bed." I swallow and try to regain my composure. I look at the floor, the ceiling, the diaper pail, anywhere other than the nearly naked woman standing just a few feet away from me. Keep it together, Henderson.

Gia pushes off of the wall and walks toward me. Her hair is pulled up into a yellow scrunchie on top of her head, wild dark brown tendrils fall around her face like a halo. The impure thoughts I'm having about her in this towel are anything but holy.

"Good, I'll feed her before I get dressed and then you can lay her down if you want?" She reaches to take Astria from me.

"Sure, I'll just go get ready for..." I rock back on my heels, preparing to make my exit. They need privacy and I need to go hide my semi-hard cock before it gets me into trouble.

"Stay." Gia places her hand gently on my forearm. I

immediately look to where her skin connects with mine, and I know I'd do whatever she asks of me. My need to satisfy this woman clearly knows no bounds. Self-preservation be damned.

"Are you sure I won't be a distraction?" My eyes remain locked on the way her fingertips send tiny bolts of lightning shooting erratically beneath my skin.

"No, she's exhausted. She didn't nap much today. Look at her, she's asleep already. She'll dream feed, and then you can give her some snuggles before you lay her down. Your early class is tomorrow, right?"

She pulls her hand away and I feel the loss of warmth throughout my entire body. I try to shake it off. This isn't unusual. This level of comfort between us is normal. I'm the one making this into something it's not. Don't be weird, man. Do not be weird.

"Yeah, and I've got to be at the rink early. I picked up an extra shift."

I pick up every shift they'll give me. The exhaustion in Gia's eyes doesn't go unnoticed by me. I want to do whatever I can to provide a comfortable life for Gia and Astria. That starts now. I wake up every day and work to fulfill the silent promises I've made to both of them. I hope that we'll look back on the days when we shared a bathroom in a small apartment on campus with a smile. This is just the beginning. I want to give them the world.

"Sit. Tell me about your day. I feel like I haven't seen you in ages." She nods to the neatly made bed that she sleeps in at night. As if I needed another reason to think about her in bed.

I take a seat on the edge of the purple quilted

comforter and pray she can't see the way my dick presses up against the zipper of my jeans. This is not the time.

She sits in the rocking chair adjacent to me with Astria in her arms, crossing her legs and allowing the towel to split on either side exposing miles of long silky brown skin.

So smooth. I want to run my hand up the apex of her thighs and see if her skin is as soft as it looks.

With one flick of her hand where the towel is knotted at her chest, the material releases, and her breasts are out on full display. My mouth waters. I fucking stare like a deer caught in the headlights of oncoming traffic.

I have no strength left. I'm weak. So, fucking weak for this woman.

Her breasts are more than a handful. They're full and tight. Her nipples are a deep shade of purple. I couldn't look away if I wanted to. I'm a fucking barbarian.

This isn't the first time I've seen her nurse, Astria. There's nothing sexual about the ability of a mother to feed her child. It's natural. It's an accomplishment to be celebrated and proud of, not sexualized.

Doesn't change the fact that the woman sitting in front of me is the sexiest woman I've ever seen.

Despite what I know, what I feel is entirely different. As Gia sits in front of me with her breasts exposed so openly, I can't help but be in awe of her beauty. She feeds and nourishes our child in a way that I can't, and over the last six months, I haven't heard her complain once about it. She just…does it. She's a boss.

"You said you have some things to work on?" Gia's soft question as Astria begins to nurse breaks me from my trance. I look up to find a knowing, crooked smile on her plump lips.

"Huh?" I stumble, unable to get my thoughts together quickly enough to answer coherently. I swear, this woman reduces me to a cliché at best.

"Earlier. When you got home from practice. You said that you've got some things to work on. From what I'm hearing through the *mom*-vine, you're having an amazing start to the season. What are you working on?" She doesn't miss a beat, and I welcome the easy conversation.

I'm so happy that she's formed friendships with the other spouses. We're not a big team, and this is college, most of my teammates are still single. There's only a small group of women here, and they don't welcome newcomers into their circle easily.

Gia met most of them when she was still pregnant with Astria. They allowed her in without hesitation. She's easy to love. Even when she insists, she's better hiding behind a camera lens.

Tonight is real. This is our life. Discussing our day. Debriefing with each other. Talking about things that aren't just parenting.

"Precision. Speed. Agility." I think back to the things I discussed with Coach tonight. Our team looks good as a whole going into the season. We're still a relatively new team, but we're starting to drum up some chatter. Rumor is, we might even get some scouts from the big leagues this season.

I'm the goalie. The buck stops with me. It's a lot of pressure, but it's the type of pressure I thrive off of. I need that pressure to drive me. As long as I'm working harder and smarter than my opponents, I'm winning. Losing isn't an option.

She lifts her eyebrow slightly. "So, you're aiming for perfection, then?"

"Something like that." I shrug it off because she's not wrong.

Perfection is what it takes to get called up to the next level. Even if I only get a few years. I should make enough with signing that we'll have a comfortable life. I don't want wealth and mansions. I want comfort and happiness.

I don't want Gia to struggle if something happens to me. We did this together, we're in it together. I want their future secured no matter what our future looks like.

"You know, I happen to know a little girl that's going to grow up thinking you're pretty great." Gia smiles down at Astria and my heart melts into a puddle in my chest.

"Yeah?" My lip curls up at the corner as I watch them together.

"Mhmmmm." She hums as she rocks slowly back and forth.

"And what do you think?" I tilt my head to the side and ask a question I have no business asking.

"Me? Doesn't matter." She answers honestly, but I can't let it go that easily even though I should.

I run my hand absently over the stubble on my jawline. "You're my best friend, Gia," I admit openly.

"By default." There's that eyebrow lift again. "Your best friend was my brother. I'm basically him with a vagina."

My eyes widen to the size of saucers. I choke on my

own saliva. I sputter and cover my mouth with my hand before I speak too loudly and wake up our peaceful daughter.

"For the love of God. Never say that again." I shout in a loud whisper.

I run my hand down my face, still not believing she'd say something so…so brash. And dammit, why am I now thinking about her vagina. My line of thought is completely fucked up.

Gia's shoulders begin to shake. Her nose crinkles and her eyes close to near slits as she tries and fails to hold herself together. The more her body shakes with her laughter, the less skin her towel covers. Tears roll down her cheeks. She's all but naked at this point. I'm dying a slow death.

Fucking.

Hell.

"What's so funny? Get yourself under control, woman. You're going to blind Astria with milk to the eyeball." I focus on our daughter, and not my naked wife.

Astria somehow manages to continue eating her meal through an apparent dead sleep all the while her mother laughs at my attempt at an honest and open conversation, only proving what I already know, she sees our relationship as purely friendship.

She sucks in air and tugs the towel over her exposed thigh, which only pulls material from covering another piece of skin. I can't win.

"Are you done?" I ask.

I'm annoyed with myself. I shouldn't allow it to get to me, but it does. I begged for this. We're in this situation because I put us in it. It's no one's fault but my own, and now I get to suffer the consequences.

She sighs, "Oh, God. The look on your face was priceless. Why am I never prepared with my camera when I need it the most? We could have framed that one for the living room."

Using her free hand, she fans the tears that mark her face.

"I'm glad you find my discomfort so amusing."

Gia shifts Astria from one breast to the other in one fluid motion, never waking her.

"I'm sorry. You and I both know T and I are two totally different people. I was kidding. I apologize. And, as an aside, Astria's fast asleep, but breast milk is totally safe for her eyes. I actually put it in there regularly when she wakes up and they're crusted over with sleep." She shrugs and I feel the skin between my eyes pucker as I try to decipher what medical voodoo she speaks of.

"You put boob milk in our daughter's eyeballs?" I wonder aloud.

Seriously? That's a thing? Where have I been when this has been happening?

"Yeah. I do. Want some for your eyes? It's great for dry skin too. Got an earache? It'll cure that too." She counts off cures for ailments like they're common knowledge.

"Shut up. Seriously? We should be bottling that stuff up." I halfway tease, but can't stop myself from wondering why this isn't advertised more. I had no idea breastmilk was a miracle cure-all.

"And that sir, is illegal."

"Huh. There's still so much I need to learn." I make a mental note to step up my breastfeeding research. What else is there that I don't know?

"Tell me about it. We're doing a good job winging this parenting thing though, right? I mean, she's pretty spectacular." Gia supports Astria's head as she unlatches in a sleepy blissful state of what I like to refer to as *milk drunk*. A light stream of off-white liquid trickles from the crease in the corner of her tiny, puckered lips.

"Yeah, she's pretty spectacular." I stare at my two girls, they're so perfect…*both* of them. I never could have imagined this life.

I stand and walk to where Gia sits, lifting Astria from her arms. I pull her into my chest and inhale the sweet scent of innocence from her hair. I try to soak in this moment with them. I want them all. Every single moment.

"Just like her Mama," I say under my breath as I turn and lay our daughter down gently into her crib.

CHAPTER EIGHT
GIA
One-ish years later

"**A**stria! No ma'am. Give it back. *Now.*" I emphasize the last word using my very best mom voice.

It's amazing how naturally that tone comes. I thought for sure I'd have to watch YouTube videos or something to teach myself all the tricks of the trade, but that's not the case, the minute I need it it's there, sounding so similar to my mother that I almost fear for my own life when I hear myself.

Astria pauses mid-crime with the contraband in question, a book about a construction worker and a magical hotdog named Larry. We stare at each other, a silent battle of wills, where she determines at a mere eighteen months of age whether or not her theft is worth the potential consequences of her actions. Do the crime, do the *time-out* chick.

"It's fine, really. Camden needs to learn to share. I'm

sure he deserved it. That boy is his father made over. He's so *damn* stingy with his toys." I watch Sylvia from the corner of my eye as she mouths the word damn behind her hand while I continue to stare down at my own mini-tyrant with the most threatening face I can conjure.

Camden, who is two, takes advantage of Astria's apparent distraction and snatches his book back. Astria stomps her foot in his direction, but then gives up and picks up a toy truck from the floor. The two seemingly forget their disagreement and begin playing like nothing ever happened.

"Carter? Stingy?" I angle my body toward Sylvia where we sit on the couch in her living room.

Carter Tolar is the starting Center for the Rafferton Rams. It's the same position T plays. Carter's a senior this year. Carter and Sylvia were high school sweethearts that married just as soon as they could legally do so. Together, they have one son, Camden, who has become somewhat of a best friend/playmate to Astria.

Sylvia went through a six-month technical program and became a licensed cosmetologist as soon as they got married. The woman is a magician with a hot oil treatment. I won't let anyone else near my hair. She's the sole reason I no longer have to braid it and can allow it to live out it's best life in its natural state. Otherwise, I look like I was trapped outside in a hurricane with a faulty electric transformer, and I was *not* the last man standing.

They live in the same building as we do, and Camden attends the same childcare center Astria does. Sylvia was the first woman to befriend me when we moved in.

She's kind of the leader of the pack when it comes to

the other wives. We're a small group. This year is a big year for Carter. He transferred here right after the birth of their son. The team was brand new. If he's going to get picked up without having to go to a small farm team, this is his year. He's got a lot riding on it.

"Mhmmm. I'm his favorite toy, and that man does not share." She smiles slyly.

I would be a big fat liar if I said I wasn't completely jealous of what they have.

Damien and I keep to ourselves when it comes to the details of our relationship. We've learned that it's better to say nothing. People assume we're just private, and we are. But not for the reasons they might think. It helps that our schedules are totally opposite because we're constantly juggling Astria between work and attending classes.

We've found our rhythm now. Life is getting a little easier, if there is such a thing. Either that or we've just gotten used to the weight of the world constantly sitting on our shoulders.

Astria is no longer attached to my breasts. That in itself has offered me freedom that at the time I didn't realize I missed. She attends the childcare center more now, which gives me more time to work on my schoolwork. I was able to take on a full load this semester, and still manage to have time to continue to build my online photography platform.

"Trust me, I have seen the way that man looks at you. I get hot just thinking about it." I fan my face with the travel pack of baby wipes that sits in my lap, ready to go to war with whatever mess these two can conjure up at a moment's notice. I make it a rule to never leave the house without them.

Sylvia brushes me off. "Please, like Damien doesn't look at you the same way." She rolls her eyes, and a wave of sadness hits me out of nowhere like a ton of bricks. People see what they want to see.

"Yeah." I smile, but it doesn't crease the corners of my eyes. I'm a fraud.

"Seriously, girl wake up, your husband is so gone for you it's not even funny. And the way he brags on you constantly? Please." She pushes, and the words of truth bubble up into my throat.

How long has it been since I've been able to share any part of my life with anyone other than Damien? My own mother doesn't know the truth about our marriage.

Damien was right, it works. We're co-parenting Astria, and she lives a happy and full life. But at what cost? I'm losing myself. Every day, another piece of me is chipped away.

I'm mom. I'm student. I'm Damien's best friend.

I've lost me...I've lost Gia, and I'm not sure I'll be able to find her again.

"So, are you traveling with them this weekend?" Sylvia's question takes me by surprise because it's not something I even considered.

"As in, three days from now?"

I never travel with the team. Ever. I'd have to leave Astria behind, and the season is almost over. We've almost made it through a second one, and somehow this is still working.

And the game this weekend...well, it's one I've been

trying to pretend was never going to happen. This isn't just any game. It's *the* game.

"Obviously, it's a huge game for them!" Sylvia echoes my thoughts, but not in the same way. "The Chambliss Lions are legendary for their hockey team! If our boys beat them…this could be it. This could be everything Carter has been working toward. Gah, that man works so hard. I just…I want him to see his dreams come true. You know? Of course, you know. I'm sure you feel the same way about Damien." Sylvia bounces on the couch next to me with excitement that I just can't conjure up.

Tyler and Damien are going to be on the same ice again. Sylvia's not wrong. This game is huge, and I already know how stressed Damien is about keeping his emotions under control. He's been brooding about it for days already. The tension in our apartment is enough to suffocate an elephant.

I've got this nagging voice in the back of my head telling me that he needs me. But why? How? In what capacity? He hasn't come right out and said it, not in those words exactly.

I mean, he asks me to go to every game. Always. But we have an agreement about traveling, and we're both on the same page about leaving Astria with anyone overnight. Neither one of us are comfortable with that yet.

When do you get comfortable with that as a parent? Just the thought makes me feel sick to my stomach.

"I think I'm going to stay back. I need to stay with Astria, and…" I start.

"Girl stop. When was the last time you had a date with

your husband?" A date. Um.

Control your face, Gia. Control your face. This is basically your only female friend, be cool.

"It's been a while." I watch Camden and Astria play with trucks on the floor in front of us with an intensity that isn't warranted for a playdate with toddlers.

"A while as in last month?" She pushes, and I can't help but get annoyed with her. I'm immediately defensive. How is it any of her business? This is my relationship. Or lack thereof.

"Maybe a touch longer." My shoulders stiffen, as I feel myself begin to physically close off from the conversation. I'm alienating myself. I have to protect our family and our secrets.

"Last year?" She pushes a little bit more, and I dig my fingernail into the side of my palm in a failed attempt to check my temper.

"You know, I don't remember exactly." I pop off with more attitude than I intend.

"You don't remember? You don't remember the last time you and Damien were actually alone together?"

My hands curl into fists. Who is she to judge to my marriage?

"It's not a big deal, okay? We both agreed to make sacrifices while Astria was young. This is just another sacrifice. It's a means to a bigger goal. It's a decision we made, together, for our family." I hate the words as I say them. Because, while they're true, they hurt. Somewhere buried deep beneath the words of sacrifice and grown-up decisions is a woman that just wants to be seen as someone other than a mom, a friend, or worse – a little sister.

"Can I be honest with you, Gia?" Sylvia sighs, and I dread whatever it is that she's about to say next.

"I'd rather you weren't." I roll my eyes and lean back into the couch, glaring at the ceiling tiles above my head.

"We're friends. Whether you like it or not." I'm going with *not* right at this moment. "You can sit there and close yourself off from me all you want, but friend to friend...you need an *o*. It's written all over your face. I know how hard it is to get alone time with the tiny *o-blockers*. Trust me, it takes some creativity. I'm offering you the weekend. Two nights alone with your man in a hotel room. I'm not taking no for an answer."

Two nights alone with Damien? I can't say the thought of spending even one night alone with him in the same bed hasn't crossed my mind, a time or...thirteen thousand four hundred and sixty-two.

"You make it sound so glamorous." I exaggerate.

"Marriage isn't glamorous. You know that. But sometimes we just need to get dirty in a hotel room and remember what it was like before we swapped out our name for Mama. You know? Keep the arguments clean and the sex dirty, it's the only way to survive this thing."

No. I don't know what any of those things feel like.

"So, you're saying if I say no, you'll kidnap my child? Is that what I'm hearing?" I cross my arms over my chest, refusing to allow myself to consider the possibility.

"Semantics. Take the offer, Gia." She demands.

Honestly, I trust Sylvia. A tiny thought begins to take hold somewhere in the deep recesses of my brain.

I could take my camera and my laptop and get a ton

of work done over those forty-eight hours of freedom. I wouldn't have to worry about keeping another human alive. I wouldn't have to make snacks. I could sleep in. I could get my own hotel room, and there will be no one to wake me up in the middle of the night demanding a drink with no words, just blood-curdling shrieks.

"Why aren't you going?" I volley the question back in her direction.

"I can't. I'm totally booked up at the salon on Friday. Don't worry, though. I'll take the kids to their regular playgroup at the center while I work. Afterward, I'll pick them up and bring them back here. It'll give Camden someone to play with while Carter is away. What's going from one to two? They'll occupy each other. Actually, it's the perfect solution."

Perfect, for who exactly? I don't even know if Damien would go along with it.

"I don't know." I chew on my lip, unsure as to why I'm even considering this. Damn peer pressure is what this is.

"Just think about it, okay?" She eases off just slightly, but I hear what she's not saying.

"Or else you'll kidnap my child." I finish for her, knowing her exact intentions. She means well, but she can't understand what she doesn't know. She has no idea. Nobody does.

"I didn't say that." She bats her eyelashes at me innocently, and I know she's teasing. I appreciate her friendship, and her advice, even if it is unwarranted and misplaced.

Sure, it sounds like a great idea, but it just won't work.

CHAPTER NINE
DAMIEN

I slip my key into the lock and slowly open the door to our apartment. I stayed late after practice tonight to work on tightening a few things heading into our games this weekend, but not so late that I'll miss bedtime.

Fucking Chambliss. I knew if our season was as good as everyone was predicting we'd end up here eventually, but I tried not to focus on that. I knew if I let it get into my head early on, it'd affect my game. So, I pushed that knowledge to the side and continued to work my ass off for my team. We're all working our asses off, and we're so close.

Nobody knows my connection to Tyler Patterson, starting center for the Chambliss Lions. They don't know he's Gia's brother. They don't know that we may as well be brothers. They sure as fuck don't know that he hates me with the ferocity of a thousand angry hornets.

I know he's bringing that shit to the ice, and that

knowledge has been weighing on me heavily this week. We head out tomorrow, and it's my job to keep my emotions in check. I have to be the bigger man. I have everything to lose and nothing to gain by starting shit on the ice with Tyler.

I smile to myself when I hear the music of a familiar show playing on the television. Astria's giggles are loud and joyful. The sound immediately eases the building tension in my shoulders. Honestly, I'm feeling better after my practice today than I have all week. I'm resolved in my ability to do this. I know our team can pull off a win. I'm confident.

I see Gia's reflection in the mirror that hangs in our living room, as she picks up toys and places them into a basket.

I close the door behind me gently. I slowly bend and place my bag down on the floor remaining as quiet as I possibly can. I'm a voyeur in my one home, but I'm not ready to interrupt them just yet. I kick off my sneakers and walk on just the balls of my sock-covered feet as I inch my way near the living room.

I pause near the wall that separates our kitchen from the living space. I take a minute to study her, while she doesn't know I'm watching. She mumbles to herself, probably running through the list of things she thinks she needs to do before bedtime. She's the hardest-working woman I know. Somehow, she balances everything, and she makes it all look effortless when I know it's anything but.

She bends down to pick up Astria's favorite blanket, just a few feet away from me. She's so damn pretty. I don't know who to credit for the invention of leggings, but damn if the black leggings she wears don't hug every single curve of her hips. She wears a cream-colored tank top that barely contains her ample breasts. With each movement, they nearly topple from the top, and send my heart racing.

Her skin is radiant. Her hair is pulled up into a scrunchie on top of her head. I want to tug that scrunchie out and watch it fan out around her.

She's my best friend, but she's more than that. So much more than that. We might be two independent people working together for a common goal, but what she doesn't realize? In my quest for our independence, I became dependent on her. I'm dependent on waking up to her brewing coffee for us every morning. I'm dependent on watching her rock our daughter at night. I'm dependent on her soft laughs at my teasing and her long rants about the gaps in humanity.

I'm an addict. Our co-parenting has turned into my co-dependence, and I don't know if I can see a future without my girls in it. To hell with a five-year plan, I want forever, and that line of thinking is terrifying.

Gia steps into my space, without knowing it. Her scent invades my senses and fills me with contentment. It's now or never.

"Honey! I'm home." I call out as I swoop in, catching her from behind and wrapping her in my arms.

She squeals and immediately pulls her arms up into defensive mode, but it's too late, I've got her.

"Oh, my God! Damien!" She half-heartedly tries to elbow me and fails. I wrap my arms around her and tuck her body into mine.

"How are my girls today?" I lift her off her feet and twirl her in a circle before placing her back down again and releasing her.

"You could have asked that without scaring the living, breathing life out of me." She pops her hip out, and places her hand on her chest, heaving to catch her breath.

I watch the rise and fall of her breasts, with a hunger that I can never truly satisfy. I've been starving for years.

"But then who would save you? Nah, I like scaring you. Then, I can be the one to swoop in and save you. It's the best of both worlds. I'm the hero. Isn't that right, Astria baby?" I glance over Gia's shoulder as our daughter watches us with a brief fascination before turning back to her show.

Gia's eyes dance with humor as she smiles up at me. I dart in before she can stop me and place a platonic kiss on her cheek.

The kiss is friendly enough. It's not the first time I've kissed her over the last year or so. I steal a kiss here, a touch there. The stolen moments are all I have. Those moments are the only thing keeping me from losing my damn mind.

The taste of her skin on my lips widens my smile. I feel lighter with each moment that passes between us.

"What's got you all giddy? This morning you were pissed at the coffee for not being strong enough. Last night it was the hot water, not being hot enough." She's not wrong.

I've been a brooding asshole lately, but it has nothing to do with them, and everything to do with me.

"Nothing, I had a good practice today. And I get to come home to the two most beautiful girls in the whole world." It's the truth. I might be an asshole some days, but I'm a lucky asshole and I know it.

Gia eyes me suspiciously before stepping into me and placing the back of her hand on my forehead.

"Um, Click, what are you doing?" I don't move. I'll take any reason for her skin to touch mine.

"Checking your temperature. Are you sick? Did you take candy from a stranger?"

I chuckle to myself as she slowly removes her hand.

I lift my hand and wrap my fingers around her wrist before she can pull away completely.

"No, I'm fine. I just…I was thinking about some things today, and I guess it sort of put my thoughts into perspective. I've been living inside of my head too much. I've been bringing home my stress about this weekend…about my game in general. It's not fair to you or to Astria. Dealing with my broody ass wasn't part of our agreement." I shrug it off.

"Booty." She doesn't hesitate to correct me even though Astria is very clearly preoccupied again behind her, smiling and laughing contently at her show.

"Right, my broody booty." I tug her body to mine with her wrist. I continue to smile like a damn jackass.

She falls into me easily, laughing at the silliness of my words. It's all part of parenthood. The made-up curse words on the fly are some of my favorites.

"Has your broody booty eaten dinner? I can make you a sandwich." She props her chin on my chest and looks up at me with thoughtful brown eyes.

It's funny how something like making a sandwich can make you go all warm and tingly on the inside. I want to tell her that there are a million things I'd rather eat right now than a sandwich, but I don't think that would be appropriate. Especially since our daughter is just a few feet from where we stand.

My hand rests on her lower back, and it takes every ounce of my strength not to allow it to travel lower. Pregnancy and childbirth only made this woman's body sexier, and her curvy backside is no exception to that.

"That's okay, you've done enough today. I'll make something when I get done packing. We're leaving out early tomorrow, and I'd rather have everything ready tonight."

We fly out in the morning. We normally travel by bus, but Chambliss is too far, and this is a big game for us. Coach booked us flights, which is a luxury we don't typically get. The alumni support for an up-and-coming hockey team is severely lacking.

"You sure? You know how good I am with a turkey sandwich. I've got a reputation with meat. They know me by name at the deli counter." She wiggles beneath my hand, and I pray she can't feel the inappropriate things she's doing to me through the thin material that separates us. I know how good she is with *all* meat. That's the problem. I can't fucking forget. Maybe I need to have a talk with the butcher at our local market.

I clear my throat and try not to say anything that I'll have to explain away later.

"I'm sure, let me get my things together and I'll come lay Astria down for bed, I want to put her to bed tonight since I'll be gone this weekend." I pause her wrist still in my hand. "You sure you won't come watch me?"

I throw out the question as a last-ditch effort. I know she's not coming. She won't travel with Astria, and she won't travel without her. It's fine. It was all part of our agreement. Doesn't matter. I ask her every single game anyway. Truth be known? It's kind of become a superstition for me.

Astria is getting older, but I don't want to remind Gia of that for multiple reasons. One, I don't want to admit that my little girl is growing up too quickly. And two, I don't want Gia to put an expiration date on our arrangement. I'm not ready for that conversation. I convinced her to stay once. I'm not sure how I'd manage to do it again without admitting how I truly feel. Which is what? Conflicted? Is it lust? Is it love by proximity? Or have I somehow managed to truly fall in love with my wife – my best friend?

I am already well aware of the obvious answer to the aforementioned questions, and that does nothing but create more problems. I'm a solutions guy. Problems don't fit with the plan.

"You never give up, do you?" She bats her long black eyelashes up at me.

"It's a big game." My voice sounds rough for no reason at all.

I'd love to have her there with me, but I don't want to throw fuel on an already smoldering flame. If Tyler found out she was there with me…I don't want to think about what might happen. I can't put the team at risk like that. I can't put her at risk. He would never hurt her physically, but emotionally – I'm not sure what seeing him after all this time would do to her.

"Don't remind me. You heard from, T?" She asks casually, like she's reading my mind. Honestly, given the trainwreck happening in my brain tonight, it's a good thing she can't.

"The better question is, have you? I know he tried to call."

Tyler hasn't stopped trying to reach out. He calls every so often. If Gia doesn't want to talk to him, we won't. If I don't have her back, who will? She's the mother of my child. I was in the room with them the day everything went down, and I don't know how you heal from that level of heartbreak. He broke her. He broke her and she and I had to work like hell to put the pieces back together. I don't know if I'll ever be able to forgive him for that.

"And you know how I feel about that. I'm not ready." Her eyes widen, but she knows I'd never betray her trust. We're solid.

"I respect that." I nod, as I look down at her with a seriousness that I know she understands.

"You're a good man, Damien. You know that?" She turns her head and lays her cheek against my chest. I hold her to me and place my chin on the top of her head. Her wild curls tickle my nose. I savor having her in my arms. I wish I could hold her like this forever.

"You're making me blush." I tease as I smile into her hair.

"Don't let it go to your head, big boy." I can feel her smile against my chest.

"Big boy? You like em' big don't you, Click?" The

words are out of my mouth before I even realize what I'm saying. My mind races with the implications of what I've said. This could go so many different ways.

I brace for her reaction, but she surprises me. She laughs…hard. She giggles and snorts until Astria joins in behind her. The sound of their laughter is contagious. Before I know it, we're all doubling over in laughter together. Gia's body shakes in my arms with joy, and Astria's toothy grin is the cutest image I think I've ever seen.

These are the moments that I know we've made the right decision. This is why I can't mess this up with my own feelings.

I want to keep them. I *have* to keep them.

CHAPTER TEN
GIA

Big boy. Really? I can't believe I called Damien a *big boy*. I need a social media break. At least he laughed about it. That was my only saving grace.

"You were laughing at me too, weren't you girlie?" I help Astria into her pajamas. She chats away, mumbling things, half of which I do not understand.

I can't stop thinking about the text Sylvia sent me earlier today, reminding me of her offer to keep Astria for the weekend.

I would need to leave tomorrow. It's too soon. I'm not packed. I'd have to pack Astria.

It wouldn't work.

But…he did ask me to come.

Who am I kidding? He always asks me to come. He's a nice guy. Too nice. He probably feels guilty leaving me here alone with Astria all the time. Which, he shouldn't. He does so much. Considering I was dead set on doing this whole thing alone to begin with.

It's funny how life works out sometimes. Not funny in a comical sense. More like funny in a life will fuck you sense, and you can't do anything but laugh about it…but still. Funny.

I've been a married woman for about two years now, and one thing I've learned is that I think a defining factor in the failure of a lot of marriages is unmet expectations. I'm not an expert at this wife thing, but let's be real. What Damien and I have works, and that's because I don't have expectations. I am totally and completely flying by the seat of my pants most days.

I don't expect things of him. He doesn't have to give me anything. He owes me nothing. Every day, every hour, he's working for our family. He's working to better himself. We have a common goal, and without expectation, we both work to achieve that goal.

"Snug, Mama." Astria tugs on a curl that's come loose from my untamed hair.

"I think Daddy wants to snug tonight."

I turn on the lamp that sits on her nightstand and turn off the bright overhead light. I flip the switch on her noisemaker. Something that I've become oddly addicted to since we still share a room.

Astria is getting ready to transition to a toddler bed, and I'm not ready for that yet.

So, most nights I let her snuggle into bed with me until her eyes begin to get heavy with sleep, and then I lay her down in her crib.

That's not the case every night. Damien and I take turns. Especially when it's hockey season and he's spending more time at the rink than he is at home. On those nights, I sneak out and read in the living room or take a nice long hot bath while he rests with her in my bed.

Those nights I don't sleep. I can't. Not when his smell is all over my pillow. It infiltrates my sheets. I'm restless, unable to think of anything other than wanting him when I shouldn't. And when I finally do give in and close my eyes, I dream of him. Tonight will be one of those nights.

I peek around the doorframe and see the broad expanse of his shoulder blades as he stands in the kitchen. I bet he's making a turkey sandwich. Stubborn broody booty. I could have done that for him. Astria tugs on my hand, and I turn and climb into my bed. He'll still be a minute, and I can go ahead and help her start winding down.

She wastes no time jumping in beside me and making herself comfortable, stealing the majority of the mattress and almost busting my lip in the process. Oh, the joys of having a toddler. There is no such thing as personal space anymore.

The only person I truly wish was all up in my space can't seem to stay there long enough for anything to happen. This marriage thing is a joke when it comes to having alone time. Honestly, I don't know how people that truly are married for, you know love and whatnot, make this work. Damien and I couldn't do anything if we wanted to. Every time I think something might happen between us; there she is.

The air thickens with lust, he kisses my cheek softly, and bam, just like that Astria is screaming bloody murder for her snack.

She's not hungry. She didn't need anything in particular. She just happened to lose her snack cup beneath her blanket and couldn't find it. The world almost ended. But so did the moment I thought I might have with Damien. Or, maybe, I could have imagined it all. Maybe the moment was only in my head.

I twirl her hair in my hand. She's got soft hair, like Damien's. It's dark like mine, but the texture isn't the same. I love the feel of it between my fingertips. She's lucky she'll never have to deal with the wild and crazy locks that are my hair.

Speaking of luck. She's lucky she's so darn cute because this child is a menace to my love life, or lack thereof.

"Hey, girls, you still up?" Damien whispers from the open doorway.

Astria sits up in the bed, confirming that we are, in fact, still awake.

"Daddy!" She squeals. He's easily her favorite. I understand, I can't blame her. He's my favorite too, girlfriend.

"Well, don't you two look cozy already? Can I have some kisses before bed?" Damien walks over to the bed and stands beside where Astria is lying next to me. I know he wanted to cuddle, but he won't push it if he thinks he'll disturb her bedtime routine. I know him too well.

"Daddy stay." Astria yanks back the covers and pats the spot next to her, which is obviously much too small for Damien's large frame.

"Mommy is here already. Kisses and then sleep. I

promise to bring back surprises when I come home." Damien tries to cover Astria with her blanket, but I can already tell where this is going. I sit up and start to climb out of bed, wanting to give them the opportunity to snuggle and already dreaming of a hot bath.

"No!" Astria yanks off the blank and grabs my tank top before I can make my escape.

"Daddy and Mommy snug!" Astria exclaims, and I freeze.

Damien looks from Astria to me, where I sit with my tank top askew awkwardly kneeling halfway on and off of the bed.

A look of panic crosses his features. He doesn't want this. We've never been in this situation before. Somebody has to say something.

I try to think of anything to say that will get me out of this room before things become even more awkward. "It's okay, Astria. Daddy will snug until you fall asleep. Mommy just got your snugs. I'm all full up. Let's let Daddy have a turn."

"Daddy and Mommy snug!" Astria repeats, and my eyes widen at Damien.

Why isn't he saying anything to help the situation? He stands there in his gym shorts and t-shirt, looking even more handsome with every passing day. His hair is down and falls on his shoulders in wavy blond locks. A light dusting of hair coats his sharp jawline. This man is my husband, and it hurts my heart that he's mine but he's not. And it shouldn't. Sometimes I wish I saw him as a big brother. It would make my life so much easier.

"Daddy stay! Daddy stay!"

His eyes search mine for answers I don't have the heart to give. We can both snuggle in this bed with Astria and be civil about it. It's fine. It will be fine. We're adults. Mostly. Most days I don't feel like an adult at all. I stare at Astria at least once a day and wonder how I'm keeping us both alive.

Ugh. I can't turn him away, and Astria has a grip of steel on my tank top.

"Okay, tonight we can have a family snug. Only tonight. Okay?" I repeat, and I don't know if I'm saying it for Astria or as a reminder to Damien and me that we can't blur the lines. I can't risk my heart that way. I won't risk our family.

"You sure?" Damien watches me from the edge of the bed with hesitation.

No. I am absolutely not sure.

What's the worst thing that could happen? Astria will make sure she takes up every available spot between the two of us. She'll fall asleep. Damien will lay her down in her crib and then go to his room. Easy enough.

"Yeah, it's fine." I give in.

Astria yanks me back down with the strap of my tank, and Damien climbs in next to her.

She can't leave any room for me on the small bed when it's just the two of us, but she has ample room for Damien to join us. I see how it is. Again, no surprise here. She's a daddy's girl through and through.

The bed dips with the weight of his large frame, as I try to make myself smaller, curling into the wall at my back.

"Daddy and Mommy snug!" Astria giggles and curls

into Damien, who has to be teetering precariously on the edge of the small mattress.

Damien wraps her up under his muscled arm. His fingers find the skin of my shoulder, where he rests them. He stretches out beneath my sheets and his bare foot brushes against mine. He touches me from top to bottom, and my stomach swirls with flutters. I want more than anything for this to be our reality.

I scoot closer to the wall, but it's no use. There's nowhere else to hide.

"Story!" Astria requests, and for a moment I'm thankful she didn't ask for a song.

Damien doesn't move to get a book from her bookshelf though. Instead, he settles in, sighing in thought before he finally begins to speak, his tone soothing even to me.

Once upon a time, there was a beautiful princess.

This princess wasn't just any ordinary princess though, she was a magical princess. You see, she had a special gift. She could see things that most people could not. She saw beauty in even the ugliest of ogres.

Astria giggles at the word ogre, and the sound melts my heart.

One day she got lost deep in the forest. She was scared, but she didn't cry. She was the bravest princess in all the land.

She searched and searched for her path home, but she had no luck. The sun was starting to set. It will be dark soon. She was starting to worry that her family would be mad at her if she were lost.

Astria gasps quietly. I watch the two of them in the faint light of her lamp enraptured by the story that

Damien weaves for her. I sit in awe of the man that fathered my daughter.

I don't recognize this story as one I've heard before.

Along came the biggest, ugliest ogre of the entire forest. All of the townspeople feared him. Everyone except the princess.

He was nervous to approach her.

Damien brushes his thumb along the skin of my shoulder, slowly, as he takes his time.

The ogre had been warned to never speak to humans, especially the princess. Her magic was sacred. She wasn't like the others.

When he noticed she was in danger, he knew he had to stop her. She was wandering too far into the dark forest. Not even the ogres go there.

Danger. Something in the way he says that one word triggers a memory buried somewhere in my mind.

Suddenly Damien's story begins to feel familiar.

Despite every warning, he approached the beautiful princess.

At first, she was angry. She didn't want help. She wanted to save herself, but the ogre persisted.

Is my imagination too much? Or is there so much more to this story than an ogre and a princess?

He took her hand in his, and she followed him in the opposite direction, to the edge of the forest nearest town.

The ogre watched the princess. He could not believe just how beautiful the princess truly was. When the princess finally saw a road that she recognized she kissed the ogre on the cheek with excitement.

The ogre was stunned. He'd never been kissed by such a beautiful princess.

He fell in love with her instantly, but the ogre knew he could never have the princess.

Love. I tug Astria's blanket over my body. I do my best to hide from the emotions that are suddenly swarming me. It's just a children's story, right? This is make-believe.

He was an ogre after all. He was destined to live his life alone in the forest.

To the ogre's surprise, the princess returned the following day. She brought mushrooms and onions, the ogre's favorite.

"Ewwww," Astria yawns as she speaks, and I can tell that she's fighting sleep.

That night instead of returning to her castle, she stayed with the ogre.

You see, the princess saw the beauty in the big ugly ogre too.

Damien's foot brushes my calf muscle, and my eyes start to water for no reason at all.

Her magic allowed her to see his heart.

Sometimes, love grows from the messiest of situations.

There is beauty in all life.

I run my fingers through Astria's silky hair. Her eyes are closed. She's fast asleep, but Damien continues.

Sometimes, all it takes is a little magic to find that what you've been looking for has been in front of you the entire time.

I hold my breath.

And more often than not, the story that leads you there is nothing at all like you thought it would be.

You see, the princess fell in love with the big ugly ogre. The ogre loved her from the very first kiss. Together, the princess and the ogre lived together happily ever after.

Silent tears fall from my cheek. I've fallen in love with the ogre. But the thing is, he's not ugly at all. He's the kindest, most beautiful man I've ever known.

And the whole kingdom soon learned what the princess knew all along. Beauty is in the eye of the beholder, and real, true beauty lives in our hearts. We just need a little magic to find it.

My heart beats wildly in my chest as I lay still beneath my armor, Astria's blanket, fearful that moving will break the beauty of this moment. Is it true? Or is it merely a fairytale?

I was never supposed to develop feelings for Damien. That was never part of the five-year plan. I wasn't supposed to crave his touch or go melty at the sound of his terrible singing voice. None of this was ever supposed to happen. But, it did. And things have changed.

I owe it to myself to find out what this is between us. I owe it to Astria. I owe it to our little family and the future that I know in my heart that we can make together.

Damien breaks the trance. He rolls from the bed, lifting Astria's small, sleepy body effortlessly to place her in her crib.

I sit up, and watch him, knowing I need to say something, but unsure of how to say it.

"Hey, Damien?" I want to come to your game this weekend. The words are on the tip of my tongue, but when he pauses to look at me, they refuse to leave my lips.

"Yeah, Princess?" He prompts.

My lungs stop working, and every coherent thought I had proceeds to vacate my mind. A small smile lifts at the corner of his lips as he patiently waits for me.

Astria shifts in his arms and we both freeze, fearful that she'll wake up. The moment is lost.

"Goodnight." It's all I manage to say before Damien lays Astria down for the night.

CHAPTER ELEVEN
DAMIEN

"Good game tonight, Henderson." Carter Tolar clasps me on the shoulder as we step into the elevator of the hotel, we're staying at for our series this weekend.

We won game one. Two more games decide if our season ends here or not.

"Thanks, you too." I nod, not wanting to get into a conversation. I'm tired. I just want to go back to the room and call my girls.

We might have won tonight, but I was on edge the entire game. More than usual. I did everything I could to play my best game and simultaneously ignore Tyler every time he skated past me. Somehow, we managed to get out of there without any bloodshed or cheap shots thrown from either of us.

It wasn't easy, and now I'm exhausted.

"You headed in for the night?" Tolar asks, clearly not

catching the hint that I'm not in the mood to chit-chat.

I shove my hands into the pockets of my slacks and watch the lights on the elevator as they move at a snail's pace.

"Yeah, you sound surprised?" I look at his reflection next to mine in the mirrored wall of the elevator. I never go out with the guys after a win. I go home. Or, if it's a home game I stay to work at the rink and pick up a few extra hours. He knows that though. So, what's with the interrogation?

"Not surprised, just thought you might be out celebrating with some of the other young guys, that's all. You're smart to stay back. We still have two more games. Now isn't the time to celebrate, we've still got work to do." He shrugs, but there's something else there that he's not saying. I see it in his eyes. I brush it off. The whole team is hyped after our game tonight, and we're all handling it differently.

"We do. Two more games. I'm not celebrating yet. Young guys, really? You're funny." I'm only a couple of years younger than he is, and as far as life goes, well I'm decades ahead of most of the guys on our team. He knows that. Our stories carry a similar timeline, although the way we arrived at this point was very different.

Tolar snickers. The man literally snickers to himself in the corner of the elevator like a fucking schoolgirl that just found out her best friend is crushing on the new boy in class and nobody knows but her. I look around, but we're only surrounded by mirrors. I don't get it. What am I missing?

"You got something to say, Tolar?" I tilt my head to

the side in confusion.

"Nope." He crosses his arms over his chest as if I'm the one that's being weird.

The elevator dings alerting us to our arrival, fucking finally. We both step out into the hallway at the same time. Tolar turns left and I make a right. The whole team is staying on the same floor, but our rooms happen to be on opposite ends of the hallway.

"Hey, Henderson." He calls out after me before I can get two full steps into the corridor.

"Yeah?" I ask over my shoulder, even though I truly could care less what he has to say. I'm so close. Just a few more feet and I can seclude myself in the sanctuary of my hotel room.

"Sweet dreams." He smiles widely before turning and swiping his room key over the panel on the door to his room and disappearing behind it.

What the fuck has gotten into him tonight?

I turn back toward my room and that's when I see her. I forget everything. Tolar's strange remarks from the elevator, our win over Chambliss, Tyler's watchful eyes on the ice…everything except the woman standing in front of my door with a backpack slung over her shoulder and a rolling overnight suitcase parked at her feet.

Three long strides and I'm standing in front of her. Every worst-case scenario plays through my mind in fast-forward until I reach her.

"Is everything okay? What's wrong? Where's Astria?" The words burst from my lips the moment I finally reach her. My heart beats so hard that it thunders in my ears and makes it nearly impossible to think.

She wrings her hands together nervously, which only makes my heart race faster. My stomach sinks to my toes. A light sheen of sweat breaks out over my skin.

"Yes!" She says quickly, an odd look on her face. What is it with tonight? "We're fine. I didn't mean to worry you. I didn't know how to come right out and say it. So, here I am. Surprise!"

She smiles and throws up her hands, waving them in the air awkwardly. I can't remember there ever being an awkward moment between us. Why the nerves? Why now?

"Surprise? Say what?" I grip her shoulders and physically move her to the side. I look around where she stands for any sign of our daughter and see none. No stroller. Nothing.

Realization clouds her features. If only I could find the same fucking clarity because I'm still seconds from losing my shit here.

"Take a deep breath, Damien. Astria is with Sylvia. I saw you get off the elevator with Carter, I was sure he let it slip when I saw the two of you together." She speaks quickly, answering my questions, but not quickly enough. Her answers only create more questions in my mind.

"Why is Astria with Sylvia, Click? You're not making any sense. Did she need an emergency haircut? I don't get it. Help me understand before I die. Jesus, woman." I try to calm my voice, but I can't rid it of the worry that is draining years off my life every second we stand in this godforsaken hallway.

"Sylvia is keeping Astria for the weekend." She pauses a beat before continuing. "For us."

"Are you pregnant, Click? Because the last time you surprised me you were pregnant, and I know for a fact…" My voice trails off. I know I shouldn't ask, but damn, tonight just keeps getting wilder with each passing minute. Is it a full moon?

"What? No! Why would you think that?" Gia looks horrified that I would even make the suggestion. The thought makes me feel sick on my feet, and not because I wouldn't want to see her pregnant again, I do. Just not with anyone's babies but mine.

We agreed not to see other people, and for almost two years now I've had intimate relationships with no one except my fucking hand.

"Then why are you here?" I don't mean it the way it comes out, and judging by the look on Gia's face, she's not hearing it the way I intended either. I'm fucking this all up. Whatever it is that's happening here.

"You asked me to come." She whispers and her smile dips.

"I always ask you to come." I stand in front of her like the idiot that I am, still unable to reconcile the events that led up to this moment.

"This was a mistake. I'm sorry, Damien." She grabs the handle of her suitcase, clearly exasperated with me, and takes a step past me when finally, my brain decides to catch up.

"Click, stop." I reach out and wrap my fingers around her small wrist.

We stand in the hallway of the hotel, alone, and I realize that it might be the first time we've been truly alone in well, years.

My green eyes search her brown ones.

My heart races for an entirely different reason as we say a thousand words with a single look.

I'm wearing slacks and a blazer. When I got dressed in the locker room earlier, I was quick to resent the fact that I had to wear a suit to walk from the locker room to the hotel room, Coaches' rules. Now? I'm thankful I'm not in my usual after-practice sweats.

I take a minute to really look at the woman standing in front of me. If I had paid closer attention earlier, maybe I would have put the pieces together sooner. She doesn't look frazzled or in a panic. Actually, she looks the complete opposite. She's fucking stunning.

She's wearing a black, fitted t-shirt dress that hugs her every curve. The hem skims the top of her thighs and begs me to run my hand beneath it to explore what she's wearing underneath. Her hair is combed out. I love it when she wears it that way. Gold sneakers adorn her feet. She looks young and full of sass that I haven't seen in a long time. Suddenly, I'm reminded of how young we truly are, and the people that we were before life got so fucking hard.

The fear that was just eating me alive is suddenly replaced with a desire and need I typically don't allow myself to feel.

"I'm sorry I missed the game. Late flight." Her smile returns.

She pulls her plump bottom lip into her mouth and bites down on it with her teeth. The dark purple pigmentation of her lip turns pink beneath the added pressure. I want to lean in and run my tongue over it. I want to taste her. It's been so long. I don't even remember what she tastes like. That doesn't mean I haven't dreamt of my memories of that night more times than I can count.

I lift my thumb to her lip, and tug it free, running the pad of my thumb over her moistened skin.

We're approaching a line, that once crossed, we will never come back from.

Danger. Danger. Danger.

It's a fucking neon sign flashing in my brain.

"Click, I need you to be honest with me. Did you come to watch the game or are you here for something else?" I want so badly to come right out and ask her, but I tip-toe around it like a damn pansy.

Is she here for me? Am I crazy to even consider it?

Not for the game. Not for her photography. Not because she's worried, I'll have a confrontation with her brother. None of that, just me.

She takes one step into my space. My hand tightens around where I still hold her wrist.

Standing up on the tips of her toes, she's almost able to look me in the eyes - almost.

"Well, you see, I got lost in the forest. I'm looking for a big ugly brute of an ogre. Have you seen him?"

Her breath fans my face. Her words light a fire in my soul. *Our fairytale*.

I don't say another word, I've said enough already. The next words out of my mouth need to be said in private. I don't want to risk one of my teammates walking up on a conversation that is meant only for the two of us.

I pull my room key from my jacket pocket and swipe

it over the door without breaking eye contact. I push the door open with my elbow, and yank Gia behind me through it, into the dimly lit room. I'm thankful I had the forethought to leave a lamp on because I need to see her face. I don't want to miss anything.

I need to know this isn't just another dream.

I don't want the fucking fairytale. I want our reality. I want my wife.

She drops her suitcase and bag just inside the door, and I quickly shrug out of my jacket.

Turning into her, I push her against the nearest flat surface, pinning her on either side with my hands against the wall. The material of my white button-down shirt pulls tight around my biceps. My brown leather loafers are planted on either side of her gold sneakers.

Our chests rise and fall in unison with heavy gasps for air. I want her air. I want her oxygen. I want her. All of her.

"Tell me what you came here for, Click." I lean in, getting into her space. I'm assaulted by her scent, and it makes me dizzy. That scent has haunted me for years.

"I hear there's a hockey game in town. Thought I might get some shots for my website. It's been a while."

A coy smile plays on her lips. Her intentional avoidance of my question causes my hands to clench into fists against the walls of the hotel room. This isn't the time for games.

"Don't play with me, Gia. Say it." She looks up into my eyes as I bite out the words, barely holding onto my control. I've been so tightly strung all night. So careful. I can't be careful anymore.

Four Score

The tension is so thick in the space between us that you could cut the lust with a knife and serve it up like fucking birthday cake.

"I came for you, Damien." Her hands find purchase on my hips. She tugs my shirt from where it's neatly tucked into my slacks, but that's not how this is going to go down.

The first time we were together was rushed and messy. I can't guarantee this won't be messy, but I can assure you I am going to take my fucking time wringing every single ounce of pleasure from her.

"Why?" I move long enough to grab her hands and pull them up above her head with one of mine. Her shoulders lean into the wall and her body arches, causing her center to press flush against my hardened length.

She rocks into me, and my hand tightens around her wrist. We're in unchartered territory.

"Because I want you. Because I couldn't sleep another night in that damn apartment without you next to me in bed. Because every time I touch myself, it's your face that I see."

Thank fuck. A deep, possessive rumble rips through my chest.

"Jesus, Gia. Do you realize what the last two years have been like for me? It's been torture. Living in the same apartment with this constant need pulsing through my veins and no way to satisfy it. It's purgatory, having these feelings and not being able to do a damn thing about them." I barely recognize my own voice.

"Trust me, I know. I've lived it too."

I look down between us and notice just how high her

dress has ridden up her thighs, I still have her hands pinned above her head, stretching the material of her dress, and taunting me with miles of dark, tan skin.

"I want to fuck you, Click. Dammit, I want to fuck you until your screams wake every person in this building." The truth in my words physically pains me. If she says no to what I'm about to ask, and I have to walk away from this, I don't know that we'll fully recover. I don't know how you come back from this.

"We do this on one condition."

My dick throbs to be inside of her, but I will shut it all down if we can't agree to the terms.

"It doesn't have to be…" She starts, but I don't let her finish.

"One fucking condition," I repeat.

"What?" She asks and the word is breathy. She's already close and I haven't even touched her yet.

I prepare myself for what I need to say. This is the only way tonight works out for everyone.

"No matter what happens after tonight, I get to keep you. I need you to promise me that no matter what happens, you'll stay. Both of you. I'm not ready to let you go, and I refuse to risk losing our family because I can't keep my dick in my pants. I've waited two years already. I can wait longer. Hell, I'll become a damn monk before I risk losing what we've built. The two of you mean more to me than one night in a hotel room."

CHAPTER TWELVE
GIA

I love you.

I practiced those three words over and over again in my head on the flight here. I told myself I'd wait until the right moment. I promised myself that I would know when it was right.

But now I'm not sure that moment is going to come after all. Or ever.

What's the protocol for when you fall in love with your husband? I wish I knew.

Need courses through every last inch of my body. Damien holds me hostage against the wall of his hotel room, and the only barrier between the desire wreaking havoc on my nervous system, and the blissful high of ecstasy I'm certain will come the moment he touches me is hanging in the balance of one single word.

Yes.

The problem? The consent he wants is for one night. I don't want only tonight. If I agree to his condition, where does that leave us? Will I be tormented by the memories of this night for the next sixteen years? Is this it? Is this all there is for us? There has to be more. He said it himself last night. I might not be a princess, but I deserve my own happy ending.

"What do you say, Click? Are you in?" His voice is gravelly, and the sound makes my skin tingle with awareness. When was the last time our bodies were this close without a toddler screaming for attention?

Are you in?

I spiral down a black hole of memories, transported back in time to what feels like a lifetime ago. How different is this moment? Really? Because both times this man stood in front of me and asked me that question my life was about to change. I get the feeling it's about to change again. Ready or not.

He holds my hands up above my head with one hand, and the other finds my thigh, slowly inching up the skin beneath my black dress. I bought this dress on the way here. I didn't have much time after I dropped off Astria with Sylvia. It's been ages since I went shopping. Thankfully, the outlet store next to the airport had exactly what I needed to feel sexy again.

My thighs are slick with my desire for him. A low ache has already begun down deep in my belly. It wouldn't take much. I'm desperate for some relief.

His fingers reach the thin material of the black lace thong I picked out specifically for tonight. He drags one finger beneath the lace and my breathing stutters. I'm already nearly gone for him. Maybe he's right. Maybe we can just fuck this out of our systems tonight, and all of the other feelings will go away. A girl can dream.

Don't get me wrong. I love being, Mama. I love being, Click. But for once I want Damien to see me as Gia. I want him to see me as a woman. I want to feel desired. Even if all we have is tonight.

I'm taking back my fucking name.

"Yes, I'm in." I give in.

Everything happens so fast.

Damien swallows my words as he slants his mouth down onto mine. His tongue slides over my teeth and down my throat demanding he take what is rightfully his. He groans as he moves his lips against mine, and the sound is like an electric shock to my system. His lips are the perfect mixture of firm and thick. His tongue is demanding, but gentle.

This is a kiss you remember for a lifetime; it brands your soul and steals air from your lungs.

The walls we've so carefully constructed come crashing down around us in a flurry of hands and lips and tongues.

My head slams up against the wall, but I don't care, I want more. I crave it.

He wraps the hand that was just skimming the skin beneath my dress around the lace material that I meticulously selected for tonight, and with one swift flick of the wrist, it falls from my body to the floor at our feet.

My dress is yanked up around my ribcage. I press my body against the wall and use the leverage to lift myself and wrap my legs around Damien's waist. I kick off my sneakers and cross my ankles at his back, pressing my now exposed clit against Damien's belt, searching for pressure as he continues to assault my mouth with his tongue. The cold metal feels so good against my heated flesh.

Finally, Damien releases my hands and they immediately go to the base of his neck. I tangle my fingers in his hair. God, how I love this man's hair. My hips take on a life of their own. I writhe against him. I can feel how hard he is through his slacks. I relish the fact that I did that. Maybe he doesn't think of me as his best friend's little sister after all.

Suddenly, he reaches up between us, gripping the slender column of my neck. His fingers cover my throat, and he pushes me away, pressing my head against the wall with a force that takes me by surprise. My eyes flare wide, fear skates down my spine. I trust Damien, but I don't know what's happening. This is so different from the first time we were together.

His fingers tighten a little more, and his eyes dilate as he watches my reaction in the dimly lit room. My legs remain securely wrapped around his hips.

I can feel my heart beating in my throat.

I can breathe. I can still breathe, I remind myself. I work to calm my nerves.

He tightens his fingers a little more, and suddenly I feel a gush of warmth between my thighs. My pussy begins to slowly pulse. Damien looks down between us. My arousal coats the front of his pants like a fucking badge of honor. His lips quirk up into the boyish grin I'm familiar with, and the fear turns into something else.

"Play with me, Click?" He asks, and I'm not sure what he's asking of me, but I want more.

"My name is Gia," I whisper, barely about to get words out with his hand still firmly gripped around my neck.

His eyes darken.

"Okay. Play with me, Gia. Do you trust me?" His hand tightens again, and I know I won't be able to speak.

I feel my orgasm teetering on the edge of total obliteration.

I trust him.

I nod my head once, and he releases me. Spinning us, and tossing me to the bed. I take a deep breath and swallow before grabbing my dress where it's bunched up around my waistline and pulling it off over my head. I toss it to the floor, followed by my matching black bra, leaving me completely naked and exposed in front of him.

Damien unbuckles his belt and slowly pulls it from the loops. His eyes watch me hungrily. This might be the first time in the history of ever that I've thought a piece of leather was sexy. His dress slacks are marked by me. I did that.

I scoot back on the still-made bed as he continues to peel off his clothes, layer by layer.

I lean back on the pillows and open my legs up for him to see exactly what he's doing to me. Having a baby changes a woman. I'm not the same young girl he slept with that night years ago.

My body is entirely different, and I wear every scar and stretch mark like a fucking badge of honor. This is the body of a woman that's created life. It's something I'm proud of, and I try to channel that confidence as I slide my hand between my thighs and begin to stroke my aching clit.

I don't want to come yet; I'm not ready for this to be over. I want to draw this out as long as I possibly can. And I definitely want to explore his hands around my neck again, because that level of intensity is not what I expected from the golden boy of hockey, Damien Henderson.

He's a good guy. A good man. And good guys don't choke their wives into orgasm. Right? Because fuck if that's the fantasy I never knew I needed to play out.

"Good girl, touch yourself, Gia. Show me what feels good to that pussy." Damien's dirty words shock me.

I've never seen this side of him. I don't hate it. His words heighten the sensations that are currently taking over my body. He licks his lips as he steps out of his boxer briefs one foot at a time.

His cock is hard. It stands rigid between us the moment it's released. My throat is sore as I swallow. I can still remember the feeling of him inside of me, but we didn't take our time. I never got to truly see him, and this is well… it's impressive.

I use two fingers to spread the lips of my slit and my other hand to continue touching my clit.

Damien stands at the edge of the bed, taking his cock in his hand. He strokes himself from base to tip, all the while never taking his eyes off of me. Pre-cum drips from the tip and he catches it with his finger. At first, I think he's going to use it as a lubricant, but instead, he lifts it to his lips, and opening his mouth he sucks it off his fingers.

I moan. Fucking hell, I've never seen anything so erotic. I'm fascinated by the movement of his hand as he pleasures himself.

"You said, you see me when you get yourself off. Tell me, is this how you imagine me, Gia? Is this what you see? I want you to tell me your fantasies. I want to make them come to life for you." Damien fucks his hand in front of me, and I try not to focus on his words. I try hard, because fuck if I'm not going to come without him touching me, and then this will all be over. I can't let that happen. I slow my strokes and allow my own warmth to drip onto the comforter between my legs.

"I thought you were going to fuck me. You said you were going to fuck me, and I swear to God if you don't put your dick inside of me Damien, I'm going to come anyway. I'm so close." I beg him. I use words that I've never thought to use in a million years, but I need him to understand how desperate I am for this - for him.

"Baby, I promise I'm going to fuck you, but first I want to watch you come. I want you to show me how you come when you think of me. I want you to tell me your fantasies as you slide your fingers into your pussy and explode around them. I want to watch it all, and then, you'll come on my mouth. I'll drink every last drop. And only then will I fuck you. We're not even close to done. So, tell me, what do you want, Gia?"

A fresh wave of lust hits me. I remove my hand, afraid that if I touch myself again, it will be game over. I've never come more than once. Not ever. That's the stuff of fairytales, not real life. We left the fairytales on the other side of the hotel room door. They don't exist here.

"I can't, I can't do that." I shake my head back and forth in complete denial of what he's suggesting.

"You can, and you will. Come for me, Gia. Now." The demand in his voice as he says my name rocks me to my core.

I close my eyes and toss my head back, placing my fingers back on my clit. I press down, knowing that with just the right amount of pressure… "Fuck! Damien!" I scream out his name. I move my fingers from my clit to where my orgasm pulses violently. My body shudders on the bed, and I temporarily lose all of my senses as every nerve inside of me is laser-focused in one single place.

Shit. I gasp for air. I collapse back, content to bask in my euphoria, but Damien's not having that.

My eyes fly open when his tongue swipes my sensitive clit. One lick. Then two.

"You taste so fucking good, Gia. So sweet." His words vibrate against my skin, and I nearly climb from the bed with the intensity of it.

"Oh my God, Damien. Oh my God, you're going to kill me." I wrap his long hair around my hand and tug until his eyes glance up to meet mine.

"I'll bring you back from the dead just so I can make you come again, baby." His tongue tracks from my clit to my opening with long, languid strokes. I arch my back off of the bed. It's all too much.

He strokes me with his tongue through the aftershocks of my orgasm, until the electric shocks begin to lessen, and the pleasure begins to build in my core again.

Fuck. Me.

I rock my hips into his face, looking for more. More of his filthy mouth. More of his tongue. More of everything.

"Nuh uh, not until you tell me what it is that you want. What are your fantasies, Gia?" He slowly pulls back. He's got to be fucking kidding me right now.

"You're serious?" I ask incredulously. This is not the time for a conversation.

"Mhmmm…" He hums, and the sensation of just barely touching my clit makes my eyes nearly roll back into my head. But then he stops. Nothing. He was serious.

So, now is not the time to tell him that I love him. Absolutely the fuck not.

"Damien, please," I beg as I try to think of something, anything else.

"You first, give me something to work with, Gia." He turns his head and bites down lightly on the inside of my thigh. This is torture.

Dear Lord, forgive me. I guess I'm headed to the confessional. If this man only knew the number of times, I've thought of him as I've touched myself over the last two years.

"I, um, well…sometimes when you work late after practice, and Astria is already asleep I sneak out into the living room." I feel so awkward right now, but I continue, my need for more of his tongue spurring me forward. "I spread my legs wide on the couch and I imagine you walking in on me like that. I imagine that you'll catch me, and then demand to finish me off."

"You like it when I take charge?" He brushes his lips over my slit lightly, barely teasing me.

"In bed, yes." I physically tremble beneath his touch as I speak.

"In this fantasy, do I ever eat your pussy?" He asks as he slowly spreads my lips with two fingers.

"Yes," I answer breathlessly. There are so many versions of that damn fantasy I could make a *Passionflix* movie out of them all.

"Do I drag my tongue along your clit, like this?" The warmth of his tongue glides across my slit from top to bottom.

I make a noise at the back of my throat involuntarily.

"Gia?" He pulls back, waiting for my answer.

"Yes," I answer. God, this feels so much better than anything I have ever imagined.

"How about like this?" His mouth descends upon me, eating me relentlessly. He sucks my clit into his mouth and I squeeze my eyes shut. I swear fireworks explode behind my eyelids.

"No, we aren't doing that. Look at me, Gia. Watch me." Using two fingers he slaps my clit, and a warm gush of my arousal coats my thighs. The relief is only temporary as he slides those fingers into my opening, and closes his mouth down on my clit again, sucking down the warm liquid.

He curls his fingers inside of me, managing to hit the exact right spot.

"Ahhhhhhh!" I cry out, screaming at the top of my lungs. My pussy clenches down around his fingers and my abdomen tightens as wave after wave of pleasure completely wrecks me. My pulse drums in my ears like a stampede of wild horses.

When I finally open my eyes, I see Damien between my legs. Wide smile. The dirty blonde facial hair coating his chin glistens with the remnants of my second orgasm of the night. *Two*. How? I don't know, but I'm not complaining.

"So good, Gia. So, so good. What comes next?" He asks, and I almost hate to answer him. I don't know how much more my body can take. That's when I remember the condition.

If this is only one night, I want every single minute of it.

"Do you have a condom?" I ask, knowing I brought some with me if he didn't. Good girls always come prepared, even when they're preparing to do bad things.

A brief moment of panic passes in his green eyes, and I know he doesn't have one. For some reason, that makes me happy. I blindsided him, but he wasn't prepared for anyone else either.

"It's okay, I do, they're in my backpack. And I'm on the pill." I got on the pill after I stopped breastfeeding Astria. Just in case.

I was wholly unprepared last time. I love our daughter, and I firmly believe things happen for a reason, but I also know that I'm not ready to bring another child into this world right now. Period.

"Good idea to double up." Damien nods, and hops off the bed, grabbing up my backpack where I dropped it in the entryway.

He hands it to me, and I pull out the unopened box

of condoms I picked up at the airport.

"Been there, done that," I say as I open the box and hand him the foil packet.

"Got the toddler to show for it." I laugh at his words as he raises an eyebrow and simultaneously rips open the packaging with his teeth, spitting the remnants of foil on the floor next to the bed in a move that should not be sexy, but…

My laughter is cut short as he begins to roll the condom onto the tip of his cock and up the full length of it in one motion. He grips the base of his cock, and I swear I see it throbbing between us. His muscles contract. His chest rises and falls. He's an Adonis, and tonight, he's all mine.

He kneels back between my thighs, rubbing the tip of his cock over my clit, moistening it.

"And in your fantasy Gia, how did it feel when I slid my cock inside of you? Was it like this?" He inches the tip inside of my opening and I feel myself stretching to accommodate him.

I grip the sheets on either side of the bed as he slowly inches his way in.

"Was it like this, baby? Tell me, Gia, is this what turns you on?" He asks again.

"Yes, but this is so much better. I want it all, Damien. All of you." I lift my hips and he takes them in his hands. He pulls me to him, and I take him to the hilt. Fuckkkkkk.

His immediate satisfaction leaves his lips in a hiss.

"What do you want, Gia?" He asks, and I'm over the talking. Done.

"Fuck me, Damien."

I'm no longer capable of speaking.

It's all the permission he needs. His green eyes turn molten. His long hair flies wildly around his shoulders, and his muscles flex with each movement of his arms as he pulls me to him.

Sweat glistens on the hair on his chest, down the path of his abdominal muscles. He looks like a Greek God. I've never seen a man so beautiful, and yet so fucking feral.

"Gia, baby, you feel so damn good. I've thought about this moment so many times." He grunts as he creates a punishing rhythm that quickly begins to build my orgasm for a third time. Every thrust feels better than the last.

The pressure continues to build low in my abdomen until I don't know how much more I can take.

"Tell me you've always been mine, Gia. Say it." He demands and I see the tight leash of control he's still holding onto about to snap.

"I'm yours, Damien. Let it go. Take what you need from me." His fingers dig into the skin on my thighs and hips as he holds my weight. He's all consuming. There's nothing slow or gentle about the way he thrusts into me, taking what I know he wants and giving me exactly what I need.

The sound of his skin slapping against mine echoes throughout the room, and quickly becomes the soundtrack to my impending orgasm.

He slams into me once, twice…

"Come for me Gia, come on my cock." He slams home one final time, and I'm overtaken with pure sensation. His filthy demands push me over the edge.

Everything about this is erotic, and sexy.

"Damien…oh my God…Damien," I scream as my orgasm rips through my body and clenches around his cock. My muscles quiver with exhaustion from the overwhelming pleasure that this man has rung from my body in such a short span of time.

"*Mine*. You will always be fucking mine." He roars and I feel him release inside of me. His muscles jerk rapidly with the intensity of his own orgasm. He repeats my name over and over again before he collapses into me. *Gia.*

I found her. Now I just have to give her a voice.

He rolls us both to the side so as to not crush me. Our breathing is labored as we watch each other in the dark.

No one says anything.

He takes my hand in his, lifting my wrist to meet his lips, he softly kisses the faint flutter of my heartbeat beneath my skin. Emotion begins to overwhelm me, but I refuse to cry. I wanted this. I got what I wanted. I have to believe that despite the conditions of our agreement, everything else will come in time.

We have time.

CHAPTER THIRTEEN
DAMIEN

Game three.

It's tied up and there are only seconds left in the third period.

We lost last night. We played hard, but they played harder. It wasn't enough. Tonight, decides our future this season. Emotions are running high on both sides.

She came.

I'll be the first to admit I'm struggling to keep my head in the fucking game.

Gia's wearing my jersey in the stands tonight, and it feels *so* good. She's here for me. A fact I've been brutally reminded of both times Tyler's scored on me tonight. Asshole.

We've played together our entire lives. Small things, things that most people wouldn't pick up even after hours of studying film, he knows about my game. I guess he

Four Score

could say the same thing about me, but there's only so much I can do and maintain my position. It's doing me no fucking favors tonight. He's on fire.

I have a feeling I know why.

I'm in love with his sister. It must be pouring off of me, and ricocheting off the ice directly in his face. Judging by the way he looks at me every time he gets near me? He knows it. I know it. Truth be known? I've known it for a long time. Too long.

The only person that doesn't know it is the woman that sits in the stands tonight wearing my number, watching the game behind the lens of her camera. I thought this weekend would be a one-and-done thing. I thought we could purge this from our systems and go back to the way things were.

That's a fucking farce if I've ever heard one.

We can't. I don't want to move backward. I'm never giving her up. It's not happening, and that's all there is to it. I just don't know how to tell her, and I'm terrified of the repercussions of confessing my feelings to her after I was so adamant that we could do this and maintain what we had before.

Seconds tick down on the clock. Jesus, who the fuck gave this asshole the puck again? Tyler skates toward me for what feels like the hundredth time tonight. He lines up the shot, and I prepare to block it. His eyes lock onto mine. He hesitates. The fuck? He hasn't hesitated all night. Something is off.

The arena rumbles around us. I drown out the noise and try to focus on watching the puck with the precision I'm known for. We're so damn close. We can save this trainwreck in overtime, if only I can…

Fuck. He's going right. I feel it. I stay quick on my feet and wait for his move. He's going to run out of time. He pivots. Shit.

He takes the shot over my left shoulder, and I'm fast but not fast enough. The puck finds the pocket and I miss it. The buzzer sounds, and the feeling of defeat washes over me.

Was I distracted? Is this my fault? Did I let my emotions slow my game tonight? Last night?

What's different?

This loss sits on my shoulders. My head was in the stands, not in the game where it should have been.

The crowd erupts into complete anarchy.

That's when I see him. He's waiting for me.

I skate out of the net, preparing for a moment that was always inevitable. He wants this, fine.

If we're going to do this, let's do it. It's better we do this here and leave it all out on the ice. I'm not taking this back to Gia; she doesn't deserve that.

"You're hurting her, Tyler," I say through a clenched jaw.

I pull off my helmet and drop it to the ice at our feet as I approach him. I'm pissed. I want him to see it. I want him to look into my eyes. I'm pissed that we lost. I'm pissed that Gia was here to see it. I'm pissed that he knew I was going to think he was going right, so he went left.

I'm just so damn mad at him. How could he hurt her like this? How could he hurt us? He was my brother. It's his fault that our family is broken.

Every emotion I've held back for two years bubbles

to the surface.

I see Carter skate closer out of the corner of my eye as our teammates begin to take notice of our impending confrontation. They have no idea what's at stake here. A hush falls over the crowd as they too start to notice something unusual happening on the ice.

"Me? I'm hurting her?" He reels back as if I've punched him. Him? He's got to be fucking kidding me. As if he has a right to feel wronged in this situation. He lost that right years ago when he threw it away like it meant nothing to him.

"Damn right, you're hurting her. You abandoned her when she needed you the most." I move closer to him, getting into his space. He needs to hear this, and if I don't get this off my chest I just might explode.

I stood back and let Gia handle this when we were on her turf. I let her call the shots. But tonight, we're on my turf. We're on the ice, and all bets are off.

"You're one to talk. She's the one that cut me off. She's the one that won't return my phone calls. And she's the one that turned to you when things went sideways." His gloved hand hits the front of his jersey as he annunciates every word.

Sideways...that's a classy way to talk about your sister and niece, asshole.

"You know why she turned to me, Tyler." I try to keep my voice even, but it's nearly impossible to keep the emotion from bleeding into every word I say.

He knows good and damn well that he'd have done the same thing in my position. He should be thanking me for stepping up and handling my responsibilities like a man, not pushing me away because he thinks I stole what belonged to him.

I broke the fucking cycle. I am not my father, and that's something I will never not be proud of. He can take that trash talk somewhere else.

"She was never yours to touch. She was a fucking baby. She was your sister." Fire lights his eyes, a direct match to my own.

Maybe he's right, maybe I shouldn't have touched her, but she was a legal fucking adult. Sometimes things happen, and we can't change the consequences of those actions. I wouldn't change a damn thing about that night. And I sure as fuck wouldn't change the outcome.

He doesn't even realize what he's missing out on. He doesn't realize that my daughter has his nose. He doesn't know that she giggles when you tickle her toes or that she loves avocado and blueberries, just not mixed together.

"Your sister. Not mine. She was never yours to keep. Get off your damn high horse. She was eighteen. We were all kids."

I won't touch him. I won't throw a punch because I know it's important to Gia. I'm already crossing a line here, and I hope I don't screw up all of the progress we've made in the last forty-eight hours just by having this confrontation.

I can feel her watching us.

"It's a good damn thing we're not in a fucking court of law because you'd be convicted of perjury for that bullshit lie." He seethes.

Now he's goading me. He wants me to react. I need to calm the fuck down. We both need to calm down.

One of Tyler's teammates tries to step in, but he shakes him off.

"She was eighteen, Tyler. Gia was old enough to make her own fucking decisions." I reiterate the facts. No crime was committed. We were both legal adults. Sure, maybe I broke bro code, but I stood by her. I didn't abandon her like he did. I didn't walk the fuck away.

I am not my father. The words thunder in my head and squeeze the air from my lungs.

"You lied to me. You told me you didn't get into Chambliss. But you didn't even apply, did you? You stayed back. Why? So, you could rob the damn cradle while I was away at school?" He's talking about things he doesn't know anything about.

"It's not what you think," I emphasize.

"Then what is it?" His words are filled with venom. He's too far gone.

"This isn't the place." I try to de-escalate a situation that's already gone too far. We need to take this somewhere private. Tyler is spiraling. I see it in his eyes. He's past losing control. He's lost it, and I'm right behind him.

"You stole my family."

My family. Gia might be his sister by blood, but she chose me. She chose Astria. She chose our future together. My blood pumps right next to his through Astria's veins. He doesn't have a claim over her. That's my daughter, and I'll be damn if anyone tries to say otherwise.

I should walk away. I should be the bigger man.

"No, Gia gets to choose. She's a fucking grown-ass

woman, trust me." I know what I'm implying as the words leave my lips, but I don't stop. "News flash, she chose me."

That's when it happens. He shoves me.

It takes me less than a second to move from shock to rage. The excess adrenaline pulsing through my veins from our game floods my system.

He's left me no choice. I won't allow his actions to go unanswered a second time. I have to fight back.

It's funny, at first it kind of feels like we're kids again, grappling on the ice over something stupid. It's all part of the game. It's part of the reason we love the sport. It's ingrained into every single hockey player from the time they grip their first stick.

The fans love bloodshed. Right?

I take the first swing. This one's for Gia. This one's for his inability to see past his anger and reconcile a broken family.

His helmet hits the ice and skids to a stop somewhere off in the distance. Tyler's blood speckles the white ice with red.

Tyler looks stunned for a brief second. Then his eyes track to the stands and I know he sees her. I don't turn my head. I can't look at her. Shame washes over me because of my inability to control the situation. I made a promise to myself that this wouldn't happen, It's too late for regrets though. What's done is done, and now we have to settle this once and for all.

I hear Coach yelling in the background. Whistles are blown. Fights between our corresponding teams break out around us, and the fans cheer us on. They think it's a show, and they just got upgraded to VIP. Unfortunately, this is all too real to me.

Somehow, Tyler gets a steady grip on my jersey, and I falter on my skates. I swing again, and miss, catching nothing but air and losing my footing completely.

I hit the ice, hard. The fall is jarring. I'm weighted down with my gear. I'm like a fucking turtle stuck on its' back in the middle of the highway.

Everything from that moment forward transpires in slow motion. I see Tyler coming down on top of me. I try to roll out of the way, but I'm too slow.

I hear the thud as he lands on me awkwardly before I feel it. Then, I don't feel anything.

I see blood in my peripheral. Lots of blood. Whose blood is that?

Suddenly, I'm cold. Colder than I should be in my gear. I'm soaked with sweat, but I'm freezing. Tyler is screaming something, but I can't hear him. The noise fades around me and all I hear is the sound of my heart beating in my ears.

It occurs to me briefly how strange it is to hear your own heart beating.

Blood pools around me, coloring the white ice a dark crimson.

That's a lot of fucking blood. Those stitches are going to be a bitch. Somebody should call a medic.

I open my mouth, but no words come out. Why won't my voice work? Huh. I need a nap. Just a quick little nap right here on the ice, and then I'll be good to go.

The last thing I see before I slowly drift off to sleep is the fear in Tyler's eyes.

CHAPTER FOURTEEN
GIA

Something's not right.

I've been around hockey my entire life. I don't love sports. I've always been more of a creative mind, but I know hockey.

I've taken thousands of shots of players over the years. They're some of my favorites.

Raw, unfiltered emotion. Stills of the body doing amazing things, defying the odds of what should be humanly possible. It's a beautiful thing to watch, even if I think that the sport itself is rather barbaric.

I grew up watching Tyler and Damien.

I grew up at the rink.

Fighting is par for the course. It's what keeps the fans coming back for more.

This is different.

I race from the stands. I take the stairs two at a time, trying to get to the rink.

Four Score

He wasn't getting up. Damien wasn't getting up. He just laid there, still, on the ice, as blood pooled around him.

"Ma'am you can't go past this line, I'm sorry." Someone grips my arm, and my momentum is halted as I attempt to enter the closed-off area that surrounds the rink.

"My husband. Damien Henderson is my husband." I screech at a man that's clearly just doing his job.

Any other time I'd be thankful that he takes his job so seriously, but right this second, I need him to not be such a hard ass and let me get to Damien.

"Yeah right, and I'm an underwear model for Calvin Klein. Go home, game's over."

Well, sir, I gave you the benefit of the doubt. I appreciated your very tiny position of authority at this rink, but you clearly have an ego problem and I do not have time to deal with your shit today.

I fumble for my identification, anything that will prove I am who I say I am. I need to get to him. I need to make sure everything is okay. Things always look worse on the ice than they truly are. Right? It's probably nothing. Just a few stitches. Maybe a missing tooth.

Two medics rush past me with a stretcher into the arena.

Somehow, I manage to locate my Rafferton student I.D., but the asshole doesn't give it a second look when I shove it in his face.

I'm seconds from taking my chances, and risking arrest when the medics rush back in our direction. I see Carter skating up behind them.

The color drains from his face the moment he sees me.

The medics rush past me in a flurry, one of them holding something firmly against Damien's neck, but all I see is the blood coating everything.

"Go, Gia! Follow the medics. Now!" Carter screams at me. The fear in his voice coats my insides with a nasty sludge that settles like lead in the pit of my stomach.

I turn and run. I chase after them. They're already climbing in the back of the ambulance by the time my feet catch up.

"Gia Henderson!" I shout my name at them.

They completely ignore me, but they don't stop me when I climb into the back of the ambulance just before someone slams the doors closed.

Within seconds we're in motion. I huddle in the corner, completely petrified. I try to remain invisible, it's not difficult. Not a single person in that ambulance so much as glances my way. Their attention is focused on Damien.

The medics scream things back and forth to each other that my brain struggles to comprehend.

Two words.

Two words register.

"No pulse."

I repeat them over and over again in my head like the most nauseating mantra known to mankind.

"Less than one minute out." The driver shouts at us over her shoulder.

Dread creeps up my spine and wraps its knowing, long arms around my lungs and heart, squeezing me until I feel like I'm suffocating.

It's both the longest and shortest few seconds of my life.

The medics hurry out of the ambulance meeting a team of people in scrubs who take Damien from them and leave me standing in the emergency bay of an unfamiliar hospital alone.

I want to crumple into the fetal position on the concrete. I want to fall asleep and pretend like this is just some bad dream. I want to be anywhere but here, living in this moment.

I shouldn't have come. This is my fault. This loss. The fight. The blood. *All of it.*

I'm seconds from falling apart.

"Ma'am?" A soft voice breaks through the chaos inside my head.

I stare at her. A woman that looks not much older than me wearing a pair of pale blue scrubs. When I don't say anything, she repeats herself again.

"Ma'am? Do you need help?"

"I…I don't know." I stammer through my words as I answer her honestly.

I don't remember where we are. I barely remember my own name. I can't think of anything except Damien on that stretcher and the medic saying that they couldn't find a pulse.

"Oh my God, he's dead." I bend over and throw up on the concrete at my feet.

"It's okay. You're going to be just fine. My name is Lyla. I'm a nurse here." She places her palm on my back and rubs her hand in slow circles until I finish dry heaving.

She drops her hand when I stand back up and face her again.

"Where is here?" I ask as I look around for any indication of where we are. It's a hospital, clearly. It seemed like we were here within seconds, almost. Two minutes tops from the arena.

"Chambliss Health, you're at the University hospital." The answer is obvious, but my brain can't understand obvious right now. I'm unable to process anything past what I already know and what I know is that the medic said *no pulse*.

"Are you a student?" I'm not sure why it matters, but it's the only thing I can think to ask.

I don't want her to leave me. I don't want to be alone, but I don't know how to ask her to stay. She doesn't know me. I'm a stranger to her.

"No, I'm not a student here. I just got off my shift. I'd be happy to take you in and get you cleaned up. Do you need something to eat or drink?" The thought of food sends another wave of nausea hurling at me like a Mac truck. I heave, but there's nothing left.

"I need Damien." I shiver and cross my arms over my body.

"Is this about the hockey player they just brought in?" She asks gently.

Sirens sound off in the distance and cause my heart to jolt. It's like they're coming back and we're going to have to relive the last few minutes all over again. I won't survive it.

"He's my husband," I answer, and I realize tonight is

the first time in maybe, forever, that I told someone Damien was my husband and truly felt like I was his wife. But, it's too late for all that.

"Tell me a little bit about him. We'll go inside while you talk, okay?" She takes a step forward and lightly places her hand on my arm.

She's wearing a name badge, which means she's probably telling the truth. Why would she lie to me? I'm a crazed-looking woman standing under the emergency bay of a hospital all alone with barf covering her shoes. I'm totally approachable.

"He's an amazing father." I hiccup.

"You have children?" She slowly turns us toward the sliding automatic doors to the emergency room and I follow her. What choice do I have? It's the only way I'll get answers. Answers that, truthfully, I don't think I want.

"A child - one. A daughter, her name is Astria. She loves her daddy more than she loves me. He's her favorite." My voice trembles, and my throat burns. Tears fall from my cheeks to my shirt. I'm still wearing Damien's jersey. We walk through the open waiting room together, and I try to keep it together as curious eyes follow us.

"I bet he is. What else?" We approach a door, and she scans her badge over a panel on the wall, and the door swings open in front of us. She nods to another woman on the other side of the door, and we keep walking.

"I love him," I confess to a complete stranger, words that I've been too scared to say to Damien. Words that have been on the tip of my tongue so many times over the past forty-eight hours, but I never could quite find the right moment.

We had time. I thought we had time.

"I'm sure you love him very much. I bet he loves you too."

I laugh and the sound is broken, it's filled with bits and pieces of my shattered heart.

It's like I'm in a daze. "I'm not sure," I say as I follow her through what feels like a maze to me. So many hallways and elevators. We walk together, her hand never leaving my arm.

"I am. I think he loves you very much." She says with confidence that I struggle to believe.

"Really?" I ask as if she has any idea.

She doesn't.

But for some reason the thought that she might believe that Damien loves me like I love him, well, it feels good. I'm willing to hold onto anything that feels like something other than misery at the moment. Anything. Even if she is just being nice to me.

"It's complicated," I answer before glancing down at my phone.

I pause in the middle of an empty hallway. Missed calls and text messages light up my phone already, but I can't deal with any of it right now. I just can't.

I see Sylvia's name on the screen and swipe to open the message. That's my only other priority.

Sylvia: *We were watching the game. I turned it off before, you know, but I needed to check on you. Carter says you're at the hospital. Are you okay? Is Damien, okay? The coach isn't telling them anything.*

Sylvia: *I know you're probably busy. Astria is fine. She's* *asleep right now. I just want you to know that I have her and that she's comfortable and taken care of.*

I begin to cry again as I read her text messages. I miss my baby. I miss our family.

What have I done?

Gia: *At the hospital. I don't have an update yet. Thank you. Thank you from the bottom of my heart. Please hold her tight and give her all my love. I promise I will call when I can, but for now, know that I'm doing the best I can to get us both home quickly.*

I type out the text and hit send. I hide the truth of our circumstances down deep in my heart because I need to know what we're up against before I can make a plan of action. Damien is our solutions guy. He's the one that always has the plan. I don't want to do this without him. I'm thankful for Sylvia tonight. I'm grateful for our hockey family.

I set my phone to do not disturb for now and look up from the screen as my new friend begins speaking again and we continue our walk, to where I'm not sure.

"Complicated or not. You're his wife. You're the mother of his daughter. He loves you." She says it so easily, like it must be true. Who is this woman?

We continue together down a long white corridor until we reach a small room with a vending machine. There are ten plastic chairs inside. It's completely vacant.

"How about I sit with you for a little while?" She motions to one of the chairs in the room.

"You don't have somewhere you need to be?" I ask, still not sure where we are or why we're in here. Where have they taken Damien?

"Right here. Right here is where I need to be." She sits down when I don't move and pats the seat of the chair next to her.

With no other choice at the moment, I take a seat. "Thank you…what did you say your name was?" My hands shake as I place them on my lap.

"It's Lyla, but that's not important. Tell me a little bit more about Astria and how much she loves her daddy." She nods for me to continue, and her voice is so soft, so reassuring.

I don't know what comes over me. I sit in the hard plastic chair in the waiting room of a hospital I'm completely unfamiliar with and tell a total stranger all about Damien's fairytale bedtime story and the way he loves to sing to Astria, but that he sings completely off-key.

I tell her that we grew up together. That he was my brother's best friend. Until I kissed him, and that's how we ended up here. Maybe I skipped a few years, or maybe I didn't. I can't be sure.

Time ceased to exist in our little bubble of waiting, and for that I'm thankful.

It's not until I notice the sun shining through the hard plastic blinds on the window of the waiting room that I realize it's morning. It's a different day.

Lyla's tired eyes catch movement over my shoulder, and I turn my attention to where her eyes remain locked.

A man in what I have to assume were once crisp blue scrubs, like Lyla's, and a white coat stands at the entrance to the waiting room.

He's covered in dried blood. His shoes have covers

on them. They're coated in blood too.

Damien.

"Are you Gia Henderson?" He asks and I wonder for just a second how this man knows my name. Did Damien wake up and ask for me? Is he okay? A brief moment of hope fills my heart, but it's short-lived.

Lyla places her hand on my thigh in a silent show of support. The moment feels somber, but I also don't feel like it's me living it. It feels like I'm watching a movie. This can't be my life.

"I, uh, I am," I answer reluctantly. I'm scared. The last time I was this scared I had Damien with me. He promised me that we would be okay. He promised me that we would do this together. I can't do any of this alone. I don't want to.

"Mrs. Henderson, your husband suffered a laceration to one of his carotid arteries last night. That's a major artery that provides the blood supply between your heart and brain. He lost a lot of blood quickly. When he got here, he didn't have a pulse. The survival rate for this type of injury is very low."

I choke on air. Tears fill my bloodshot eyes, and snot drips from my nose. I think of our daughter. I think of how she'll never know the man her father was. The good man he was.

I think of my mom and how she must have experienced a moment just like this one. God, is this what she felt like? This complete and utter sense of helplessness. I can't help but feel like history is repeating itself. It's like I'm stuck on a merry-go-round of hell and I can't get off.

I bend at the waist and stare at the floor. I ball my sweating palms into fists. I brace for the words I know are coming next.

"He's alive, Mrs. Henderson."

I cry out when his words register. I release some of the pain through my screams. Lyla wraps her arms around me and when I look at her face it's stained with tears of her own.

Why didn't he lead with that? Jesus. My heart thuds back to life. It's a slow thud, but I feel it all the same.

The doctor continues to speak, as my lungs slowly begin to work on their own again. "We got him back, but he's still unconscious. He's in a medically induced coma. We need his body to heal. He's not out of the woods yet. Not by a long shot. He had to have a blood transfusion. We won't know if the blood loss caused any permanent damage to his brain until we're able to wake him up. And even if he's fine, it's a minimum of three to six months of recovery time. There's a risk of stroke. He's got a long road ahead of him."

"He's alive," I say, my voice wobbly.

I grasp onto those words and hold on to them with all of the strength that's left in me.

"He is, and as soon as we get him situated in the unit, we'll let you see him, okay?"

My body is flooded with relief. Damien is a fighter. He's alive.

CHAPTER FIFTEEN
TYLER

"Just checking in. He's sleeping like a champ. Everything looks normal, Gia."

Who's sleeping? Am I dreaming? It's like I can hear this unfamiliar voice, but I'm in a dark room without any light.

"Thanks, Lyla. You have no idea what it means to me that you're here."

Lyla? I don't know a Lyla. Do I? Geez, I'm so tired. Sleep feels good. Maybe I'm the one sleeping like a champ. Naps are good…I'll just sleep for a little bit longer.

-o-

"Gia, good to see you. You're looking better this morning. Get some rest last night?" I hear a man's voice.

Fucking hell, my head hurts. Who is this man and why is he looking at my wife?

I try to move, but can't. I try to open my eyes, but nothing happens.

"Thanks, Doc. Damien and I had a riveting conversation last night. He nearly kept me up all night. Honestly, I can't believe I look so refreshed." She laughs lightly, and the sound soothes me.

We did? She said my name, take that motherfucker. But…I don't remember any of that. Did she call him Doc? I must have gotten my dome rocked at practice or something. Shit, my head. Maybe if I fall asleep, I'll wake up and feel better.

-o-

"Mom, she doesn't need cookies before bed! Absolutely not. Put the cookies down, woman. You're a menace." Am I dreaming? That voice. It's familiar. It sounds like Gia.

Why is Mama Patterson here? She hates flying. Is it Christmas already? Panic ensues. I don't remember buying anything for Gia recently. Did I forget Christmas?

"He's okay, still resting. When he wakes up, we'll have a better idea of what we're dealing with." What are we dealing with? Who is resting? Did something happen to Jeff?

"Listen, Mom, I appreciate you staying with Astria. You don't know what it means to me. Can I see her? Hold on, let me Facetime you guys back." Astria. My baby.

Facetime? Why does Gia need to Facetime her? That doesn't make sense.

The hotel. We were at our series at Chambliss. I thought Sylvia was keeping Astria. Is it time to go?

Bits and pieces of what feels like memories flash in my mind, but they're all fragmented and meshed together. I can't see them clearly nor can I decipher between what is reality and what might just be a distant dream.

I definitely took a hit to my melon. I feel like I've been asleep for years.

"Mommy! Mommy!" I hear Astria, but I don't see her. Why can't I see her?

"Hey, baby! I miss you! Don't take the cookies from Grandma, they have broccoli in them!" Broccoli, Gia is so full of it.

"Daddy!"

I'm here baby girl, Daddy's here. But my voice won't work. Why won't my voice work?

The questions only make my head pound harder.

Fuck. The fight. My voice wouldn't work. Where's Tyler? There was so much blood.

"Daddy has a boo boo, but we're getting him all better. I promise." Gia's voice sounds so calming. I could listen to her talk for hours. Maybe I'll go back to sleep for a while longer.

Wait.

Me? I'm hurt? I don't feel hurt. I feel tired. And I can't see a damn thing. Why is it so dark?

"Astria." I croak, and it works. Finally, my voice works. Damn, I sound rough. My mouth feels so dry, and I'm thirsty, so thirsty. I feel like I've swallowed razor blades.

"Daddy!" I hear Astria's sweet squeal. Gia gasps. I crack my eyes open enough that I can make out her silhouette in the chair next to me.

Where am I? My eyes burn. I try to move, but can't.

"Gia? Was that Damien? Was that Damien, Gia?" Mama Patterson. Where's the fire? She sounds panicked. What is going on with everyone? This is the strangest dream I've ever had.

"Mom, I'm going to need to call you guys back. Oh my God. He's awake. Oh my God!" Gia jumps from the chair, dropping her phone on the floor in the process, but instead of picking it up she slams her hand down repeatedly on a button on the wall. I just barely can make out a red flashing light through the burning slits of my eyes.

"He's awake!" She screams over and over again. So much for a calming and relaxing.

Damn, my head hurts. Is the yelling necessary? I took a nap, it's not revolutionary or anything.

"Gia?" I manage to say her name, but words are hard right now. My throat feels tight.

"Damien, you know my name? You know Astria?" She asks in disbelief, standing beside me.

That's a ridiculous question. Why wouldn't I know who they are?

"Yeah, did we win?" I can't remember if we won the final game. My team needs me. Did we advance? Was the fight before or after the buzzer? The timeline is all mixed up in my head.

She doesn't answer me immediately, instead, she lets out a laugh. It's a loud, full-body laugh. She laughs so hard that tears stream down her face, and she piggy snorts through her nose.

I blink over and over again, trying to clear the burning

sand from my eyes.

I'm still trying to figure out what the hell is going on.

"Gia? Is everything okay? You called for us?" A woman in a pair of scrubs peeks around a light blue curtain.

"He's awake! Lyla, he's awake!" She continues to laugh. Her laughter borders insanity, and it makes me a little anxious.

Lyla, that name sounds strangely familiar to me. It's like I'm having de ja vu. The woman looks from Gia, who is in a fit of complete hysterics at the moment, to me, and her smile widens.

"Mr. Henderson, welcome back. You gave us quite the scare. How are you?"

Welcome back?

"Thirsty, I'm parched. Did we lose the game?" I ask again, this time a little annoyed with myself that I can't remember.

"I'll get you some water soon, I need to get your vitals first. I'd say you won, Mr. Henderson. You won the game of life."

The game of life?

The woman that Gia referred to as Lyla hovers over me. It's like they are familiar with each other, friends even, but I've never seen that woman before in my life. As my vision begins to clear, I look around, realizing for the first time that I'm in a hospital room. I'm hooked to machines that continue to beep in the background and do nothing to help my throbbing head.

Gia, despite her smile, looks like she hasn't slept in days.

"Gia?" I look to my wife for answers.

"You had a cut and lost a lot of blood. We're at Chambliss Health, the University hospital." Gia explains. She looks at the woman, Lyla, who I'm now assuming is a nurse, and nods. There is something they aren't saying.

I wiggle my toes and my fingers. I'm sore as shit, but they're all there. I can move them. That's always a good sign, right?

"I'll grab the doctor; he's making his rounds now. He will be around to explain everything very soon." The nurse finishes up, giving Gia a quick hug before leaving us alone again behind the privacy of the curtain.

"You're out of the playoffs." Gia finally says with a nervous smile.

"Damn, I played like shit. That was my fault. I'm sorry about the fight, Gia. Do you, um, do you know what happened? Where's Tyler? Is he okay?" I ask questions as the fog in my brain begins slowly clearing, much like my vision, unfortunately, it's taking longer than I would like.

"He's out of the playoffs too."

"How?" That doesn't make any sense.

"Chambliss dismissed him from the team." She glances toward the floor and then back up to meet my eyes. Again, with the secrecy. It doesn't sit well with me.

"Why would they do that? Is he injured?" I'm immediately concerned for T, despite where our relationship is right now.

I can't just shut down on family. I can shut you out, but I can't shut down my love for someone I grew up with my entire life, the brother to my wife. It's just not the way I'm made. We might fight like hell, and I will always back Gia's decisions, but my worry for his well-being won't disappear.

"He's fine, I guess. He didn't die, if that's what you're asking." Huh, she seems saltier about T than usual. I don't have much time to dig deeper.

Knock. Knock. Two brief knocks sound off on the wall of the room.

"Damien Henderson, the man – the myth – the legend, or so you've come to be known in this unit. How do you feel?"

A man, probably in his late fifties' steps into our space. His hair is silver and combed neatly. His jaw is coated in a matching silver beard that's clearly been trimmed with precision. He's tall and fit, and he wears a white coat like he owns the damn hospital. I like him immediately.

"Like shit, honestly," I grunt and try to sit up, but pain shoots down my neck and into my shoulder, sobering my movements.

"Good, that's what I'd expect. Do you recognize this woman? She's been hanging around here for a few days. Says she knows you." He smirks in Gia's direction, and it annoys me that she smiles. Who does this fucker think he is? I take it back. I don't like him at all.

"That's my wife," I growl, and his smile only magnifies, showing off what are surely overpriced store-bought veneers.

Gia snickers, and then recovers when she realizes I'm watching her, and I do not find him amusing.

"And your daughter's name is?" He continues as if he didn't just blatantly flirt with my wife using his fancy-ass doctor smirk.

"Astria," I answer, still irritated with the guy, and paying very close attention to his flirty face and silver beard that I'm starting to think he colors to make himself look more sophisticated than he is.

"And your favorite sport is?"

"Hockey." Which means I know how to check your ass in less than two seconds. Or I could if I wasn't strapped to this damn hospital bed, flirty-doc'flirterson.

"And ten plus three is?"

"Thirteen. What does this have to do with anything?" I finally ask.

Doesn't this man understand I have a headache from Hades? And his googly eyes and pop quiz are only making it worse.

"Well, Mr. Henderson, we'll have to do some scans to confirm, but my preliminary assessment is that I don't think you suffered any permanent brain damage from your injury."

"What injury? Did I get a concussion?"

Concussions are pretty common in any contact sport at this level. I've had a few. Far less than some of my teammates, mainly because I spend most of my time in the net.

"I don't think he, um, remembers all the details of that night." Gia cuts in.

"Short-term memory loss is normal. It's the body's way of protecting our minds from trauma. Residual shock, if you will. Your memories might stay foggy. They might not. You didn't get a concussion, Damien. Your carotid artery was nicked during your confrontation with the opposing team."

"My what was what? I answered every single question you asked me correctly." I'm going to need a little more clarification. So, what, I don't remember who won the game. Big deal.

"You were cut. Just barely." Please, all this over a cut? "The cut lacerated one of the main arteries in your neck. Hell, you might be one of the luckiest men I've ever met." Do not give my wife eyes again, fucker. "Had the incision fully punctured the artery you would have completely bled out within seconds. We lost you twice that night before getting you back. You underwent surgery and a blood transfusion. You have been in a medically induced coma since."

"You lost me?" I ask, still confused.

"When you arrived here you had no pulse." He answers with zero bedside manner. Zilch. Who gave this guy a medical degree?

"I died?" I ask him incredulously. Not possible. I look at the machines that are hooked to me again and have to wonder if this isn't just a touch dramatic.

"Yes. But you aren't dead, and we intend to keep it that way. That's why we have a lot to discuss before we can get you ready to transfer back home. I'm not sure how much anyone has told you, and it's not our policy to bombard you with information after such a traumatic event, but you have been here since last weekend's game. It's Friday."

Friday? *Fuck*. I'm tossed a piece of humble pie by the good doctor, and it's not going down easily. It's been an entire week already? I lost an entire week of my life.

"Where's Astria?" I ask Gia, suddenly realizing that

she's here and we've been without our girl for almost a week. We've never been away from her for that long.

"She's with my mom. They're at our apartment. She's fine, I've spoken to her every day. I promise." That explains the phone call - the voices.

"I want to go home, Doc. I want my baby." A feeling of helplessness washes over me, and I forget all about my irritation with the guy. I just want my family.

"I understand completely, but you're going to have to stay with us a little longer. We need to make sure you're stable and get your care plan worked out. You'll need rehabilitation."

"Rehab?"

"You're looking at three to six months."

We're at the end of the season. It's time for summer. Most of the guys will be taking off for a few weeks anyway, especially since we lost. I'll miss some practice and conditioning, but three to six months sounds reasonable. I'll have it done in three.

"Good, I'll be ready to play next season. I might miss a few games, but I'll work harder. I'll be ready."

Gia and the doctor exchange a look that makes my stomach sink.

Doctor Silver Fox looks over at Gia, but this time I see nothing in his eyes but pity that I don't want to acknowledge.

"I'm sorry son, but the likelihood of you playing hockey professionally again is, well, it's not likely at all."

Not a fucking chance.

CHAPTER SIXTEEN
GIA

We haven't spoken a word about what happened between us at the hotel room in Chambliss. Not a single word.

It's maddening.

I mean, I know I have more important things to be worried about. I literally have a list a mile long of things that need to be done, and I swear that list is growing by the day, but I can't stop thinking about it. I can't stop thinking about him.

I do the dishes, and suddenly I'm imagining his tongue on my clit, demanding I tell him my fantasies.

I unload the laundry, and I'm daydreaming about his hand around my neck, my body pressed up against the wall, pulsing with need.

I was at the supermarket yesterday morning, and I picked up a cucumber, and dammit if I wasn't immediately picturing Damien entering me, stretching me. Right there in the produce section, I was soaking my panties holding a damn cucumber.

I'm a mess.

What's worse? I'm not even sure he remembers. His memories from that weekend are a scattered mess, even though he tries to pretend they aren't. The doctor said he might get them back, but he might not.

What if he forgot? Every touch. Every kiss. They're seared into my soul. I couldn't forget if I wanted to. I don't want to forget. Not yet anyway.

It's not just about how good it felt to finally be with him. Or how hard the man made me come, over and over again. It's about intimacy. It's about finally feeling like we got it right after so many years of thinking that it was never going to happen for me…for us. I love him, and I am still holding on to the hope that there's something there for him too.

What if I never get to feel that way again?

It took another week in the hospital before they felt like Damien was stable enough to return home, and even then, they required transport by ambulance to our local hospital, and then another night stay there to verify he was still, in fact, stable. Damien's usual patient facade was slipping with every passing day. He's frustrated, and he has every right to be.

Once we finally made it home, he was required to spend one more week on bed rest until he could resume what would be considered light-normal activity for most humans. Not super hockey humans.

It broke my heart to hear the doctor tell Damien that his hockey career was probably over. Something about the potential for restraining the artery and an increased risk for stroke.

That's another thing we haven't talked about yet. We've done an excellent job of avoiding all of the important topics.

Instead, we spent our time away watching game shows and Facetiming with Astria. I'm so thankful she won't have memories of any of this. I think my dreams will forever be haunted by the sound of those sirens and the sight of Damien's blood on the ice. So much blood.

Damien's mother flew out to see him as soon as she heard the news. She didn't leave until Damien finally convinced her he wasn't going to bleed out in the middle of the night, and the team of doctors and nurses overseeing his case were completely capable. She is still calling daily to check in, and I can't blame her. I'd do the same in her position.

My mama stayed with us in our tiny apartment at Rafferton until she felt we were completely situated. She cooked chicken and waffles for Damien no less than five times.

She never once questioned my bed in Astria's room. Thank God. In fact, I think she thought it was a guest bed because she was totally comfortable and set up in it when we arrived.

I set Damien up securely in his room, a straight shot to the bathroom and back. Doctor's orders.

I slept on the couch, using the excuse that I was afraid of hurting Damien in his sleep. We pulled it off, but now I'm even more exhausted. I thought I'd finally rest when we made it home. I was wrong.

I'm playing catch up on my classes, and my website. I have orders coming in, and that's great, I just need the time to fill them. I'm playing nurse for Damien, and not the sexy kind. I've distributed doctor's excuses to his classes and picked up all of his finals so that he doesn't miss anything in the last few weeks of the semester. I've hosted his team as they've come in and out to check on him since we made it back. Our apartment has been a revolving door, which has been fine, I'm so glad that Damien has that level of support, but I'm lonely despite the chaos.

I'm in full-blown survival mode. I can't stop, because I know the moment I do, I'll collapse and I'm not sure I'll be able to get back up again.

Astria is at her playgroup today, I just hit submit on my last final for the semester, and now I'm unloading the dishwasher, cue inappropriate daydreaming.

I'm counting down the hours until bedtime already, and it's barely early afternoon.

"Gotcha!"

I jump and squeal when a pair of lips land on my neck out of nowhere.

I whip around quickly, prepared for battle in my own kitchen, "Damien, oh my God. Get your ass back in that bed. This isn't the bathroom. You aren't supposed to be out here. From the bed to the toilet, you know the drill. You should have called me if you needed something. You could hurt yourself. Oh no! Did I hurt you when I jumped?" Panic builds in my chest as I try to catch my breath. My heart races from being caught off guard, and quite literally caught fantasizing about the man standing in front of me, and then because I'm worried, I might have hurt him, or he might have hurt himself.

He stands there, freshly showered, and grins at me, which only sets off more alarms in my mind. Did I give him the wrong medication this morning? God, did I overdose him in my state of utter exhaustion? Is he high?

"It's Friday." He says, slowly, taking the clean bowl I was holding out of my hand and setting it down gently on the countertop behind me.

"I know, I've got to pick Astria up in two hours and then I'll cook dinner. You, sir, should be in the bed." I point toward his open bedroom door, but he just continues to grin at me, his green eyes dance with a lightness that I haven't seen in weeks. I didn't realize how much I missed it until just now.

"Nah, I think I'll stay here, thanks for the offer though."

My God, I forgot how ruggedly handsome he is. Seeing him here, standing in the kitchen in his grey sweatpants and faded Rafferton Ram's t-shirt, his hair still damp from the shower is doing things to me that only make the proverbial elephant in the room that much more suffocating.

The *l-word* elephant, not the hockey elephant. One elephant at a time. You know what a herd of elephants is called? A parade. As if elephants stampeding in your kitchen should be cause for celebration. Parades are fun. Parades are a good time. Nope. Not mine.

"Can I help you with something? You're acting strange, Damien. Should I call the doctor?" I eye him skeptically; his usual scruff is more of a beard than scruff lately. He let it grow during his hospital stay, despite my numerous offers to shave it for him. Something about not trusting me with sharp objects near his face.

I think he just wanted to torture me, really. Because this beard is doing all kinds of things to enrich my fantasies. It's almost like I can feel him between my legs just standing here looking at him.

Damn parade.

"Nope. It's Friday, which means my bedrest is up. Mama Patterson is gone. Astria is at her playgroup. And I just took the best damn shower of my life."

"Shit, it is Friday. You're up, like up - up. How are you feeling?" I realize suddenly that he's right. How did I not remember? I've been counting down the days, and somehow, I still managed to forget.

"Want to know a secret?" Damien steps into me, ignoring my question. He places his hand on my hip and I nearly melt into a puddle on the floor at his feet with the contact.

This is not a normal reaction, right?

This isn't how you react to your brother's best friend, a man you saw go through his onion armpit, yellow braces phase.

This is how a woman reacts to her husband.

Only this isn't what we agreed to when we signed our marriage certificate. Get it together, Gia. Remember the onion. Do not simp on me now.

"You stole too many pain meds this morning?" I ask nervously, my heart skipping along happily on the yellow brick road, but my mind short-circuiting with his proximity.

The parade. Where the fuck is the parade route right now. I need a map. Somebody get me a map because I fear we have veered off course.

He works his thumb slowly under the stretchy fabric of my tank top, skimming my bare skin and sending chills skating down my spine and prickling the tiny hairs on my neck.

We can't do this. Not now. His heart. His brain. The injury. I don't know what the protocol is. He just got off of bedrest today. He hasn't even been fully cleared by the doctor yet. He still has rehab. What is he doing?

He leans into my body until his mouth is right beside my ear. I can feel the heat from his breath. I can smell the soap he used in the shower, and *Dial* has never smelt so damn delicious.

Just when I think my legs will give way beneath me, he whispers into my ear, "I remember."

-o-
DAMIEN

I've been good. I've obeyed the doctor's orders, and despite what he said about my hockey career I am planning a full recovery.

That decision has already been made in my mind. Much like this one.

"What exactly is it that you remember?" She tries to act nonchalant like she's not sure what I'm referring to, but I can tell by the slight tremor in her voice and the hitch in her breath that she knows exactly what I'm talking about.

I slip my hand fully under her shirt and slowly move it around to the base of her spine, just above the waistline of her black jogging pants. I feel the lines that I know are etched into her skin, dipping just above her plump ass. An ass I have done nothing but dream about every damn day since I woke up immobilized in a hospital bed.

I'm like a deprived child. I was given a brand-new toy only to play with it once or twice and then have it snatched away. I'm taking back what's mine.

She made me a promise. I fully intend on her keeping it.

I lower my mouth just far enough to allow my lips to brush the delicate line of her neck before bringing them right back up to her ear. Her breathing quickens and I smile because we haven't even scratched the surface yet of what I plan to do to her.

Not today. I know my limits, but I want her to know that just because we haven't talked about it does not mean I've forgotten the promises we made to each other.

"We can pretend like the fight never happened, Gia. We can pretend like my hockey career isn't hanging in the balance of fucking medical release. What we aren't going to pretend about though? The fact that you made me a promise. You promised me that our relationship wouldn't change."

"It hasn't. It's exactly as it was before we went to Chambliss."

"That's not what I meant, Gia. I think you misunderstood." I nip at the lobe of her ear with my mouth before placing a kiss delicately behind it. Electricity skates up my spine with our proximity.

I walk us back one more step until I feel her back bump the countertop.

"Your condition. You said…"

I look her directly in the eyes, pressing my forehead to hers. I want her to hear me loud and clear when I say this.

"What I said was that I was going to keep you. That you couldn't run. That the two of you stay here, with me. A family." My nose brushes up against hers and my lips are just a breath away from touching hers.

"We're here, Damien. We aren't going anywhere." She whispers in the space between us.

"Good answer," I say just before closing my mouth down over hers.

God, I've missed this woman.

I slide my tongue into her mouth, and she opens up for me without hesitation.

My hand slips below the fabric of her sweatpants and I run my palm over the smooth skin of her ass. She's not wearing any underwear, and the thought nearly makes me come unhinged.

I grip the cheek of her ass in my hand, and pull her body into mine, pressing my pelvis against her so there is no question as to how much I want her.

"Damien, we can't!" She tries to push me away, and it doesn't do anything but make me that much hungrier for her. I don't budge.

"Kiss me, Gia. Just fucking kiss me, that's all I'm asking. I need this. Please." My balls will hate me for this later, but I just need to taste her.

She gives me a worried look, glancing at the bandage

that still covers the incision on my neck. It's mostly healed, but the wrapping won't be removed until I'm cleared by my doctor. I'll have a scar that I'll live with as a reminder of that night for the rest of my life. A physical manifestation of the consequences of my actions. The loss for my team is on me. My inability to walk away from a confrontation with T, on me.

I understand her concern, but the consequences of waiting to touch her now that I'm up and moving again are outweighed by the feel of her tongue as it fights for dominance with mine in my mouth.

She twists the back of my t-shirt with her fists. I use my free hand to reach up and grip her neck, tilting my head to the side to gain a deeper angle on her lips. I swallow every pant and soft moan she gives me. My dick throbs against where I swear, I can feel her heat through the material that separates us.

If anything, all of the blood has left my neck and traveled south for the foreseeable future.

We stand there, in the kitchen, with the dishwasher open, and make out for what feels like an hour but isn't long enough.

I slow the kiss, even though I wish it would never end, and finally bring myself to pull away. How is it that one kiss and this woman has my world spinning like a top? I place my forehead back on hers and gasp for air. When I open my eyes again, I see her swollen lips and big brown eyes staring back at me.

I swipe my tongue out and run it slowly over where her lips remain slightly parted, needing one more taste.

"You remember," she says with disbelief.

I answer confidently, "I remember," not wanting to leave even a shred of doubt in her mind.

"Damien, I…"

She starts, but I cut her off with one more chaste kiss. I don't want her to question what's happening between us. I don't want her to turn me away because of my injury. I've lost so much already. I can't take anymore. I need her here with me. I need to know she's with me. *Mine*.

"Thank you."

"For what exactly?" She looks at me curiously, her brown eyes searching my green.

"For saving me."

CHAPTER SEVENTEEN
GIA

He's wrong.

I didn't save him. This whole mess is my fault, all of it.

I don't regret kissing Damien that night, all those years ago. I will never regret it, because the sweet, softly snoring little girl in my arms was a result of our actions. I will never regret our daughter. I won't regret the love that has grown in my heart for her father.

What I struggle to live with is the fact that our little girl almost lost her daddy and I'm to blame. I grew up without a father, and to be honest, I didn't fully understand what I was missing until I saw the way Astria looked at Damien. I never knew how special that bond was until I watched it unfold in front of me. Her innocence is sacred, and whether she realizes it or not, she was so close to losing it.

I lay in bed and steal all of Astria's sleepy snuggles. I

hold her innocence in my arms and try to soak it all in. I prolong getting up and laying her down in her own bed.

God, when I close my eyes, I can still feel his lips on mine.

He got back about ten minutes ago. I heard the door to the apartment open and close, and then my phone lit up with a text letting me know it was him.

He's not wasting any time now that he's off bed rest. He was on the phone all afternoon, making appointments with his doctor, getting a referral for rehab, and setting up an appointment to meet with his coach.

I just hope he's not trying to do too much too soon.

Increased risk of stroke. Potential for reinjury. Deadly blood clots. I've spent more time using Doctor Google than I care to admit, and that search bar is a bitch.

Ugh. I'm thirsty.

I need a glass of water. Dammit.

I wait until I hear the shower cut on and get up and put her down for the night. Luckily, I think we've moved past the sleepless nights of constant wakeups. I lay her in her bed and pull her favorite blanket up around her.

My sweet girl, she's growing up too quickly. It's so strange being a parent. My mama had a saying she liked to repeat to me when I was a little girl. She'd say, "Gia baby, these days might seem long, but I promise you that the years are short." At the time I wasn't sure what she was talking about. I know now.

I watch her for a moment longer, and then slowly sneak out of our bedroom, closing the door gently behind me.

"Boo!"

I jump ten feet in the air and quickly cover my mouth with my hand. If this were a horror movie, I'd be dead, because I was damn well flying instead of fighting.

"Dammit, Damien! Why are you always doing this to me?"

I smack his bare chest and the moment my skin ricochets off of his I realize my mistake.

He's not wearing clothes.

Damien is propped against the wall in our hallway wearing nothing but a white towel, slung low around his waist.

"Why are you always so skittish, Click? Afraid of the boogeyman?"

His eyes dance in the dim light, but all I can think about is how much thirstier I just became.

"Why aren't you in the shower?" I shout in a whisper back at him.

"Got hungry and needed a snack." He shrugs, and his abdominal muscles dance with the movement.

My eyes are glued to the light dusting of hair over his pecs that trail down the line of his abdomen and to…I gulp. *Holy Hell.*

"For the shower?" My eyes are nowhere near looking at his.

I stare blatantly at the deep v that disappears beneath the towel and taunts me.

"Sure, why not? No better place to eat a turkey sandwich." He laughs lightly, and the sound draws my eyes back up to his. My God, this man is beautiful.

"Maybe I should call back over to Chambliss. I think the doctor missed your brain damage." I try to remain unphased, but this isn't a fair fight. I'm completely unarmed, and he is well, very well-armed with all the right equipment.

I just needed water.

"You will not be calling Doctor Silver Fox." He says adamantly, and now it's my turn to laugh. Doctor who?

"Excuse me, what did you just call him?" A small smile tugs at my lips, as he shifts his feet ever so slightly, showing the first sign of discomfort that I've seen from him since I stepped out into the hallway.

"Doesn't matter. No need to call him. I do not have brain damage, and that was only reconfirmed this afternoon when I got my official release to stand and walk like a normal human again."

"You did what? When?" How did he get a follow-up appointment so quickly? I knew he made some calls, but I figured it would at least be next week before he saw the doctor again.

"Don't ever underestimate a man with a blazing set of blue balls."

My eyes widen, and I try to contain my smile. Whoops. Did I do that?

"What are you saying, Damien?" I ask and my voice sounds breathy.

Why am I panting already? *Get it together, Gia.*

"I'm saying that I have been released to light-normal activity."

"Oh, okay, great." See, light-normal. A stroll in the park. A brisk walk to class.

I take a step toward the kitchen. I'll just grab my glass of water, and he can get his sandwich and we can go back to doing what we were already planning to do this evening. The shower is still running, I would hate to think of the water we're wasting.

"Come to think of it, I don't want a turkey sandwich anymore." He steps in front of me. A brick wall of naked man chest immediately halts my progress.

"You said light-normal." I swallow and look up into his eyes. So far up. Did I shrink or did he somehow grow taller over the last few weeks he spent on bed rest?

"Doc said I can fuck my wife."

"Damien Henderson, you did not ask the doctor that!"

"Oh, I damn well did. He said if I have a stroke, it's on you, now come get in the shower with me."

I don't move. I'm torn between giving myself permission to give in to what I want, and making up an excuse because I'm scared. I'm a big chicken. But I have zero excuses.

"You're scowling, Click. It's cute," I immediately release the pinch in my brow.

He sighs, and reaches forward, gripping the waistline of my shorts and tugging my body to his. "I'm just teasing. He didn't say that about the stroke. What he said was that I should be mindful of my limitations."

"And those are? Because nothing about what we've ever done has been um…light to moderate." He laughs at my words, but I'm being serious.

Every time we're together it's explosive. It's fireworks and dynamite not a fucking sparkler at New Year's. He's not a damn cat, it's not like he's got nine lives to play with. The man has already died more times than the majority of the human population. Death is not something you tempt more than once.

"How about this? You be easy with me, and I'll be easy with you. It's just a shower. Don't overthink it." He runs his fingers over the elastic of my shorts, and my stomach flips, reminding me just how much power this man holds over me.

"I don't want to hurt you, Damien." It's a plea for mercy because I know in my heart that I'm about to give this man anything and everything he wants.

"Look at me Gia, the doctor said I'm okay. I promise you won't hurt me, and if anything feels off at all, I promise to tell you. Okay?" The sincerity in his eyes steals the very last bit of my resolve.

I succumb without further argument, "Okay."

Placing two fingers under my chin he tilts my head up. Leaning down, his lips brush mine in the softest, sweetest kiss I think I've ever felt.

Releasing me, he takes my hand in his, and instead of going to the kitchen as I intended, I follow him into the bathroom, my thirst completely replaced with a different, much more all-consuming need.

He turns to face me, in front of the shower, steam billowing around us in the room, God help my hair.

He pushes the straps on my tank over my shoulders, and I slide my arms out. He leans in and again kisses my lips, then my neck, blazing a trail until he tugs my tank below my breasts and pulls one into his mouth. He gently massages the other with his hand as his tongue draws circles around my nipple.

I breathe out his name, "Damien". He takes his time,

working one side and then the other. My breasts swell beneath his touch. My nipples harden, and my orgasm begins to torturously build in my belly.

Gripping the towel around his waist, he releases the knot and allows it to fall to the floor, exposing his carefully sculpted, naked body.

I study every hard line. I allow myself to take a moment to appreciate the beauty of the man that stands before me as he worships my body. I almost lost him. The realization steals the air from my lungs. Emotion claws its way up my throat and cinches off my oxygen.

His cock throbs angrily between us. It's thick and covered with veins that I want to be inside of me. I'm desperate for his touch.

He drops to his knees in front of me, yanking my tank and shorts down my legs. I step out of them, and he moves them out of his way.

He kisses my belly. He brushes his lips over the stretchmarks left from my pregnancy with Astria. His lips don't stop their descent until they reach the trimmed patch of hair just above my clit.

"You are magnificent," he says the words just before his mouth descends on me. He places open-mouth kisses on my clit, my thighs, and my soaked opening. His lips and his tongue stoke me until I find myself gripping his hair in my hands and writhing on his face unapologetically.

The hair from where his stubble has grown into a beard does all the things that it promised in my fantasies and more, everything about this moment feels magnified.

With one hand tangled in his hair, I reach for the

shower door with the other, needing something to stabilize myself. My legs feel weak, but that only makes me fuck his face that much harder. My hips move erratically as I feel orgasm threatening.

Like he can read my mind he says, "That's it, baby, come for me. Let it go."

With his permission, my pussy contracts and my orgasm rips through my body. God, it feels so good. I was worried I would never feel this again. Fuck.

Before I can finish riding out my pleasure, Damien stands and pulls us both into the shower. Hot water hits my already scorching skin. The water cascades over our bodies, bonding us together in a way that feels ethereal.

"Damien," I whisper his name as we stare at each other. Does he feel it too?

"Gia, baby, I see you. I see all of you." He says just before lowering his mouth to mine and consuming me.

He presses my back against the wall. I prop my leg on the bench and open wide for him.

He breaks away from our kiss, "I know your hesitation, Gia, but I want to be inside of you with nothing separating us." I understand. I know what he means. He needs that connection.

I want him to mark me. I want him to brand me as his. The game has changed since that night in the hotel room.

I'm playing for keeps.

"Please, Damien." It's all I manage to say.

He lines the tip of his cock up with my entrance. Water splashes around us.

He stretches me slowly. He doesn't stop until he's

fully seated inside of me. He rests his elbows on either side of my head. We both gasp for air in the humidity.

"You're so beautiful, Gia." He slides out and back in.

"You're so caring, and thoughtful." Out and in.

His words are intoxicating.

"You're an amazing mother and wife." Out and in.

My first orgasm still pulses slowly around his cock, but I can feel it building again. His praise lights me up from the inside out, filling a void I never realized was missing.

"Gia, fuck, I can't do this without you. None of this. You and Astria, you're my reason." His hips begin to move faster as he takes what he needs and fills me with something else entirely. My heart is so full that it might burst in my chest.

I reach my hands up between us. I grip his face in my hands. Water falls all around us, but he stills for just a moment.

I kiss his chest before looking up into his eyes, "Damien, I love you."

I say the words that have been strangling my heart for months. I finally release them and give them life. Relief floods my body.

"Really? You love me?" He pauses long enough to look me in the eyes. That he would even doubt he was capable of the magnitude of love I feel for him is heart wrenching.

"I love you so much, Damien." I use every emotion I hold inside of me and hope that he hears the truth behind what I'm saying to him.

"Gia, baby, I love you too. You're my world." He says the words just before he slams in and out of me two, three more times.

Without warning, my orgasm pulls me under, a tidal wave of ecstasy. I drown in it. It fills my heart and lungs as I pulse around his cock and plead for mercy in the shower.

"I love you, baby." He whispers once more he slams into me a final time and I feel his body shudder with his release.

We come together, holding each other. I try to allow my fear and anxiety to wash away with the water as it rains down around us.

My chest rises and falls against him. We stand there like that until the water runs cold.

Damien flips off the taps. He picks his towel up off the floor and wraps it around my body, drying me off before drying himself.

We walk together from the bathroom to his bedroom. We climb into his bed, and he pulls my naked body to him.

I roll, scooting my back to his front, still soaked from the shower. He wraps his arms around me, warming me from the inside out.

"Gia, I meant what I said. I love you. You and Astria are my whole world, and I will stop at nothing to make your dreams come true." It's a confession in the darkness.

"You are my dream, Damien." It's all I say as I lay there in his arms and wonder how we got here. Together. Holding each other as our daughter sleeps soundly in the next room.

CHAPTER EIGHTEEN
DAMIEN

"I'm sorry Damien, but rules are rules. The Board's already handed down their decision. We have to release you from the Rams."

Take it like a man, Damien. Do not let this break you. There are other ways.

"Yes sir," I say, my voice tight. I drop a copy of my medical release onto his desk anyway and clench my fists at my sides.

This way will be harder. It's not the path I wanted to take. Hell, none of this was on my radar just a couple of months ago. I was at the top of my game. We should be in the playoffs right now.

Life can change in an instant. Guess I like learning that lesson the hard way.

My current release is conditional. I still have weeks of rehabilitation to undergo, even then there's not one hundred percent assurance I'll be cleared completely.

I guess I thought, hell, I don't know what I thought.

It's okay. This is a minor setback.

Coach doesn't look up from his desk. He doesn't so much as glance toward the paper I've placed there. His silence is the nail in the fucking coffin of my college career. Realizing the conversation is over I turn on my heel and leave.

I walk out on my team, but I won't quit.

I won't quit because I have something worth fighting for.

I head to the locker room and thank God for small mercies when it's empty. I quickly empty my gear out of my locker. I study the wooden benches that line the walls. Rafferton is scrolled on the wall above the entrance to the showers. It was my first time playing without T. It was my first time belonging to a team that was my own. I made a name for myself on this team. This has been my home for the last two years. I've been through so much during my time here. I stand in the middle of the locker room and rake my hands through my hair.

How do I explain this to Gia?

Fuck.

How do I explain that I failed her? I failed our daughter and our family. I failed my team. I take a deep breath and pull down my Ram's jersey for the last time.

Sometimes the hardest step to take is the next one.

-o-

"How did the meeting go?" Gia asks the minute I walk through the door.

Astria is in the kitchen attempting to feed herself. Something green covers her face, her shirt, and the floor. Maybe some of it made it into her belly. Could be peas? Could be avocado? It's hard to tell.

Either way, the minute I step foot in the kitchen, the smile on her face gives me the perspective I need to say the words that need to be said. I don't want to drag this out any longer than necessary.

"I've been released," I sigh, setting my gear down on the floor at my feet. My shoulders feel tight and heavy with anxiety that's been building since I left Coach's office.

The whole way here I thought about what our next move should be. I know what I have to do, but I can't make this decision alone. I need her to back me, and if I'm being honest, I'm scared shitless.

"For the season?" She looks up from where she's cutting up vegetables at the counter.

"No, forever," I answer resolutely.

She sets down the knife and runs her hands over the front of her jeans. She turns in my direction, leaning back against the kitchen cabinets and crossing her arms over her chest.

Her forehead crinkles with worry.

"What do you mean? Did you show him your release?"

"It didn't matter. T wasn't the only one the Board came down hard on. Rules are rules, and I'm out." I spit the words out, but they taste bitter. They're not any easier to say now than they were to hear.

She pushes off the counter and in two steps she's

standing in front of me. Her hands land on my chest.

With concerned eyes, Gia says, "It's okay, right? Are you okay?" It's not lost on me that she's worried about me. There are so many other things for us to be worried about, but her immediate reaction is to worry for me.

"I will be."

"You?" The word is a question, I wish she didn't feel the need to ask.

Nothing we do is about me, anymore. It's about us. We're a team.

I reach up and wrap her hands in mine against my chest. "We will be. I have a plan, but I need you to trust me."

"What about your scholarship?"

I glance up at the ceiling. I think I hate this part the most. I debate how I want to say what I know has to come next. How can I put my feelings into words and have them make sense?

"Have you ever been faced with a valley so deep that it feels like a cliff?"

"I don't think I'm following, Damien."

"I feel like I'm toeing the line of a massive cliff, and this valley we're facing, it's so deep that I can't see the bottom. I'm scared, Gia. I want to make you proud. I need to provide for you and for our daughter. It's a lot of pressure." I don't hold back.

I need her to know that I'm willing to confide in her no matter what. All of my fears and my secrets, I'll share them with her because that's what people do when they love each other, right? As a man, I'm expected to carry the load alone, but it's too heavy right now. I have to trust her to take some of the weight, even if it hurts like hell to give it to her.

"I understand. But you're not alone. You're never alone, Damien. Do you understand what I'm saying? I see you. I see your heart. If we have nothing, it's okay as long as we have each other. Maybe that sounds cheesy, but it's true." Her hands squeeze mine. Tears sting the back of my eyes.

My lungs fill with oxygen, and from those words alone the weight begins to feel lighter.

"I see you," I exhale and regroup my thoughts. "I want to jump, Gia. I need to take a leap of faith. It's a long shot, but if I try to stay and finish my degree, I'll miss my window of opportunity. I need to focus on finishing my rehab, and I need to figure out a way to make it to the next level."

"Okay, but the doctor at Chambliss said that the risk…"

"I don't give a damn what he said. I appreciate the fact that the man saved my life. I respect his medical opinion as just that, an opinion. I've had a lot of time on my hands the past few weeks and in that time, I've done my own research. It's possible, Gia. I can get my life back. I can make a life for us."

She pops up on her toes, her eyes widening with excitement so suddenly that I have to take a step back, "I have an idea." She squeals.

"Yeah?" I feed off of her positive energy. I'll take all of it I can get. I'm tired of feeling so beaten down. I want something to be excited about for a change.

She nods, her smile only widening, it's contagious.

"Yeah, I think we should jump."

Are we losing it? Is she losing it? Have we bypassed the cliff and stepped off of the ledge of insanity?

"You're serious? What if we fall?" I start to question my own decisions. What seemed so clear on the way here is suddenly becoming muddied. Nerves and fear begin to creep in.

"What if we don't? What if we fly?" She leaps up into my arms, kissing me on the lips in front of our daughter. It seems like a strange thing to say. Astria's a toddler. She can't realize our relationship is different now than it was six months ago. But something about the moment feels significant.

My chest tightens, and then more of the pressure I've been under releases.

"I love you so damn much it hurts, Gia," I whisper as I kiss the top of her head, unable to stop smiling.

She tilts her head back with a laugh and says, "Language, Damien. Dang. Say dang."

"Is dang really that much better?" I smile down at her, glancing over at our daughter who is still trying to figure out if the spoon belongs in her mouth or if it's better used as a slingshot.

"Huh, you know, come to think of it, I've never really considered it. You might be right. It's not much better, is it?" She laughs harder and so do I.

We stand there, together, in the middle of the kitchen holding each other, and the moment feels so normal. I wonder if this is how most married couples make life-altering decisions? Or if we're missing a step or something because leaping off of a cliff and diving headfirst into uncertainty shouldn't feel this right…, should it?

Gia looks up at me, confidence shining in her eyes, "We're going to fly."

"We are."

CHAPTER NINETEEN
DAMIEN

"Pick up the pace, Henderson, you're slow as shit. Your reflexes are weak. Did you hear me? Weak ass motherfucker. Camden could get a shot in on you and he's two."

My lungs burn. I skate back and forth, covering the net as Tolar rains pucks in on me like the fucking monster he is.

"Fuck you, Tolar." I spit through my mouth guard, gotta preserve my pearlie whites, especially when Carter has made it his apparent mission to knock one, or all, of my teeth out this morning.

He smirks arrogantly, and I can see it from all the way across the ice. "I'd rather you not. Sylvia's a little territorial. She doesn't like to share, and I've never really been into dickheads."

I might have lost my scholarship, and my place on the team, but I didn't lose my job. A job that's granted me full access to use the arena to my advantage. Sure, I have to work around everyone else's schedule, but it doesn't matter. I have ice time, and I use it every chance I can get.

Carter was picked up by the LA Renegades despite our drop out of the playoffs. Most guys go home in the off-season. Not Carter, he's spending his off-season here. I get the feeling Sylvia is his home, so he doesn't much care as long as she and Camden are with him. I can respect that. Sylvia is wrapping up her business for the move, and they wanted to allow Camden as much time with his friends as they could before they had to pack up and report for pre-season conditioning.

That's how I ended up here, in this predicament, with pucks flying at my head like missiles. We ended up practicing together by accident. I'd been coming early in the mornings, and one morning he was here, and I was no longer alone. He's been waking up at the ass crack of dawn every morning since to torture me. He says it's because he tries to get his ice time in before Sylvia and Camden wake up for the day, but I think he secretly likes me. He just won't admit it.

He screams at me, and I push myself harder. "Your mom fucking skates faster, Henderson." See, he's a big fucking mush.

My doctor says I'm medically cleared to skate. Or, as clear as I'm going to get. I still have a few months left in my rehab program. Sure, there will always be risk there, which Gia likes to remind me of when she thinks I'm pushing myself too hard, but I've been working on listening to my body and learning my limitations. I'm adapting my game, and I'm getting better every day.

My heart pumps stronger. My brain reacts faster.

I practice with Carter. I get the arena cleaned and ready for the day. I go to rehab. I head back to the arena for my second shift. I practice again. Gia stops by to get shots for the social media accounts she's building for me. I shut the arena down, and go home to my family.

Sweat drips from my face as Carter shoots the last puck. He plants his foot. It's a slapshot, and I block it. Zero. Not a single puck made it past me this morning.

I skate from the net and start gathering up all the pucks that we've accumulated. Carter skates up beside me, checking me with his shoulder just hard enough to get my attention.

"What the fuck, Tolar?" I right myself and skate backward to keep an eye on him.

"Sylvia said she's ready to head out to California."

"Already?" I ask. "I thought you had a couple of weeks yet." Damn, I don't want to turn all soft here, but I thought I had a couple of weeks left with Carter. Losing my team was rough but having this one-on-one time to practice with someone I respected, well, I hate to admit that I have kind of been enjoying the torture.

Carter passes me a puck, and I pass it right back to him. "Yeah, well, the Renegades have a summer camp. They called me up early. Sylvia, she was ready, so that's it. We're out."

Just like that. I wonder if Sylvia mentioned it to Gia. Damn. Astria's losing a friend too. We're all losing somebody here, and it sucks.

"Who will berate me every morning before breakfast? I might develop a complex." I rub my chest over my pads and smile like it doesn't bother me, but fuck if I'm not a little sad about it.

Tolar stops skating. He taps his stick on the ice. "Listen, there's chatter about Henegan."

"Logan Henegan?"

Logan Henegan is the goaltender for the Renegades, and a damn good one. I've studied him for years. I think I have one of his jerseys back home somewhere at moms with some of my old stuff.

"Yeah, he's favoring his left knee."

"The one he injured last season?"

Henegan went down for two games last season. Rumor was that he'd injured his knee, but he came back without needing surgery and played out the remainder of the season, helping to lead the Renegades to the cup. They didn't win, but they came damn close.

"One and the same. He's pushing thirty." He says it like thirty is old, and I guess it is in hockey years.

"He's still young." Hell, I feel older than thirty most days. Between the shit we put our bodies through for the sport and the pressure of raising a family. Life has a way of aging you.

"I'm just saying. When I get there. I might slip your socials to a few people."

My social media accounts. I smile to myself. I didn't even have a Facebook page two months ago. Gia's idea was genius. She's made it her mission to get me in front of the scouts one way or another. If I can't play for them, she'll force them to see me.

I'm tweeting and tocking and booking and probably ten more things I don't know anything about. She's running it all, updating my accounts multiple times a day with photos and videos of me practicing. She does it in between building her own business, raising our daughter, and still attending classes of her own. I don't know how she has time to do it all.

She even had my mom send some old clips she had of me back in high school. She swears it's working. She gets excited to tell me about interactions we're getting and new followers we're gaining every day. I don't understand half of it, and I'm still not entirely sure how it's going to help my hockey career, but I trust her. It's easy to get caught up in the excitement when I see how excited she is about all of it.

She's back behind her camera again daily. She's in her element and she's thriving.

"I knew you were sweet on me, Tolar." I lift my chin in his direction and smile at him.

"That's what your mom said." He adds with a grunt, and skates around me, leaving me to clean up the remaining pucks.

"Fucking asshole, you'd be lucky to have my mom," I yell after him as he heads off the ice.

He turns just as he steps off the ice and yells back at me. "Don't give up. Okay? You're the best damn goalie I've ever played with, and you've been given a shit hand. Don't give up, and don't get yourself killed in the process."

Right. Just don't fucking die. Easy enough.

-o-

Gia climbs over me on the bed and straddles my chest. "Damien, oh my God, Damien look at this." She shoves her phone in my face, but I have a hard time seeing anything other than the miles and miles of chocolate brown skin framing either side of my hips as her silky sleep shorts ride up her thighs and leave very little to the imagination.

"What am I looking at babe?" I try to focus on her phone, I truly do, but it's hard to concentrate when she's riding my chest like a fucking pony at the county fair. Are these shorts new?

"You're going viral!" She hops up and down on my bare chest with her phone in her hand, and my cock immediately hardens. Bam, zero to sixty just like that.

"Gia, baby, fuck. You've got to stop bouncing like that and give me a second." I take her hips in my hands and still her movements. It does nothing for my hard-on, but it does allow me to see the screen of her phone without all the bouncing and jerking around.

"Oh, whoops," she blushes, and her cheeks darken with warmth. She's so damn cute sometimes it hurts.

I study the screen in her hand. "Okay, tell me what it is that I'm looking at exactly." I take the phone from her and watch what appears to be my entire hockey career consolidated into a three-minute video. Hell, I'll be the first to admit it's pretty cool. I look damn good.

"So, your mom sent me those videos of you from high school. I snagged some video footage from the Ram's YouTube channel. Then, I took some of the footage I recorded during one of your practices last week. I mashed them all up together using this new program I've been trying out, and I put that video to a trending sound then shazam you're blowing up." She rambles, her words running together, in all of her excitement.

She snatches the phone back away from me and does this little shimmy on my chest that makes her breasts bounce and my tongue go down my own damn throat. *Fuck* this woman.

I've been in here all alone in this king-sized bed for two years. It's a crying shame that we wasted so much time.

"Wow. That sounds like a lot of fucking work." I grip her hips again, and do my best to listen to what she's trying to explain to me without tossing her down on the bed and ravaging her before she can finish. She's excited, this is important.

"It is, but it isn't. I know what I'm doing, Damien. It's one of those things you figure out as you go. Anyway, I posted the video this morning and when I checked it just a few minutes ago it has over a million views. You have over two hundred thousand new followers. Today." She points to the screen, and her enthusiasm is tangible. It's eating her up from the inside out. I can see it in her smile and the way her eyes light up with each word.

"I take it that's good? It sounds like a lot."

"Good? No. Good is breaking the three-hundred view threshold and having over fifty likes. This is amazing. This is unheard of. You hit the jackpot."

I sure did, I think to myself as I take in the women in front of me. She did all of this for me. If anyone deserves recognition, it's her.

"You, ma'am, hit the jackpot. You did this. You're

amazingly talented, Gia. This is your video, your work. Most of these images are shots you got or at the very least edited. This is great. I'm so fucking proud of you." She never ceases to amaze me. She has more creative talent in her pinky fingernail than I have in my entire body.

"You don't get it." She sighs.

"My wife is a badass. See, I'm tracking. Now let me fuck you."

"I swear sometimes you really have brain damage." She taps my forehead with her fingers, and I grab them and hold them in my hand.

"Should I have said please? Because I am not above begging for your attention. When did you buy these shorts? You're killing me slowly, woman." Using my free hand, I follow an imaginary trail on her exposed skin until I reach the hem of her shorts, toying with the fabric between my fingertips.

She's not having it though; she yanks her fingers from my hand and swats at my opposite hand on her thigh.

"Damien! Focus. Every team in the NHL has their own social media team. They all have their own accounts. There are people behind those accounts. Real people, just like me. Only those people are actually employed and get paid to work." She motions wildly with her hands.

One day people are going to write out huge commission checks with her name on them. It's just a matter of time.

"Hey, I pay you," I reach out and squeeze her thigh just above her knee and she jerks. I know for a fact that's her tickle spot. I can't keep my hands off of her when she's this close to me. I spent years shoving my hands in my pockets. She was always untouchable. Now that I have free range to touch, I can't keep my hands to myself. I don't want to.

"Yeah, in dick," she rolls her eyes at me and then tosses her phone down on the bed beside us.

I scoot up on the bed, shifting her down my body just enough so that, said dick, is nestled right against the crack of her ass. She's the one that said dick to begin with. She climbed on my lap. This is her fault. "It's sexy as hell when you say dick. Also, I don't hear any complaints." I wiggle my brows at her playfully, and she tosses her hands up at me obviously exasperated.

Ignoring me, she continues her explanation, "Anyway, every team in the NHL has been tagged at least once in your video. Some multiple times. They're going to see this! They're going to see you. And the views are still climbing. We can build off of this momentum. We can get your story out there, and when we do, they're going to take notice. The whole world is going to root for you, Damien. We're going to make a comeback. You're going to get your chance, this is it. I can feel it."

I push up off the mattress completely, so that we're facing each other at eye level. Her long legs wrap around my waist.

"You're so fucking amazing, Click." I brush my nose against hers and smile when she crinkles hers up.

She's completely ready for bed. Her face is devoid of makeup. I can see the very light dusting of freckles that rest on the top of her nose, and fan out just over her cheeks. Her hair is already inside her cute bedtime bonnet.

It's like her eyes grow even bigger as she stares at me. Her legs tighten around my waist, and her chest brushes up against mine, her breasts barely contained by her tank top. "You're amazing. I'm just trying to get people to see what I see."

"You're relentless, aren't you?" I reach behind her with my hands and grip the luscious cheeks of her perfect ass, pulling her body even closer into mine. I eliminate every centimeter of space between us.

"I almost lost you." Her words are hushed as if she's afraid that saying them will give life back to them and make them true. "The world almost lost you before they even got the chance to see you soar. I'm not going to miss that opportunity again. We're doing this together. We're flying, Damien."

"You're never going to lose me, Gia. I'd defeat death a million times to be here with you, and with Astria. You know that right?" I ask her seriously. I'll remind her every day if I have to.

I know this isn't just about what happened to me. I understand that some of this stems from losing her dad. It's a culmination of the two events. They mirror each other in the most tragic way. I can't imagine what she went through that night, unsure as to whether or not she'd be raising our daughter alone after I swore to her, we were in this together.

I don't ever want her to feel that way again. Ever.

"I know. That's why I'm not giving up. I'm never giving up on you, Damien."

CHAPTER TWENTY
GIA

I close the distance between us and kiss him before I start crying. I pour all of my passion into one searing kiss that burns my lips and scalds my throat as I push down the emotion bubbling up inside of me unexpectedly with what should be a moment of pure joy.

I know he takes what I'm doing with his social media accounts seriously, but I don't think he truly understands the impact this is going to have on his career. This is major. If I can keep up this kind of momentum for him, it could be a game-changer.

I've always wanted to see history in the making. I want to live it. I want to capture it behind the lens of my camera and preserve it for a lifetime. Did I imagine that would involve professional hockey? Never. Am I now fully committed to my cause? Absolutely.

I want the world to see him. Without even realizing it he is giving me my dream. He supports everything I do wholeheartedly. The least I can do is offer the same level of support to him.

I pull back long enough to grab my bonnet off of my head and toss it to the floor. No woman in the history of ever wants to wear a bonnet while doing the dirty, I can assure you of that. Even if my hair does look a hot mess beneath it. My tank top follows quickly behind it.

I smirk to myself with satisfaction as I shimmy out of my shorts. I didn't go out and buy new shorts. Sylvia was getting rid of some things when she was packing for their move, and she offered me what she couldn't take with her. So, why not? Her loss is my gain. The shorts are sexy. I couldn't wait to wear them for Damien and see what kind of reaction he had to them.

It's safe to say, they did not disappoint. Thank you, second-hand silky shorts.

Sylvia's halfway across the country and she's still helping to get me laid. I really should have given her a going-away gift or something. She deserves it. Maybe I'll mail her something.

"I want to take your picture. Can I?" Damien speaks, and I pause, realizing just now that when he stood from the bed, he didn't strip off his athletic shorts and get naked like I thought. Instead, he walked over to my nightstand and grabbed my camera. His question slaps me momentarily stunned. I stare at him like he's grown a second head.

"Um, now? Why would you want to do that?" I look down at myself somewhat horrified.

I'm not typically self-conscious. I'm proud of the assets I have. They don't look the same as they did pre-baby, but I've got an ass for days and boobs that won't wait. Even if they do have stretch marks on them now, and my nipples tend to point toward hell more than they speak to Jesus.

I'm wearing no clothes to speak of, kneeling on the bed. The lamp beside us casts a faint glow over the room. The lighting in here is going to be terrible for this, honestly.

Damien takes the cover off of the lens I left attached to my camera when I was shooting earlier today. Without looking up he says, "Stop thinking about the lighting."

Butterflies swarm my stomach. How does he know that I'm thinking about the lighting? Slowly my nerves begin to turn into something else entirely. Excitement maybe?

"I was not thinking about the lighting, thank you very much." I lie.

He chuckles to himself as he lifts the camera up, and quickly snaps a shot, pulling it back to look at the screen as soon as it flashes. "Beautiful," he smiles down at his handiwork. Now he's the one that's lying. I wasn't even ready yet.

I do have to admit, he looks pretty cute standing next to the bed playing photographer. My camera looks like a toy in his large hands. It's only giving me a tiny eye twitch that he's touching my prize possession. All of which is easily forgotten the moment he brings the camera back up to his eye and the cords on his arm muscles pop and flex with the movement. He snaps another photo before I can react.

Click.

"Stop it! I'm not ready." I try to run my fingers through my nest of wild hair, but it's no use, they only get tangled up in the mess. I give up and drop them to my side a little unsure of what to do with them.

"I needed a picture of your eyes, looking at me like that." He shrugs, and the small smile that tilts his lips melts me into a puddle right on the bed.

"Like what?" I ask and my voice is breathy already.

From a small smile to a wolfish grin, the look on Damien's face heats me up from the inside out. "Like you're about to eat me for dessert."

"Was not." I worry my lip with my teeth and he snaps another photo of me.

Click.

"Oh, you definitely were. Now, turn around." He motions in a circle with his hand. "Put your hands up on the headboard and your knees on the bed. I want you to look at me over your shoulder but don't smile. Just act natural."

"Whoa. When did you become a professional?" I follow his instructions. I move to the head of the bed and spread my knees, popping my ass out a little and arching my back in a way that I know will translate well on film. If we're going to do this, we may as well do it up right.

I've taken some boudoir images in the past for different clients. Mostly wives and girlfriends of some of the other hockey players to earn some extra money.

I try to think back to how I've positioned their bodies in the past and attempt to mimic that in my own positioning. It's so much easier when you're not the one being photographed.

"I am a man of many talents, Click."

Click. Click. He snaps a couple of shots.

"Don't call me Click if you want to take pictures of my ass, Damien." I scowl at him, but it's playful. I know he means no harm by calling me by my nickname. He doesn't understand how the association works in my head. It's a me thing, not a him thing.

Click.

He looks at me momentarily bewildered, as if putting two and two together for the first time. "Click in the streets, Gia in the sheets. Noted."

I try not to laugh and fail, snorting through my nose. That's not going to be cute on film.

Click.

"Ass."

He's not wrong, though. So very not wrong at all.

Click.

"Speaking of cute asses. Yours looks delectable this evening."

I arch my back ever so slightly more with his praise.

"Just like that." *Click.* "Okay, now take your thong off and lay back on the pillows this time."

He licks his lips, and my eyes voluntarily follow the movement. There's something sensual that I didn't expect about doing this with him. It's outside of my comfort zone, being on this side of the camera, but surprisingly, I don't hate it, not with Damien. It feels special. I feel sexy.

I slide my thong off as directed, and toss it at him playfully, getting more and more comfortable the longer we do this. He catches it with the reflexes you would expect from a professional hockey player, bringing it up to his nose and inhaling deeply before tossing it down on the foot of the bed.

The sniffing was not expected, but, oddly, I like it. I've known this man my entire life. I know almost everything about him. But, in the bedroom? It's like we've never met. He surprises me at every turn, and the unpredictability is such a turn-on.

"You want me like this?"

I scoot back against the pillows, sitting upright, but leaning back ever so slightly. I bend my legs at the knee and prop my feet up on top of the comforter, giving him a better angle for the shot I know he's trying to get.

There's a fire burning in his eyes as he watches me behind the camera. "Spread your legs a little more, open up for me baby."

I do as I'm told, dropping my knees open and spreading my legs for him.

"Perfect. So damn perfect, Gia."

He's a voyeur, watching me perform for him. Anticipation begins to hum in my veins. I feel him touching me through the lens of the camera alone.

I will never look at my camera the same way again.

"You're amazing, Gia."

I reach up and take one of my breasts in my hands. I squeeze my nipple between my fingers and feel the zap of electricity between my thighs as if it were Damien's touch and not my own.

"What are you going to do with these photos, Damien?" My curiosity finally getting the best of me.

He pulls the camera down from his face and looks me

dead in the eyes before answering. "They're for me. Only me."

I nod my understanding, before tossing back my head and running my hand down my abdomen slowly, creating a trail to where my clit is already pulsing with need. I allow a soft moan to escape from my lips.

Hockey players travel a lot. They spend many nights alone in their hotel rooms with a ton of pent-up adrenaline and nowhere for it to go. Video chat isn't always an option. Especially when you have a tyrant of a two-year-old running around. I get it.

I won't let my insecurities creep in and ruin this for me.

He only wants me. He wants my body. I've never felt so desired.

This feeling of empowerment is intoxicating. I feel like I can do anything.

I move, crawling on all fours across the bed to where he stands.

Without hesitation, I grip the waistband of his athletic shorts. My palm brushes his skin, and I swear I can feel the tightening of his abdominal muscles beneath my hands.

I tug his shorts down just enough so that his hardened length juts out between us the moment it's released.

Click. Click. Click.

I kneel at the edge of the bed and lower my mouth down around the tip of his cock.

"Motherfucker," he grunts.

Click. Click. Click.

I swirl my tongue around the tip and then swallow him

until he bottoms out in the back of my throat.

He makes a garbled sound in his throat, and I smile to myself around his length.

I glance up just in time to see him lean and place the camera back down on the nightstand. He straightens and then moves closer to me until his shins hit the bed frame. He gives me the perfect angle to take him down my throat, which is exactly what I do, over and over again.

"Gia, baby, God, you're so good at that." One of his hands falls to the back of my head, but he doesn't force me, he steadies himself while allowing me to create my own rhythm.

I suck.

I lick.

I enjoy the feeling of control that I have over his pleasure until he pulls away abruptly, leaving me licking my lips with the taste of him lingering.

He steps out of his shorts and briefs never once taking his eyes off of me.

He steps back to the bed, and I allow him to lay me down. He rains kisses down around me, starting at my collarbone and working his way over my breasts.

"Yes," I call out as he pulls one of my nipples into his mouth, sucking until it's hardened and then moving on to the next.

He glides his tongue over my ribcage and goosebumps light up my skin.

"I wonder how long I've loved you, Gia." He says aloud as he climbs over my body, placing his hands on either side of me and hovering there.

His length teases me, barely touching my most

sensitive parts.

"I think I was always meant to be yours, Damien," I confess something I've thought about often.

Years ago, growing up together, we didn't realize it at the time, but even then, I think our souls were connected on a different level. We had our own frequency, and never realized it.

"Good answer." He positions his thick, muscular thighs between my legs, and I spread as wide as I can to accommodate him.

He takes a deep breath. "You've always been mine, Gia." His lips run over my jawline.

I pull my knees up, enticing him to come closer. I can feel my orgasm already beginning to form.

I use the confidence that is still steadily flowing through my veins from our photo session and take his cock in my hand, lining the tip up with my entrance.

I angle my ass up and slide him in as far as I can in our position, but it's not enough.

"More, Damien, please give me more." The demand in my own words surprises me.

"You want me to fuck you, Gia?" He growls, and I can tell he's walking the edge too, balancing, and just barely teetering without falling.

My eyes connect with his, "I want you to love me."

"Fuck," he slams his hips down over mine, and I'm immediately sated in the most delicious way.

"Yes, Damien, fuck yes," I move my hips against his as we both take what we so desperately need.

"God, do you realize how sexy it is when you say my name like that," he grunts, sliding out of me and then back in again. Every time he bottoms out in me my orgasm climbs higher, and I'm that much closer to nirvana.

His muscles flex around me, protecting me, guarding me as he makes love to me in a way I never even realized existed. It's as if we've entered another realm - a new dimension. Every time with Damien is new and different. Every time I learn something about myself that I didn't know before. It's euphoric and exhilarating all at the same time.

Our hips kiss again and again, and when I don't think I can take any more I say, "Damien, baby, fuck me," knowing good and damn well what I'm asking for.

He drives home, and a feral cry rips from my lips as I completely fall apart beneath him. One more thrust and he's coming down with me. Pleasure rips through my body as I pull every ounce of his orgasm from him, and internalize it in my own.

Our gasps for air mingle together until we slowly begin to come down from the high. He slips out of me gently before he rolls to the side and we lie side by side on the bed.

"Thank you," he says, still breathless. I turn my face to the side and meet his green eyes.

"For what?"

"For letting me love you, Gia." He kisses my lips softly with his, and I close my eyes, allowing myself to feel every second of this moment.

Somehow doing the mundane daily tasks that slowly drown out time and steal days and years from our lives, I fell in love.

In the middle of the night while the baby cried, and I cried, and he held me.

I fell in love.

In the midst of reality, changing diapers and soft coos that were never meant for me but for a child that we mutually adore. I fell for the man that helped create the best part of me.

I was forced to grow up quickly. So was he. We did it together.

I don't think I realized it at the time, but looking back, becoming a mother was so much easier than growing into a woman and discovering that the boy you gave yourself to all those years ago became the man you don't want to ever have to wake up without.

CHAPTER TWENTY-ONE
DAMIEN

"They're up by one, but there are still two minutes left in the third period." I bounce Astria up and down on my knee, while we sit on the loveseat in our living room watching the Renegades take on the Megalodons.

Gia, looks up from where she's been editing images on her laptop for the last hour, "How's Carter playing?"

"Like *shi*-garbage." I correct my language quickly before Astria starts repeating shit over and over again. She won't hesitate to tell you who she learned it from either, ask me how I know.

She's a ball buster of a two-year-old. She definitely gets that from her mama.

"Seriously?" Gia quirks her head to the side and starts actually paying attention to the screen. I can't blame her; my girl only cares about hockey if I'm the one holding the stick. Doesn't hurt my feelings any.

My lips curl into a knowing smile, got her. "Nah, he's killing it."

And he is. Carter looks like a beast out there tonight. The Megalodons are favored to win the cup this year, but the Renegades are giving them a run for their money.

The camera pans up into the stands briefly as they reset the play after a penalty on the Megalodons. They're starting to get desperate for the win and it shows.

Gia squeals, "Oh my gosh, look, it's Sylvia! How cute is she in the family box? And Camden. Look, Astria, it's Camden!"

Astria claps her hands, mimicking Gia's excitement. My girls are still missing their friends, and it makes my chest burn. Camden was Astria's best friend, even if they did fight like brother and sister most days. And Gia, I know she was close with Sylvia. She pretends like she is unaffected by all of this because she's constantly trying to put on a brave face for me, but I know it's getting to her.

It's wearing on me.

"Why do you look so worried?" Gia interrupts my thoughts, as I stare blindly at the television.

I glance over at her; her brown eyes watch me carefully. "What makes you think I'm worried?"

"You're doing that thing where you twist your hair up." Astria hops off of my knee and grabs one of her toys from the floor.

I release my hair from my hand.

"Am not." I counter. She knows my tells, and we both know I'm lying.

"Mhmmm." She sighs, but she doesn't stop watching me. She sets her laptop to the side and gets up and walks over to where I sit.

She sits down beside me and stares at the television. She mimics my body language, leaning forward and placing her elbows on her knees. She tugs at her hair, and it bounces back. Mine doesn't bounce. I smile to myself, but I stay focused and so does she. It's like she's trying to see what I see. She watches the Megalodons skate toward the net.

I hold my breath as they set up the shot.

"It's Henegan. Watch him closely. He's half a second behind them every time. Something is wrong." I pick the piece of hair back up I was just twirling between my fingertips.

Henegan's showing his weakness. That doesn't bode well for the remainder of the season for the Renegades. We all have our weaknesses, but when an injury starts affecting the entire team, and anyone with a set of eyes can see it, that's not good for the home team. A hockey team is only as good as their goaltender. Maybe that sounds arrogant, but it's the truth.

We are the lifeblood of the fucking team.

"That sucks." She bumps her shoulder into mine, and I drop my hair from my hand again. "Hey, you hear back from Raleigh today?"

Henegan blocks the shot, fuck. It was messy. The entire game has been messy. If they want to keep up their hot streak the Renegades are going to have to do something else and quick. They can't keep playing like this. The team's a ticking time bomb, and it's only a matter of time before the commentators start talking.

The chatter has been circulating for a while now. It's

not much of a secret anymore.

"I called them back, but once they got my medical records they passed."

Fucking Raleigh. Add that to the list of teams that won't even let me touch the ice. You die one fucking time, I swear.

"Again?"

You're a liability son.

"It's the third team this month."

Sorry, but we can't take the risk, Henderson.

"It's also the middle of the season, Damien." Gia places her hand on my thigh and squeezes. She tries to reassure me, but I'm starting to doubt myself.

Doubt isn't something I'm used to dealing with, and I don't fucking know what to do with it. Gia's viral video got me loads of attention. I'd be lying if I said it didn't inflate my ego a bit. I was confident. My phone was ringing off the hook. She was right, it was a game-changer. The problem? Even with full medical clearance to play, when it comes down to it, I'm a risk that no one is willing to take a chance on.

"Yeah, but this is after they've reached out to me first. They see the film. They see the shots, and my portfolio is stellar, all thanks to you. Then they get my medical records and run for the hills."

Renegades win. That was too close. I turn off the television and drop my head down into my hands. I run my hands through my long hair. It's even longer now than I usually keep it, my beard too.

I just want a fighting chance. I blew through my rehab program. I've more than surpassed every milestone the doctors wanted to see from me. Hell, I might be in better condition now than I was before the fight.

I just need game time. I need to get back on the ice. I need to feel the adrenaline from a game rushing through my veins. I want to be a part of a team. It's part of who I am, and I'm not ready to give that up. It's not time. My career has only just begun.

"Not the right team, not the right time." Gia draws circles on my thigh. I take her hand in mine and lace our fingers together. This is something she's said multiple times to me over the past few months. Every rejection I've faced, she's answered it with logic and reason that I can't seem to find.

I don't deserve her. I want to show her that I can be more than the man she married. She's never asked me for more, but she deserves it. They both deserve it. I want to show her that I can be more for Astria. I want to give them the world, and right now it's not happening no matter how hard I try to force it.

"You keep saying that, but this is the first season since I was old enough to hold a stick that I'm a spectator to the sport that I love. God, I hate it, Gia. I'm sorry, it's not fair that I unload all of this on you, but I'm starting to rethink my decision to wait it out." I scrub my free hand down my face.

My phone lights up and buzzes on the couch next to me with a familiar number. Gia pats my thigh one more time before standing up and picking up Astria. She positions her on her hip as if she doesn't weigh over twenty-five pounds.

"Astria, baby, let's go get ready for bed, and then

Daddy can come to tell us a story, okay?"

"Daddy, story! Daddy, snug!" Astria blows kisses in my direction over Gia's shoulder as she walks from the living room and into Astria's bedroom, giving me some privacy. I'm a lucky bastard.

I hit answer on my phone before it can go to voicemail. "Hey, Carter, what's up? Shouldn't you be celebrating somewhere? You guys just won." I flip back on the television but mute it, curious as to whether I missed something important after the game ended.

They haven't even had time to make it out for the press conference. He's got to be calling me from the locker room, which is weird as shit. It's just not something we do. Maybe shoot a text or something, but there's no reason for him to call me right now.

"Don't worry, I've got a pretty little thing waiting for me out in the hallway." I can hear his smile through the phone, and I know for a fact he's talking about Sylvia. "Listen, I need a favor."

What could be so important that he needed to call me from the locker room?

"Whatever it is, you got it. I owe you, man. You pulled me out of the slump I was in after my accident. Whatever you need, I'm there."

I'd never admit to anyone else that I struggled after my accident, but I did. I was scared. I wear more pads than any other player on the fucking team because it's my job to stand in front of a puck flying ninety-plus miles an hour. How the fuck a slice to the neck almost ended my life is beyond me. It's hard to get past that.

"Can you be in California by Friday?" he asks quietly

as if trying not to be heard over the chaos that I can hear in the background. The locker room might be loud, but the gossip mill in that room is louder. Trust me, I know. You'd be surprised at how much can be heard through the whispers. Few secrets survive.

"Awe, thanks babe, you got me tickets to a game, I'm flattered." I lean back on the couch, unsure of where he's going with this, and why now.

"No, fucker, we need a goalie." My heart stops beating - cold turkey. I reach two fingers up to my raised scar and feel for a pulse in my neck. "Henegan's down again. This time he's going to need surgery, and it's not looking good. Our second-string guy is shit. I showed Coach your footage, and he wants you. Show up Friday and do your thing. If he likes what he sees you've got a chance at being called up as a free agent for the remainder of the season. Who knows what that could lead to."

My heart feverishly pumps blood into my veins; a welcomed reminder that I am very much still living. A luxury I almost couldn't afford.

"Stop fucking with me, Tolar." It's all I can manage to say.

"The only person I plan on fucking is my wife. Which reminds me, she's waiting for me. Be here on Friday, Henderson. This is your chance, don't fuck it up." And with that, he hangs up. I drop the phone down on the couch next to me and stare up at the ceiling.

This is your chance, Damien. Prove yourself.

This is my chance. Prove it.

-o-
GIA

The television plays in the background as I try to set Astria up with her dinner in the living room so that I can watch the game and make sure she eats at the same time. I've had two different commission requests come through my website that need my immediate attention. No biggie, I've got this, I can multitask.

Damien is in California. I can't believe it. Freaking California. I knew it was only a matter of time. Finally, he's getting his turn. I know some people wait much longer, but given how quickly his world was rocked, and his future was stolen from him, he needed this. This might very well be his only shot. Chances like this one are one in a million. The future of his hockey career is hanging in the balance of one single game.

It might sound dramatic, but it feels very real.

We couldn't all afford to fly out to California. Damien is spending the weekend with Sylvia and Carter, and I'm here with Astria. I can't up and leave my classes this close to the end of the semester. Especially not knowing what the future holds for us yet. This whole dangling-in-the-balance thing is a little unsettling, but it's better than the alternative. We have hope. This is what we've been working toward.

The game hasn't started yet. Commentators for the game are debating on who might win the matchup tonight between the LA Renegades and the Washington Capitals.

I thought about wearing my Rafferton jersey tonight,

but I couldn't bring myself to do it. The last time I wore it we were in Chambliss. Maybe it's a little superstitious, but I'm not willing to risk that kind of juju on tonight's game. Instead, I've dressed Astria in one of Damien's old practice t-shirts as a nightgown. It still swallows her, but she's adorable. I sent him a quick text with a picture of her before the game and wished him luck.

"Yeah, Reggie, the LA Renegades are big news tonight. In an unprecedented decision, they've called up Damien Henderson as a free agent to play in tonight's game against the Capitals."

I freeze when the commentators mention Damien's name on national television. I stand in the middle of the living room and wait on bated breath for what they're going to say about him.

"Henderson's the former goaltender for the Rafferton Ram's. With only a couple of years under his college belt, he had a promising future, until a fight on the ice nearly ended his life and cost him the remainder of his college career. Since then, he's been making a name for himself on social media, of all places."

Oh God, I swallow hard. I know he's going to rewatch this later.

"We'll see how social media translates over to ice time, Reggie. It's a big step up for such a young kid, and it's a big risk for the Renegades if you ask me."

Well, that was uncalled for.

"Nobody asked you, Glenn, I think we'll see that a big risk for the Renegades might end up with a big reward for the entire home team. I'm a fan of the kid. We might just be gearing up for a historical comeback. Back to you on the ice, Alison."

Thank you for that, Reggie. I don't have a clue who you are, but I like you. I make a mental note to look these guys up and check out their backgrounds. I bet Glenn has a bone to pick with the Renegades. He's definitely a prude. His purple velvet jacket is two sizes two small…if you ask me.

I take a deep breath and try to calm my nerves. Without anywhere to direct my sudden onset of nervous energy I pick up my phone and type a text out to Sylvia.

Gia: *You there? How's the energy?*

I watch and wait as bubbles appear on the screen.

Sylvia: *It's booming in here. He's warming up with Carter. They look good.*

I bet they do. I smirk to myself. I know what she's doing. It's working, and I'm grateful for the mental distraction.

Gia: *Keep your eyes on your own husband's backside.*

Sylvia: *He's doing the splits, Gia. Give me a break. A woman only has so much self-control.*

Gia: *Fine. You get a pass for the splits.*

Damn that man and his flexibility. Hockey warmups are their very own form of foreplay. My mouth waters just imagining it. I'd have much rather been watching the warmups down on the ice than listening to the commentating.

Sylvia: *How are you holding up?*

Good question.

Gia: *Good. Nervous, but good.*

Sylvia: *Understandable. He's ready. You both are. This is what he's been working toward.*

I know he is. I just need him to be confident in his own ability. This is the first time he's been out on the ice for a game since the accident. He's physically prepared, but the mental game is a whole other issue. He thinks he's unstoppable. To some extent, he's proven that he is. It doesn't make me worry for him any less.

Gia: *He is, now if he'll just remember that.*

Sylvia: *He will. I need you to remember that for me too. Okay?*

She's right. I need to take my own advice. It's a hard pill to swallow. I want this for him so badly, because I know what this opportunity means to him. Hockey gives him something I can't. The sport is his passion, and the team is his brotherhood. That night in Chambliss stripped him of so much of his identity. I'm so grateful Sylvia and Carter are there. I'm thankful for their friendship and their unyielding support. Carter is a true leader, and I'm so happy that he's there with Damien tonight.

Gia: *Thank you for this, Sylvia.*

I don't think I realized how much I needed the reassurance.

Sylvia: *You did this. You both did. Now, let's show them what our boys can do.*

Our boys. Her thoughts mimic mine. Somewhere along the way it kind of feels like Sylvia and Carter adopted us, and I don't think I realized it when it was happening but now that we're here, living it, I don't think I'd want it any other way.

I grab a blanket and my laptop and sit on the floor next to where I've set Astria up with her dinner. Intro music plays and I grab the remote and turn up the volume. I don't want to miss anything. The players skate out onto the ice and I quickly scan them. I don't breathe until I see him on the screen.

It's strange, seeing him in a new uniform, but he looks so good. Who am I kidding? I'm not getting any work done while the game is on. I close my laptop and push it to the side. I wrap the blanket around my shoulders and cross my legs in front of my body.

"Astria, look, it's Daddy," I point to where they show him skating back and forth in the net on the screen. I know she doesn't comprehend that it's truly Damien underneath all of those pads, but I can't help but show her.

I'm so fucking proud of him.

Tears form in my eyes, and I don't try to hold them back. The camera zooms by him, and I don't miss his smile. His eyes say that he's serious, but his smile tells me everything I need to know.

He's ready for this. Just like I knew he was.

It's time to make a comeback.

Four Score

SECTION BREAK

The only thing constant about life is that it changes.

And, sometimes, the bullet you thought you dodged comes back and hits you square between the eyes.

Six-ish Years Later

Four Score

CHAPTER TWENTY-TWO
DAMIEN

Gia moans softly into my mouth, as I run my hand up the back of her shirt and pull her closer to me. My lips brush hers and I inhale her scent for the first time in what feels like forever. God, I missed her.

We've been on the road for two weeks this time. I hate traveling without my girls, but it's difficult with Astria's busy schedule. Between school and her ever-growing list of extracurriculars, it's nearly impossible for them to leave.

Not to mention, my wife is a complete badass. Gia's one of the most sought-after photographers in the industry right now. It's impossible to walk by a magazine in the checkout line at the grocery store and not see a photo my wife took. Each time my chest puffs out a little further. I'm so damn proud of her. I'm proud of us. Our lives are hectic and crazy, but I wouldn't want it any other way.

The Renegades are on a hot streak right now, and it feels good. Who doesn't want to win? Personally, I think it hits different when you defeated death to get here. I've been proving that damn doctor wrong for nearly six years now. If and when we make it to the cup, I'm sending him box seat tickets.

I slide my tongue along her plump lips, and she opens for me. It never gets old. The feel of her lips on mine. The way her tongue slides into my mouth, and she takes what she wants unapologetically. If anything, it's only gotten better with time, this fire that burns between us. This woman is the best damn kisser that ever existed, and I dare someone to try to tell me otherwise. Her body and her mind are completely in sync with mine. She is my home.

"Gross! Dad stop making out with Mom in the kitchen!" A shrill screech comes from the entrance to the kitchen, and I pull away slowly, reluctantly. We're caught.

I kiss Gia on the nose and then the forehead before putting enough space between us that we're appropriate for a viewing audience of one, not-quite-yet, pre-teen.

I look at my daughter curiously, did she say the words *make out*?

Astria's getting closer to her mother's height every day, it feels like she's grown six inches in the last two weeks alone. "Whoa there, who taught you to say making out? Since when do we say that? You're like five, right? You can't walk around saying things like that out in the open for my sensitive Dad ears to hear."

Astria scoffs. Her hair is braided in two French braids down her back, they kind of remind me of her mom's braids at that age. Her backpack is slung over one shoulder. Always perfect timing, this one.

She's just getting home from school; she rides the bus to our neighborhood with Camden Tolar. The Tolars live just down the street. I like that they're getting to grow up together, but I'm also keeping my eyes on that boy. I know how this story ends already. One day they're like your sister and the next you're standing in your kitchen with a semi being chastised by your daughter for making out.

"Dad. Come on. I'm in the fourth grade, I'm almost nine. I know what kissing is. Please, just, whatever you do, don't make another baby."

My heart leaps into my throat, and I choke. No way are we prepared for this talk. It's a Tuesday. Sex talks in the kitchen do not happen on Tuesday. That's more of a weekend topic. Actually, I need another thirty years, at least, before I'll be ready for this conversation. Or never.

"Gia. Make it stop. My ears are bleeding." I squeeze Gia's hips in my hands and beg my wife to have mercy on me and get us out of this conversation and fast.

"Astria, honey, your dad was kissing me in the kitchen. This is my kitchen. If I want to be kissed in my kitchen I can be kissed in my kitchen. We are two consenting, married adults. If we want to make a baby, we will." I widen my eyes at her in an attempt to make her stop, but she only smiles knowingly. "Just not in the kitchen." *Fuck*. That's not what I meant. I can't think about making a baby while my eight-year-old stands in the kitchen next to us, judging our every move.

More like eight going on twenty-eight.

"Why not in the kitchen?" Astria asks, and now I know she's just toying with us. She's too smart for her own good. She looks more and more like her mama every day. So beautiful.

"We're not having this conversation right now. Your dad just got back. I wanted to kiss him - in the kitchen. End of discussion." Gia looks at our daughter with a raised eyebrow and dares her to test her again.

I stare at our daughter, slowly shaking my head back and forth. Don't do it. Do not test this woman.

Astria crosses her arms over her chest, a small smirk lifting the corner of her lip. I know that look. Suddenly, I'm worried for her safety.

"Camden said his baby sister threw up all over him in the backseat last week. Hard pass."

I hold my smile in. I have an odd sense of pleasure knowing that Camden has been getting his own dose of pre-teen birth control in the form of baby puke.

Sylvia and Carter added a second child to the mix a little less than a year ago. I can't imagine starting over again at this point, honestly. Even if we are still young in comparison to most parents with a child Astria's age.

The last seven years have aged me in ways that are hard to explain to anyone that didn't experience them first-hand. It's part of the reason I keep my circle so close.

That first season with the Renegades I remained a free agent while they watched and studied my every move. It was as if they were certain I'd drop dead at any second. The commentators had a field day.

I didn't die.

Henegan retired after his knee surgery, it was time. I

got called up. Gia transferred the remainder of her classes online. At the time, she was only a couple of semesters from graduating. We made the move to California on a hope and a prayer. We didn't have anything.

No risk, no reward.

The risk paid off. I guess it was finally my time. *Our* time.

Astria and Camden picked up, like there was never any time missed between them, and they've been inseparable ever since. I'll allow it. But the minute we start talking about kissing, that shit is over. I'll lock her in her room with baby dolls and tell her bedtime stories until she reverts back to being my little girl.

"What are you doing in here, anyway, Astria? Don't you need to get your gear together for practice or do homework or…something?" Gia asks.

Astria opens the refrigerator and snags a bottle of water.

"My, um, my muscles are hurting again." I don't miss the way Astria's eyes dart to the floor quickly, before shooting back up to us again.

I get a gnawing feeling in my gut that I've missed something.

I look from Astria to Gia before I ask, "Growing pains?"

"Yeah, I think so. My head hurts too. I feel nauseous. Like last time." Astria shrugs as if it's no big deal.

Gia moves from where I've been holding her against the kitchen island and walks to our designated family medicine cabinet.

"Okay, let me give you something for it." She looks

through the medication we keep on hand, and pulls out a bottle of over-the-counter pain reliever, opening it. "How about we lay low tonight for practice?" She suggests, handing her the medicine.

Astria takes the pill and swallows it down with the water without a second thought. It seems like yesterday she was taking liquid Tylenol in a miniature shot glass.

"And let the boys have another reason to say I can't be on the co-ed hockey team? I think not. I'll play through the pain. It's fine." She turns to leave, but Gia stops her before I do. This conversation isn't over.

She walks around Astria and stands in front of her, putting her hands on her hips.

"It's not fine, Astria. Your health comes first."

I have to wonder to myself how long this has been going on and I haven't known about it.

"I want to play, Mom. Tell her, Dad. Tell her I need to practice." Astria glances over her shoulder, looking for backup.

I'm not taking heat for this. Mother-daughter relationships are tricky ones and I refuse to get in the middle of it.

She's trying to pull me into their argument, but I'm not falling for it. "I'm not going to argue with your mother, Astria. She's right. Your health always comes first."

The words taste all wrong. They make me feel like a hypocrite. I play every day with risk. Sure, I'm medically clear, and I'm constantly running through a list of checkups and appointments that continue to verify it's safe for me to play, but there's still risk involved. There will always be a risk. It's something I've learned to live with. This is different.

Astria huffs, "This isn't fair! I knew I shouldn't have told you." Her words are laced with defiance that I won't tolerate. This is something we need to discuss further, but first Gia and I clearly need to have a private conversation.

I step in, placing a firm hand on her shoulder, and she winces when I touch her. That's not normal. "Astria, watch your tone when you talk to your mother."

I remove my hand, not wanting to cause her any pain. Worry swarms in my chest like angry bees ready to take flight.

"Time out. All of you. Astria, go to your room and let me talk to your dad." Astria and I both snap to attention when Gia speaks. She's using *the voice*, and it's obvious we both know that you do not argue with *the voice*.

Astria ducks around Gia and heads straight for her room. Lucky for her she doesn't slam the door. That'd guarantee her no hockey practice, and she knows it.

Gia walks back to the kitchen island and places her hands on the countertop, leaning against the polished concrete, her shoulders sink forward. I walk behind her and wrap my arms around her.

"You think it's a migraine? Is she too young for migraines?" I ask quietly. I feel lost. I feel like I'm missing pieces of a puzzle, and I don't like it.

Gia turns in my arms and places her cheek on my chest.

"No, that could be it. I don't think she's too young, but this is the third time this month that I am aware of. The school called me last week. I didn't want to worry you. I'm scared, Damien. Call it mother's intuition, but something feels off about this."

-o-
ASTRIA

I skate toward the net with the speed I'm known for. Let these boys eat my dust. I set up the shot, and my calves seize. It feels like a cramp, but worse. I hesitate as the pain temporarily paralyzes me.

"Yeet it into the net, Ria. What are you waiting for?" Camden shouts at me from behind.

"I am!" I scream back at him.

My head is pounding. My muscles burn. Finally, my brain and muscles decide they'll work together, and my stick connects with the puck. I send it flying straight into the net. *Score.*

I breathe a sigh of relief.

"Whoop! That's how it's done, boys!" I feel someone throw a heavy arm over my shoulder and the muscle twitches. I noticed it when Dad did that earlier, too. That's a new one to add to the growing list of aches and pains I've been dealing with lately. "Yes! You did it, Ria! Give a guy a heart attack, will ya?"

I shrug Camden off of me. "I was setting up the shot. Perfection takes time."

Camden and I have been friends since diapers. Mrs. Tolar calls him my boyfriend, which literally makes me cringe and want to upchuck my lunch.

Prime example? He smells like rotting fish right now. Does she even come close to her son while he's sweating?

Gross.

Anyway, my dad says I'm not allowed to have a boyfriend until I'm thirty. I don't disagree with him. It seems like a giant waste of energy. I have more important things to focus on. Things that don't make my head hurt.

"Yeah, time that we don't have when the clock's ticking. If that was a real game, you'd have been checked before you ever connected with the puck."

He's right. I need to be faster. I'm already faster than most of the boys. Well, all of them, except Camden. But, to my credit, he's got six months on me and a full foot of height. That's saying a lot, I'm the tallest girl in our class.

"I know." I skate to the bench, ready to take my skates and pads off, and get into an ice bath. Maybe that'll help.

"I know you know, so what's up? Why the delay?" Camden sits down beside me and starts unlacing his skates. He just won't give it up.

"Can I ask you something?" I turn and look at him, the hair that's come loose from my braids flies into my face and annoys the heck out of me.

"Always, you're my bro." He smiles, tapping his sweaty, sock-covered foot into mine.

"You do realize I'm a girl, Camden? Right?" I look at him, slightly irritated, but what's new? I may play with the boys, but I'm not one. It annoys me that they want to categorize me as a boy because by doing so they don't have to admit they're getting their butt whooped by a girl. It's a cop-out.

"Nah, no way. You're a dude, Ria. Girls don't handle a stick like that. Even my dad says you're good, and he doesn't say that about just anybody."

I roll my eyes so hard they nearly fall out of my head.

"Yeah, sure, anybody but you. My dad's a professional athlete, just like your dad. I think we were skating before we could walk. Doesn't make me a dude. The answer is plain and simple. Just means girl's rule." I smirk. "You can't label me one of the guys just because you don't want to be beaten by a female."

"Whoa, whoa. Nobody said anything about you beating me. We both know who the real MVP is here, and it's me." He beats his chest like a gorilla. Sheesh, boys.

He's delusional. My dad's so right, boys this age are idiots.

"You dance to the chicken nugget song, and you cried at the end of the Mighty Ducks." I raise my eyebrows, and he straightens on the bench beside me.

He clears his throat and his voice cracks awkwardly. "You had a question?" He ignores my accusations completely because he knows I have all the evidence I need on my cell phone. Always come prepared with blackmail. Work smarter, not harder. That's what my dad always says. He probably didn't mean blackmail, but meh – semantics.

I stretch my neck back and forth before confiding in my friend, "Do your muscles hurt?"

"Like, after practice? Sure, I guess. It's normal to be sore after a workout." He stands up and strips his pads off right in the middle of the practice arena.

Most everyone's already been picked up. My mom will be here any minute to pick us up. She's been trying to help out Mrs. Tolar lately because of the baby. Camden catches a ride home with us after practice most days.

"No, like...um all the time?" I strip off my practice jersey, and then my pads, leaving me in my sports bra. I shove everything into my enormous gear bag. I snatch my favorite sweatshirt out and throw it on over my sweaty torso. Whew, I don't smell like roses either. When was the last time I washed this thing? Ugh, I can't wait to get home and get in the bath.

"I don't know what you mean." Camden grabs his water bottle from the bench, bringing it up to his mouth and spraying it in before he takes a seat down next to me again.

The Zamboni cranks off in the distance and begins its nightly run over the ice, drowning out the potential for anyone to overhear us.

The dull thud I've felt in my head for weeks is still there. Even with the medicine my mom has been giving me, it won't go away. I'm nervous to tell them. I know just as soon as I do, they'll pull me out of practice and make me go to the doctor. Doctors mean shots, and I am terrified of needles. No thanks.

"Can I tell you a secret?"

I tell Camden everything. Maybe he'll know what to do. Maybe he has the same pains, and I'm overthinking it.

"Is this one of those things that I'll get in trouble for later?" Camden scratches his cheek, looking at me nervously.

"Maybe...I don't know." I answer honestly.

Camden is the rule follower, and I'm usually the one getting us into trouble. I call it balance. He doesn't so much appreciate it when we have to face the consequences of my actions.

"Spit it out." He says when I pause for too long.

My mom will be here any minute. We should be waiting in the parking lot, not sitting on the bench inside. She'll be mad if she has to come looking for us.

"I've been hurting a lot lately. Like, all over. My head. My body. My stomach. I don't know what's up, but I'm scared." I twist my hands together in my lap.

"You talk to your mom and dad?" Camden gives me a wary look.

My eyes snap up to his. "No way. They'll freak out. They think it's growing pains."

Camden opens his mouth to say something and then closes it again. He tugs on his damp, sweaty hair, and then starts again. "Ria, you think maybe you should tell them?"

"No, and you better not say a word. Understand?" I stare into his eyes and double dog dare him to say anything about this conversation ever again.

When he doesn't answer me, I take it a step further. "Spit in your hand, Camden. Do it."

"That's gross, Ria." He reels back and scrunches his nose up at the thought. Big baby.

"Do it, Camden. Or else I'll tell everyone how you tried to kiss me on the bus in first grade and you ended up with your lips pressed up against my lunchbox when I blocked you."

I spit in my hand and hold it out between us, waiting for him.

"You wouldn't." He hisses. His eyes narrow, and he looks back and forth between my spit-covered hand and the determination that I know is in my eyes.

Oh, I would. And he knows it.

"Spit. In. Your. Hand." I demand.

Camden looks at me once more and then brings his hand up to his mouth, hocking a loogie into his palm.

I smile.

His wet palm connects with mine, and we shake.

"Promise me you won't say anything to anyone." I reiterate.

"Fine. I promise." He sighs before pulling his hand back and grimacing.

He wipes his palm down the front of his practice pants, and we both stand just before I see my mom and dad walk through the entrance to the practice arena together. That's weird.

I yank my bag up, and throw it over my shoulder, wincing when the pain shoots down my arm. "Good, now, let's go home. I can't wait to tell my dad about how I outskated you and scored tonight."

I leave Camden on the bench scrambling to get his gear together as I walk toward my parents.

"You did not!" Camden calls out after me, hurrying to catch up. "Wait up, Ria!"

CHAPTER TWENTY-THREE
DAMIEN

"I called her pediatrician today." Gia sighs, placing her cell phone down on the nightstand and plugging it up before rolling over to her back in our king-size bed and staring up at the ceiling.

After Astria left for practice, we sat down and had a long discussion about her recent episodes. We talked through the different scenarios, and what we determined was that neither one of us felt comfortable brushing it off.

I put my phone down on the nightstand, mirroring her. I'd just been catching up on some highlights from last weekend's games. When she's done scrolling for the night, I am too. Pro marriage tip.

"What did he say?" I ask.

She rolls over to face me. She props her elbow up on the mattress and her chin in her hand. "We have an appointment tomorrow morning. He wants to do some blood work and set up a referral to a specialist."

"That's good, right? I'll be here. We can all go to the appointment together." Internally, I breathe a sigh of relief. We're still mid-season and I wouldn't miss this appointment for the world. Hockey included. When I told Astria that her health comes first, I meant it. That holds true for all of us. We're a family unit.

Gia's lips tremble. She chokes out a sob that takes me by surprise. "Hey, whoa, what's with the tears? We don't know anything yet. I thought getting an appointment was a good thing?"

I turn into her, and lift her chin with two of my fingers, bringing her eyes to meet mine in the dim light of the lamp.

She takes a deep breath in and then out heavily before continuing with an onslaught of words I wasn't prepared for. "It's just, I talked to the nurse, and she immediately put me through to the doctor's personal cell phone. I normally have to wait three months for a well-check visit appointment. Tomorrow is soon. That's emergent. It means he thinks there might be something wrong. What if there's something wrong, Damien?"

I have similar concerns, but I don't say that to her.

"If there's something wrong, and that is still a definitive *if*, we'll face whatever it is head-on. It's no different than how we handle any other challenge, and we've had our share. Every time we've come out on the other side." I try to reassure her. Tonight, the only thing we know is that our daughter is sleeping in her bed, in her room, just down the hall. She's safe. She's healthy.

She took a bath when we got home and drained the

ice machine. That's telling in itself. But for now, she's sleeping. If she's sleeping, she's not hurting. She's protected from whatever is hurting her.

Something is hurting my baby. *Fuck*. Keep it together, man. Keep it the fuck together.

"I Googled." Gia blurts out her confession as if I were the priest himself, and she's committed the worst of sins.

That explains the tears.

"Did my injury teach you nothing about using Google as a form of medical reference?" Every twitch, every pain, Gia attempted to diagnose using Doctor Google. Ninety-nine percent of the time, Google was wrong. Google does not have a medical degree, and anyone can publish anything on the internet and claim credibility.

"Nope. Google was certain that it's a brain tumor." Her eyes widen with horror as she voices the fears that I know have been eating away at her from the inside out all day.

She's used to the things she loves being taken away from her at a moment's notice. Her dad, her brother, even my accident. Now this. I won't blame her for assuming the worst. I'm just glad she's willing to confide in me.

"Gia, come here." I move my hand to her hip and tug lightly, but she doesn't budge.

She shakes her head back and forth, a turbulent look filling her big brown eyes. "I don't want to. I can't eat. I can't sleep. The last time I was this worried was..." She hiccups, and this time I grab her entire body in one swift move and pull her to me. I tuck her beneath my arms, and wrap my heavy thigh over hers, not allowing her room to escape. I spoon the hell out of her because I know exactly what she was going to say without her ever needing to say it.

I lean into her ear and whisper, "I know, baby. I know." She cries softly in my arms. Her body shakes, and I hold her, absorbing her anxiety as my own and doing everything in my power to give her enough strength to get through whatever this is.

Last time she was the strong one. When I was in a hospital bed fighting for my life, she was the air that I needed to breathe. She was my oxygen, and Astria was my reason for fighting every damn day.

It's my turn to be their rock.

She sniffles and says, "I'm so scared for her, Damien. She's still a baby. She might act like she's grown, but she's not."

I pull the sheet up around us tightly, like the thin piece of fabric will somehow cocoon us from our reality.

I take my time with my reply. "We can't protect her from everything. We can only help guide her. This could be as simple as a recurring migraine caused by something she's eating or drinking. It could be growing pains. Or, it could be something else. But we're doing the right thing. We're seeking professional medical advice. We've already taken the first step. If we need to see a specialist, we will. We will do whatever we have to do to get answers, and once we have them, we'll find the best possible treatment route. I promise." I try to force myself to believe my own words. It's so much easier to say them than it is to believe them to be true.

"Can I ask you something?" The waver in her voice

destroys me.

"Anything." I bury my nose in her neck and breathe her in.

"Will you take all of the thinking away? Will you help me forget, for a minute? I don't want to have to think. I can't turn it off, and it's suffocating me." She turns in my arms, looking up at me.

I hate the vulnerability I see there. She's one of the strongest women I know. And tomorrow, at that appointment, she'll have to hide these feelings away, because we have to put on a brave face for our daughter. And we will. Even if inside, we're breaking.

"You want me to make love to you?" I kiss her tear-stained cheeks softly.

"Yes, please, give me something else to focus on. Let me feel you instead of this hurt that's building in my chest." Her hips rock into mine, and I tighten my hold on her.

I take her jaw in my hand and look deep into her eyes. "I'm going to fuck you until you're so sated that you fall asleep and don't wake up until tomorrow. Okay, baby?"

"Yes, God, yes."

My lips find hers, and I kiss her long and hard. My tongue slides into her mouth, and I do my very best to steal every ounce of worry and fear from her.

I can tell the moment she relinquishes the feelings that were holding her captive through her anxiety, and instead of overthinking with her mind, she begins to feel with her body. Our kiss intensifies. Her hands roam beneath my t-shirt, lighting my skin with every brush of her skin on mine.

She circles my nipple with her fingertips. She pinches, applying pressure and shooting bolts of desire directly to my cock. She releases one and then moves on to the other one. *Fuck* that feels good. I groan my appreciation into her mouth.

I release her long enough to pull my t-shirt off over my back. She tugs at my briefs, and I assist her by kicking them from my legs. I slide the straps of her tank top down off her arms until her breasts are released. I watch them bounce with growing hunger as she shimmies out of her boy shorts, leaving nothing to separate us.

I lay back on the bed, and she straddles me, one knee on either side of my hips. This is her favorite position, and I know exactly why.

There's no pretense, only need. Temptation unfurls inside of me. This feeling, years have passed and it's still just as strong as it's always been.

She sits up on her knees and hovers over my hardened erection.

She lifts her hand to her mouth and using her tongue she lubricates her palm. She's so damn sexy.

Lowering her hand, she uses the liquid from her mouth to lubricate herself. She's already driving me wild.

Her nipples harden as she touches herself. She pulls her hand away only to grip my length with her small hands and line the tip of my cock up with her entrance.

She doesn't ease in. She doesn't take her time or tease me. She slams down onto my cock taking me to the hilt and causing my eyes to nearly roll back into my head. I can't tear my gaze away from her. She's like a mystical, majestic creature. So curvy, so naturally beautiful, that she shouldn't exist in the real world.

She whimpers as she slides her clit against my skin. She's fully seated on my length, and it feels so good. Every movement she makes, pleasuring herself, only makes me that much harder inside of her.

"I love you, Gia. Take what you need from me, baby."

She drops forward, placing her hands on the headboard behind me and giving me ample opportunity to feast on her perfect breasts. Not needing further invitation, that's exactly what I do. Fucking hell. I grip her rip cage with one hand and use the other to massage one of her breasts while I suck the other into my mouth.

She rocks her hips on my lap again and again, rising up and down and swirling against me, creating a pattern that I know is going to pull us both over the edge. The feel of her slick, hot pussy hugging my cock is heavenly. I could live here and never be unsatisfied.

"Damien..." she says my name and I feel her tighten around me. *So close.*

My spine tingles with the beginning of my orgasm. I hear her breathing becoming heavier with each passing second.

"Take what you need, baby. Take it. Fuck me." My voice is raw with emotion that I'm holding back.

I release her breasts and move my hands around to the cheeks of her ass. I increase the pressure of her movements and spread her cheeks so that she's fully exposed. The globes of her lush ass fit perfectly in each of my hands. She was made for me. I pull her to me tighter, gaining an even deeper level of penetration. I press my hips up and pump inside of her, moving with her. I feel her arms quiver above me. Her body bows, and she cries out.

Her hips twitch as her body vibrates against mine and her orgasm pulls her under. Her pussy spasms and clenches around me, and I allow myself to fall too. I forget everything except the woman in front of me. I allow myself to get lost in the moment of unmeasurable pleasure.

The sound of our mingled gasps for air fills the room, followed by Gia's quiet sobs.

She releases the headboard and drops her hands to my chest, remaining seated on my cock. Gently, she runs her hands up my chest and cups my face. Her thumbs rake across the stubble that covers my jawline. Leaning down, she brushes a soft kiss across my lips before whispering, "Again?"

And we do, two more times until finally, she finds the peace she was searching for and is able to rest.

CHAPTER TWENTY-FOUR
GIA

"Daddy, will you hold my hand?"

My heart breaks a little bit more inside my chest. Damien takes Astria's hand in his and laces their fingers together tightly. I don't miss the emotion that passes across his handsome features in the mirrored doors of the elevator.

Her eyes are puffy and bloodshot. She's been crying on and off since we told her that she'd be going to this appointment today instead of school.

When we got here, they ran an initial panel of bloodwork and took her vitals. They also did some preliminary scans, but we've already been told she'll need a referral to a specialist for further testing. We grabbed a quick lunch, not that any of us could actually eat, and now we're getting ready to sit down with the doctor.

I don't know what he's going to be able to tell us. I'm not sure how much they can learn from the initial testing alone. I hope that they're at least able to rule out some of my bigger concerns.

Last night Damien allowed me to lose myself in him for a little while, but the relief from the crippling anxiety I feel was short-lived. Seeing our daughter so upset was hard, but seeing the fear in her eyes and knowing we couldn't take it away? That was torture.

None of the books or websites on becoming a parent prepare you for these moments. When they're small you fear for their safety. Will they choke on a grape? Will they fall down from the top of the slide and get a concussion? So many worries. But it never goes away. It only amplifies over time, and your worries become more complex with every passing day.

Just when you think you're out of the woods. Bam! It's something new and scarier than your last fear.

We walk together, through the waiting room and sign back in at the front desk, only to be ushered back immediately.

Fear gnaws at my gut. I want to cry. I want to turn around and run. I want to hide away on an abandoned island somewhere with our little family and pretend this isn't happening. Whatever this is.

But I can't.

I have to be brave for Astria. I have to be strong. I'm not sure I'd be standing here at all if it weren't for the strength of the man next to me. Maybe it makes me selfish, but I'm pulling every ounce of strength I can from him right now.

We follow a nurse in a pair of blue scrubs down a long hallway. I'm transported back in time. Why does it feel like I've lived this all before? The similarities are few and far between, but the feeling of paralysis is the same. I'm once again rendered helpless. The fate of our future is in the hands of a doctor who probably already knows the outcome.

I walk blindly into an office with burgundy and hunter-green striped wallpaper. A large mahogany desk sits in the center, and matching wooden bookshelves line the walls. A framed certificate hangs on the wall directly behind the desk, giving this man more credentials than the internet, I guess.

We take our seats across from the desk in silence. We don't have to wait long. Astria's pediatrician walks in and takes his seat behind the desk. He places a manila file folder down gently in front of him.

Despite the fear and anxiety, I can't shake the feeling that we're in the right place now. I genuinely like Astria's pediatrician, and I trust him with our little girl. Maybe this short, older man with fluffy white hair and caring blue eyes was always supposed to be here, telling us whatever news it is that he's about to deliver.

Just maybe, the trials we've already gone through have been to prepare us for this moment. I have to believe there's a reason for all of this beyond what we can see. I can't believe that this is for nothing. My mind refuses to allow me to believe we experience tragedy and harm and gain nothing.

Sensing my rising level of anxiety, Damien scoots his chair over and wraps one arm around my shoulders, while still managing to hold Astria's hand. Her dark hair is pulled up into a ponytail that falls down her back. Her tears are gone. She sits stoically, her back straight, and her features hiding every emotion I know she must be feeling. She reminds me so much of her father in moments like this. She's so much braver than I was at her age. She's so strong.

The doctor's eyes crinkle in the corner with wrinkles as he smiles softly at Astria. "Astria, it's good to see you again. You've grown nearly two inches since I saw you at your last check-up. Let me guess. You're a hockey player, like your dad?"

I see Damien squeeze Astria's hand lightly in my peripheral. My knee starts to jump with nervous energy, and I cross one ankle behind the other forcing it to stop.

"Yes, sir." She says softly, lacking her usual confidence.

The doctor drums his fingers on top of the folder before continuing. "I want to thank you all for being here today for this." He subtly shifts his focus from Astria to all three of us, making sure to make eye contact with both Damien and me, which I appreciate. "I know your schedules are very busy. When you called yesterday, I knew that we needed to see Astria sooner rather than later. Her symptoms, while not excessively concerning independently, together, give me some cause for hesitation." My heart leaps into my throat. I bite the inside of my cheeks, hoping to keep it together for just a bit longer.

"I've been doing this for a long time. I understand how difficult it is to be worried about a child. I worry about each and every one of my patients as if they are one of my own." He continues, finally opening the folder in front of him, and shuffling around the papers inside. I crane my neck to see, but all I'm able to make out is black ink and a few X-ray images that mean nothing to me.

"Thank you, for agreeing to see us on such short notice. We can't tell you how much we appreciate it." Damien speaks for all of us, which I'm grateful for. I'm nervous that if I open my mouth the tears will come out, and I'm doing everything I can to keep them at bay.

The doctor pushes back from his chair, taking the X-ray images with him. He stands and walks to a light board on the wall to our right. He flips a switch and the lights come on. Placing the film up on the illumination board I tilt my head to the side and try to make out what we're looking at.

It's definitely images of her head, neck, and maybe shoulders. I'm no stranger to film, but this is so far from my area of expertise. I look for a black circle. A shadow. Anything that might indicate a tumor or cancer of some sort.

"Tell us what we're looking at, Doc," Damien says, the assertiveness in his voice taking me by surprise.

His patience is growing thin, and that's saying a lot. He's always the optimist, seeing the best in every situation. I can tell that his emotions are starting to get to him, though. Everything changes when the health of your child is at stake.

"Everything appears to be totally normal."

"What? You brought us in here to tell us there's not an issue?" I ask, my breath escaping me all at once. I feel like I've been sucker punched...but in a good way, if that's possible. I can't decide between shock and anger, but for now, I think I'll just choose relief.

Unfortunately, the high I'm riding is short-lived.

"No, not entirely. Appearance is oftentimes inaccurate in these circumstances. I told you that I felt she would need to be referred to a specialist. That's why we're here. That's why we ran the tests this morning. I had a hunch from our conversation, but I needed to know enough about what we were dealing with so that I could refer you to the appropriate specialist. I don't see any indication of a tumor, which is good news."

"Oh, my God. Thank you." The words expel from my mouth, an answered prayer.

"We're not out of the woods quite yet." He stops my internal celebration, and my breath catches. I feel like I'm on a rollercoaster of emotions that I want off of. "You see, inflammation doesn't show on a standard X-ray. She'll need an injection of a radioisotope to give us a more accurate representation of what we believe to be wrong."

"Wait, you want me to have an injection? You want to stick me with needles, again? No thanks!" Astria jumps from her chair, clearly petrified by the thought of being poked and prodded again. It's understandable given her age, and what she's already endured this morning. This would be a lot for an adult to handle, let alone a child.

"I promise, it's a simple procedure where we inject dye into a certain part of your body to better view things like your lymphatic system." He reassures her, but I can tell from the wild look in her eyes, she's not totally convinced.

Astria slowly settles back down into her chair, "My

what?" She asks, and honestly, I was thinking the same thing. This isn't what I researched on Google.

"Astria's panel came back showing an abnormally high white blood cell count. Given the other issues she is currently experiencing, and our initial physical exam, I have reason to believe that Astria has a rare autoimmune disorder. Of course, we need to find the specific root of what's causing her body to attack itself. If caught early, we may have the ability to reverse some of the damage that potentially might already have occurred and give her a treatment plan for the future. I have a colleague that I'd like to refer you to. He's at the top of his field, and really on the verge of some cutting-edge treatment using bone marrow that I think Astria might be a candidate for, given her age and present health."

Bone marrow. That sounds invasive, but I keep my comments to myself for now. I don't want to scare Astria any more than she already is. Instead, I focus on other questions that still need to be answered.

"Why now? Why is this happening all of a sudden? I don't understand. She's always been healthy. Why did her body decide to attack itself now?" I ask, still trying to make sense of what he's saying.

This is too much information at once. I should have brought a pen and paper. Or my laptop. I need to be taking notes. I wasn't prepared.

"It's likely she's had the disorder her entire life. I've seen cases where something like this is so recessive that it never presents. Some people live their entire lives never realizing it's there. In Astria's case, given her age, I believe our culprit has to do with hormonal changes in her body. She's approaching puberty, and that's changing the chemistry in her body which may have caused what has been a dormant disorder up until this point to begin attacking her health."

"A little discretion, Doc. Please. My dad has bleeding ear syndrome." Astria says, and I can't help but smile in the midst of the turmoil inside my mind. The return of her quick wit and smart mouth tells me that she's okay. She's going to be okay. We all are. This is hope. Right?

"Ah, I have daughters myself. I completely understand." The doctor's lips tilt into a grin, and he closes her folder on his desk "Well, if you would like, I'll have our receptionist send over the referral. I'll make a personal phone call, and hopefully, we'll have you an appointment by the end of the week. Is that okay?"

"Sure, of course. Thank you." I say quickly.

I guess it has to be. I don't want to be okay with any of this, but I'm a fighter. I'm a survivor. Damien, Astria, all three of us are.

We've had our share of challenges, but we've overcome them.

Just like we'll overcome this one.

CHAPTER TWENTY-FIVE
DAMIEN

I roll over for the fifteenth time in an hour and suddenly realize I'm in an empty bed. I fucking hate sleeping in an empty bed. Gia knows that. So why is she MIA? I have a sneaking suspicion, but I'm going to have to get up in order to verify my hunch.

For the first couple of years of our marriage, I barely slept a wink. Between a crying baby and a weeping cock, I was miserable. Knowing that just a couple of walls separated me from the one person I wanted to fall asleep with was torture. When I'm on the road, I do it out of necessity. But, when I'm home? I need to snuggle. Touch is my fucking love language.

Ugh, I throw the comforter and sheet off of my body and groan. My muscles ache from practice. I hit the gym hard after our time on the ice, needing to work through my thoughts. It didn't work, they're still a muddied mess of information that I don't know how to process.

Four Score

We met with Astria's specialist this morning. It was a lot of fucking medical jargon that I don't feel qualified to understand. Scary, terrifying shit that no parent ever wants to hear.

Apparently, the guy is some sort of pioneer in his field, which is great. On the one hand, there's a level of comfort in knowing we're with the best of the best. On the other hand, I don't want to be in this position at all.

I sit on the edge of the bed, running my hands down my face. I need to shave, but I just can't find it in me to care about my appearance right now. My brain is foggy. My girls and my career are the only two things I can focus on at the moment. Everything else is lost somewhere in the abyss.

I stand and stretch my arms over my head. It's pitch black in the room. I tap the screen on my phone until it illuminates. It's just after midnight. It's too early to be awake for the day. I need to go find my comfort blanket and bring her back to bed so maybe we can get a nap before we have to be up again.

I open the door quietly and pad toward the faint light I see coming from the kitchen. That's where I find her, huddled with a cup of what I hope is tea and not vodka, and her laptop. Hell, I wouldn't blame her if it were the latter. Maybe she'd be willing to share. I try not to drink alcohol during the season, but the thought is starting to sound more and more tempting.

She doesn't move as I approach, even though I know she hears me coming. "Can't sleep, Click?" I ask.

I walk up behind her until her back is flush against my chest. I kiss her neck softly before leaning down and placing my chin on her shoulder so that I can see what she's looking at on the illuminated screen in front of her. It's not like I don't already know. She's not working at this time of night. She's researching.

"No, you?" She sighs, leaning into me.

"Thought I might grab a turkey sandwich." I turn my head and brush my lips against her cheek. I feel her jaw lift into a knowing smile. I'm teasing her. I love that we have a language that only belongs to us.

I love that no matter how hard life gets, we have each other. It feels good to be able to lighten the air around us with a few simple words. It's all felt so heavy lately. It's hard to breathe.

"Turkey sandwich my ass." She lifts her shoulder, but my chin follows. I don't let her shake me off just yet.

I snake my arms around her waist and pull her into me. "My exact thoughts. You're so good with the meat."

She gives up with the laptop, and drops her arms to her side, tossing her head back and falling completely into my embrace. She stares up at the ceiling, and I follow her eyes. "God, I still can't believe I said that. Nor can I believe you're still bringing it up all these years later."

"God doesn't care about your penchant for quality meat, babe, but I do." I pinch her hip before continuing. "Some things are just too good to let die."

The air stills between us as the final word rolls off of my tongue. Neither one of us want to say it, but we're both thinking the same thing. *Death.* It's a word that's haunted us for years.

Astria isn't facing death. But her life as she knows it is hanging in the balance of one of the most important decisions we've ever had to make. It doesn't feel like there's a right answer. Just a different set of consequences for whichever route we decide to take.

"What are we going to do, Damien? Do we let her participate in the trial? It seems risky." She turns to me, looking for answers that I don't have.

The specialist that Astria's pediatrician referred us to is heading up a clinical trial that could change the treatment of specific autoimmune diseases forever. The list was a mile long. Most of the words I'd never seen before. It was like trying to read a foreign language. The trial is still in its early stages. It's not yet been approved. We don't know the potential side effects, only a list of risks that are fucking scary.

There are very few patients that fit the criteria for the trial; Astria is one of them.

In short, she'll need a bone marrow transplant to replace the bone marrow currently attacking her body. It's a serious procedure. One that all three of us need to agree on before proceeding.

If it works, it's possible that with medication, Astria will live out her life normally. If she doesn't do it, the aches and pains she's currently experiencing will likely worsen. She'll be faced with debilitating migraines for the rest of her life, and who knows what else. Her symptoms are ever-changing, and we're just beginning to see the results of what this terrible disease is capable of doing to her body. It's a silent disease, one that doesn't present physically, and that makes living with it that much harder. It's hard to struggle with something day in and day out and yet by all outward appearances seem completely normal.

I don't want that for her. I don't want my little girl to suffer in silence.

"Did you talk to her about it, yet?" I ask.

Astria was already in bed when I made it in from practice. I was late getting home because I got a late start. Her appointment was early, and I didn't want to miss it. I try not to make getting home late a habit when I'm not on the road, and I have a gym here, but I needed the solitude tonight to think and I was already behind when we started.

"Yeah. She's doing her own research. Says she wants to make an informed decision. She's even drafting a list of questions to volley back to the specialist." She chuckles lightly to herself.

"Really? She's eight." I ask, a little surprised and a hell of a lot proud of our girl for taking the initiative to research and advocate for her own health at such a young age. Most kids her age wouldn't even know where to begin.

"Eight and three-quarters." Gia reminds me, imitating our daughter, and sounding so much like her it hurts. "I hate to admit it, but she kind of reminds me of T when she does that. The planning, and the lists. He always needed to be in charge of his own destiny, you know? Well, his and everyone around him."

I know it took a lot for her to admit those words, but she's not wrong. Tyler always needed a plan for everything. It was one of his ways of coping.

"The man with the plan," I say, and think about the plans he made for us, and how none of those worked out the way he was certain that they would. I'm glad they didn't.

"That he was. And we broke the rules." She sighs into me.

My lips lift into a knowing grin, "We did."

"You ever wonder what would have happened if you hadn't come to that party that night? If you would have never gotten that text?"

"No. Never." I say with certainty. I never looked back. Sure, I struggled with understanding my feelings, but my heart always knew. We can't change the past. We can only learn from it and adapt moving forward. Or, in our case, fall in love.

"Why?" I ask, curious about where she's going with her line of thought when she doesn't offer a response.

"Just thinking out loud. I'm sleep-talking. I don't have to have a reason." The light on her laptop goes black as if to say, it's going back to sleep too. She twists in my arms and rests her cheek against my bare chest.

"Our destiny is a direct result of our decisions. I could have ignored that text, but I didn't. I made a decision. You could have finished your assignment another way. Instead, you kissed me."

"My mama always said, *a minute on the lips, a lifetime on the hips*. She didn't say anything about getting saddled with a professional hockey player for the rest of my life and his constant need to have his ego stroked." She places a soft kiss just above my heart. Her words say one thing, but her lips tell another story entirely.

"That was the best damn kiss of my life, woman. And I'm pretty sure your mama was talking about chicken and waffles, not men." I tighten my hold on her, ready to tug her off this stool and carry her back to bed with me. Chicken and waffles would be so good right now. How long has it been?

"We need to make a decision." She props her chin up and looks into my eyes.

My eyes have finally adjusted to the darkness. Worry lines crease her forehead, it's tangible in the air.

"That's for tomorrow. Tonight, I need you to come to bed with me." I move my hands from her waist to her plump ass, and pull her off the barstool, forcing her to wrap her legs around my hips.

"I love you, Damien. I'll never regret kissing you that night. Even if you were my big brother's best friend." She smirks as I carry her through the dark kitchen and back down the hallway to our bedroom.

"Admit it, you thought about kissing me before that night."

"Some secrets are better left unsaid."

"No need to say anything, I know the truth."

-o-

"Well, now that you've had a week to think about it, have you come to a decision?"

A week has passed and here we are. Again. These offices are all starting to look the same. Unfortunately, something tells me we're going to be seeing a lot more of them.

Over the last week, we've laughed, and we've cried together, as a family. I've bonded with my daughter in a way that I hadn't before.

Gia and I both turn to Astria. We made the decision as a family, but ultimately, this is her body. We're going to let her tell him our decision.

I watch as Astria takes a deep breath. She sits tall in the chair. Her hands are clasped together tightly in her lap, but she shows no sign of fear. I've never met a braver child.

"I want to participate in the trial."

Astria wants to live her life as normally as possible. She understands that a short-term sacrifice could mean a lifetime of relief. More than that, though? What really pushed her to participate in the trial, was her need to be a part of something bigger than herself. She's selfless. She wants to be a part of change and progression. Her sacrifice could mean that others don't have to suffer. She's just like her mama. I'm so damn proud of her.

The doctor nods his head in understanding. That's one thing I like about this guy. He never pushed us to allow her to participate in the clinical trial. He presented us with all of the facts and allowed us to make this decision. He's not an arrogant ass like some of the doctors I've known in the past. I can respect him for that.

"That's very brave of you, Astria. I think you might be our youngest patient. I take it you've all discussed this and had time to review the associated risks involved. It's an invasive procedure, but one that I'm hoping will change your life as well as thousands of lives of others facing a similar situation to yours in the future. What you're doing is very courageous."

Astria smiles and seems to relax ever so slightly. I

think we all take a collective breath. It feels like we've leaped over our first hurdle. The first of many to come.

"So, what next? Where do we go from here?" I ask, knowing that we're mid-season and I'll be on the road again next week. It kills me to know that I can't be here for every step, every appointment. I know that Gia can handle it. I just don't want her to have to.

"We'll get Astria set up in the system for the trial, and hopefully be able to start looking for a match as early as next week."

Next week. We're on the road to Dallas. Two weeks on the road. Two weeks of my daughters' life I'll miss. That's never felt more real than in this moment.

That's two weeks where we could find a potential match for her. And two more weeks that this disease could possibly ravage her body even more. Who knows? Nothing feels certain anymore. I can feel myself beginning to panic. "Me, I'll do it today. I want to be the match. What do I need to sign?"

I feel all three sets of eyes on me. I'm not making sense. Somewhere, in my logical brain, I know that, but I've lost my ability to apply logic and reason to my thoughts amid the panic clawing up inside of my chest. I hate this feeling of being out of control.

"It's not that easy, Mr. Henderson." The doctor responds calmly, despite my obvious inability to remain calm.

"What do you mean? Take my bone marrow." I don't even know what I'm saying.

I've done enough research to know that I can't put myself out for that long during the season. My medical history is a shitstorm. Between not knowing anything about my father other than a name, and the severity of my previous injury, there's no way I'm a candidate for this type of procedure.

"Well, the type of match we need is beyond the standard. We can test both you and Mrs. Henderson if you would like, but that doesn't guarantee you'll meet the criteria."

He doesn't say it out loud, and neither does Gia, but they both know I'm out. Astria is my baby girl, and I can't save her. If anyone should be able to save her, it should be me. Emotion closes in around my throat and steals my words. My girls are being so strong, and here I am, breaking.

When I offer nothing to his response, the doctor continues. "The optimal donor is what we refer to as a histocompatibility-matched relative, which means they have identical HLA tissue typing. Parents are typically a half match for their children, and a fifty percent chance is all we require for a typical transfer. However, Astria's case is atypical. She has a diverse HLA tissue typing because of her ancestry. It makes finding a type match more difficult, but not impossible. This is a trial treatment, and successful acceptance of the bone marrow is imperative. We're not only looking at the percentage but more specifically the tissue typing. To meet the standards of the trial, we need both. We need at least a thirty percent match with an identical HLA tissue typing."

"Help me understand. Astria is our blood, she's, our baby. You said we're a fifty percent match. That's more than the requirement. I can understand why I'm an issue as a candidate, but why not Gia? What do you mean by atypical? She was approved for the clinical trial."

"We can be fairly certain Gia is a match. We just can't be certain she's the match we need for the trial. We can swab her today, but we need to do a panel to see if she's a fit for the trial. We need to get the blood work completed. I'm sorry, it's a necessary process. We'll get you both set up to run the samples, but I can't make any promises."

"Look, Doc, I apologize if I'm overstepping. Now that we're committed to the trial, I guess I just want her better right now. I know that's not how this is going to go down. Forgive me for being impatient. It hurts me to see her hurt, and it hurts me, even more, to know I can't fix it." My voice cracks as I allow a moment of vulnerability in the privacy of this small office with Astria's doctor and my family. I need him to know how important this is to me. I need him to understand the position I'm in.

"The quicker we take action, the more likely it is that her body will accept the new bone marrow and she won't have any lasting effects. Don't take our need for process and order for latency. It's imperative that we document everything for the trial submissions. We're moving forward immediately. If we wait, there's a possibility of permanent muscle damage. Despite her current symptoms, Astria is still very healthy. And while this isn't a cure, she will probably forever deal with the disorder, our hope with the procedure is that she will be able to manage it with medication alone, and it won't permanently impact her life. She'll be able to continue to play sports and do just about anything a normal teenager can do."

"That's all I want. I want my life back." Astria speaks up, and I couldn't agree more.

CHAPTER TWENTY-SIX
TYLER

"Tyler! Tyler! Get in here!" Casey's frantic screaming echoes throughout the lake house. I don't rush. She's been known to have a flare for the dramatics. Whatever it is, she can pause it until the popcorn finishes popping.

We're having a rare, lazy day today. We're watching one of our movies. It's a new release, but if I had to guess, someone just got stranded in a small town and they're about to run into the love of their life at a coffee shop…or a bakery…or a coffee shop that sells baked goods.

"Tyler! Now!" I swear her shrieks shake the floor-to-ceiling windows that overlook the lake.

What in the absolute fuck. I abandon my task and ensure our popcorn will burn and the kitchen will smell for at least two weeks, and walk toward my screaming fiancé in the living room.

Fiancé, I love that title, almost as much as I'm going

to love calling her my wife. Does she admit that she's marrying me? Nah. But I'll haul her ass down the aisle over my shoulder kicking and screaming if I have to. Actually, I look forward to it.

"Dammit, woman. I'm coming. I swear. You ask for popcorn; I go get popcorn. The next thing I know you're screaming at me to come…back." I pause at the edge of the room.

A news channel I recognize as being outside of Los Angeles is streaming over the sports network. She's not watching our movie at all.

A woman wearing a red sweater dress stands outside of a hospital where the screen says she's broadcasting live. "We're standing in front of LA Memorial Hospital, where just moments ago the entire LA Renegades starting lineup filed in for what we understand just might be the answer to saving a little girl's future. Seasoned Goaltender for the Renegades, Damien Henderson, dubbed the *comeback kid* of the NHL, is inside with his wife and nine-year-old daughter. Our sources tell us that his daughter is in need of an immediate bone marrow transplant. It's no secret that hockey teams are a sacred brotherhood. It's easy to see, with this show of solidarity here for a brother of their own, that sentiment holds true now more than ever. The Renegades play at home this weekend, let's see if their solidarity is just as strong on the ice. Back to you, Carmen."

My feet remain glued to the floor where I stand. My lungs stop working. I can't be certain that I know how to breathe anymore. That's my family. A foreign feeling begins to take hold inside of me, spreading like wildfire throughout my entire body. It's a feeling that I haven't felt in a long time.

The need to protect something, someone, that's my fucking blood.

I don't care about the fight. I don't care about the betrayal. None of those things matter to me anymore. The only thing that I can think of is that my flesh and blood is in that hospital, and she needs help. She needs me.

"Hey, you good? You're almost as white as me. Frankly, it's not a good look for you. Say something, Tyler." I don't know when Casey moved from the couch, but suddenly she's touching my arm, shaking me back from the initial shock to my system and bringing me back to reality.

"I need to pack," I say the first thing that comes to my mind. I have the means to get there. One phone call and a one-hour flight and I'll be at that exact hospital.

"Fucking, yes! This is the moment I've been waiting for." Casey bounces on her toes, following me into our shared bedroom.

Who am I kidding? This is her bedroom now; she just allows me to live in it. Okay, and fuck her. Sweet Jesus do I fuck her in this bed.

Her words take a minute to register as I snatch my overnight bag from the top shelf in our walk-in closet. "Cassandra, if you so much as look at Damien, I will sell your entire onesie collection in a charity auction."

"You think so little of me." She says innocently. She starts pulling clothes from hangers and shoving them into her luggage.

I pause my movements to look at her. "Even the skunk onesie, I know you keep shoved in the back of the third drawer in your closet." I raise my eyebrow as if to tell her I know where she keeps her secret stash back in her apartment in the city.

"You wouldn't dare." She hisses.

I step into her. I grab her forearm with enough strength that she's forced to look up into my eyes. "Test me, Cassandra."

"I love it when your nostrils flare, Toro. You're adorable when you get worked up. You know you're the only man I have eyes for." She snatches her arm from me, only to stand up on the tips of her toes and smack a kiss on my lips. I pull her to me before she can pull away, sliding my tongue in her mouth and marking her with my lips. I don't release her until we're both panting.

Her sass, this push, and pull between us. I will never get enough of it.

And, just like every other woman in the United States, Casey might think Damien is handsome, but I also know how she feels about men, and that trumps all. Casey fucking hates men. Trust me, I get my balls busted daily. I guess I'm just a glutton for punishment.

"When are we leaving?" she asks, still catching her breath.

She turns back to packing her things like she didn't just rock my world with one single kiss.

I adjust my hardening dick in my sweatpants and follow her lead. I quickly finish up grabbing things for a weekend trip. I don't know how long to expect to be gone. I don't have a damn clue what I'm getting myself into. I just know that I have to go.

"I'll call my mom. She'll know where we need to go to get the test done. We can't just show up at the hospital unannounced, as much as that's what I'd like to do. That won't go over well. I've tried that method before and failed miserably. I don't want to be shut out again. She's my blood too. She's my niece. Maybe she doesn't know me, but I feel like this is something I need to do. It's something I have to do." I zip my bag closed and start changing out of my sweatpants into a pair of jeans and a black polo shirt that will be suitable for the flight, and whatever we might encounter once we get there.

"And if you're not a match?" Casey asks, blatantly, not dancing around the truth.

I consider the answer to that question. That I could do all of this, and not be able to help. That we could be so close, but not close enough. Our family is already broken, it's been broken for years. What do I have to lose?

"We come home."

That's the fucking reality of our situation. I haven't seen my sister in person in nearly a decade. I haven't hugged her. I haven't been there for the important moments in her life. And my brother? The man that was my best friend? I don't even want to go there again. I can't go there. I can't let my mind take me to that place, not right now.

"Just that easy, huh?" Casey sees the truth that I'm hiding. She can see right through me.

She doesn't just want to go with me because Damien is a professional hockey player. She jokes about his good looks, but there's nothing there past that. She's just teasing. What she wants to see? Reconciliation. She's mentioned it a few or fifty times since I shared my story with her.

She has her own family drama to deal with, but for some reason, she fixates on fixing mine. Years ago, I fucked up. Regret is an ugly thing to have to live with.

"You saw his team there. They're a brotherhood. He was my brother, but that was a long time ago. They don't need me anymore. They're doing just fine without me. I'm doing this for Astria. That's it. Don't get any wild ideas." Like forming a coalition to stage an intervention and try to make us all kiss and make up. We're past that. That's never going to happen.

"You're doing something honorable; you know that?" She closes up her suitcase, placing it on the ground next to our feet, and walks toward me. She stops in front of me and runs her fingers over the lines that crease my forehead with worry.

I take her hand in mine, pulling it down and staring into her palm as if it holds all of the answers to life that I'm searching for. "It's what family does. It's what I should have done years ago. I owe it to Astria to try."

And that's the truth of the matter. I might have destroyed my relationship with my sister and my best friend, but I owe it to my niece to do what I can to try and help her.

"You're right, and I'll try too. I'd like to be tested as well." Casey says seriously. She laces our hands together.

"Really?" I squeeze her fingers and lean down to meet her at eye level. I shoot for levity, channeling the banter that flows so well between us. It's familiar and comfortable. *Easy*. I have a feeling what we're walking into is heavy, and I'm not ready for life to become heavy just yet. "Your bone marrow is probably black, like your heart. I'm not sure I want that inside of my niece." She huffs and I smile. Mission accomplished.

I kiss her on the nose before releasing her hand and picking up our bags. I need to make some phone calls.

"Why was I just being nice to you?" She smacks me on the ass as I walk by her with our things, prepared to leave. "This is why I'm mean. Men are pigs." She mumbles, but she follows me anyway.

If she keeps this up all the way to the airport, I'll show her mean. She's a frequent flyer of the Tyler Patterson Mile High Club – members' only party of one, Cassandra Elyse Stafford.

Hell, I hope she does keep it up. I need the distraction.

CHAPTER TWENTY-SEVEN
GIA

I hear the incessant vibrating of my phone against the granite countertop from across the island. I rush around the kitchen in sock-covered feet to grab it before it goes to voicemail, while also trying not to slip and fall down. I really don't need to add a broken hip to the list of things we're dealing with at the moment.

It's Saturday morning, and Astria and I are taking it slow today. I'm wearing a pair of sleep shorts and one of Damien's old practice T-shirts. My hair is an absolute wreck that I'm certain only a bird looking for a home might find appealing.

Astria woke up with a headache. A direct result of her overdoing it at practice. She insisted on attending practice. You can't tell that girl anything, and I don't have the heart to pull her from something she loves until I absolutely have to.

I skid to a stop and glance at the phone, seeing a name

that immediately puts my internal alert system on high. It's Saturday, why is Astria's doctor calling us on a Saturday?

Astria's on the phone in the living room, chatting away on the couch. The girl's head might hurt, but it's not hindering her ability to use her mouth.

We allowed her to get a cell phone because of the nature of Damien's job and because we don't live near either of her grandmothers. The only other person she's allowed to call is Camden. And those calls must be made in a public space in our home. Our inner circle is tight, and unfortunately, we have to be very strict. She has enough danger to worry about with her own body trying to attack her. Damien might be the face of professional hockey, his body plastered all over North America, but that doesn't mean our daughter has to be. It's important to us that we maintain a certain level of privacy.

"Astria, is that your daddy you're on the phone with?" I ask quickly, swiping at the screen on my phone.

She sits up slowly and glances over the back of the couch at me. "Yeah, why?"

"Put him on speaker, my phone's ringing and it's the doctor." I catch the call just in time.

"Mrs. Henderson?"

"This is she." I'm breathless from all of my running around. My palms sweat with nerves that set in the moment I saw his name on the screen.

We've been looking for a match for over a month now. I know it doesn't seem like a long time, but it feels like an eternity.

"I have good news." He says and my heart starts

beating a fast rhythm of exhilaration mixed with relief.

"You do? Hold on, we're all here. Damien, can you hear the doctor?"

I walk closer to the couch, where Astria holds her cell phone up in the air. She watches me with nervous excitement. The energy building in the room is palpable. We're all hoping for the same thing.

"Loud and clear," Damien says.

Damien's only been gone a week this time. It's just a two-game series. The Renegades are still undefeated. They're having a strong season, but Damien refuses to admit they could be looking at a cup this year. He doesn't want to jinx it. Some superstitious voodoo. We could use some good in our lives. I don't blame him for holding his breath.

"It's time. We need to have you come in; we believe we've found a match."

"Oh, my God." I cover my mouth with my hand.

Tears fill my eyes, as I look at Astria, and watch her reaction. She's crying too. She might be young, but she realizes the opportunity this could be for her. We understand the risks, but we've had time to accept them. Now we're just ready to move forward and end up on the other side of all of this. The waiting has been hard on all of us.

"We'd like to schedule the conditioning for the procedure as soon as possible, that's why I'm calling you on the weekend. I'm sorry if I'm interrupting anything. Good game last night, Damien."

"Thanks, Doc." Damien's voice sounds muffled. I can imagine he's experiencing similar emotions right now.

I wonder if he's with the boys. I glance at the time on the clock above the stove in the kitchen, they're probably down for breakfast before the pre-game meeting.

I still can't believe the show of support for our family by the entire team. Damien's medical history disqualified him from being a match, and my tissue typing didn't match the standard they were looking for. My mother and Damien's mother were both disqualified due to age. But the team, every single one of them lined up to be tested during their last home stint, despite knowing that if any one of them were a match, they'd be out the remainder of the season. They didn't care.

Unfortunately, we didn't get a match then either. Astria was put into a national database, and we've been sitting in this holding pattern since.

My mind jumps around, unable to focus on just one thing, as I try to listen to the doctor.

"Astria will need to spend a minimum of thirty days in the hospital so that we can monitor the effects the transplant has on her disorder, as well as her body's reaction to the transfer. As we've discussed before, this is a relatively new science. Not the transfer itself, but the application for her diagnosis. We're pioneering our own way, questioning what was previously thought possible, but I'm confident in the success rate of this procedure. I'm confident that we will see an improvement in Astria's quality of life."

"Can I ask who it is? Who is the donor? Can you tell us?" I'm not sure what the rules and regulations are with this sort of thing, but I'd like to know this person. I'd like them to be a part of our family. What they're doing for us is completely selfless. I want to thank them.

"I figured you would ask that. The donor has asked that he or she remain anonymous until the transfer is complete. Is that something you can live with?" My knee-jerk reaction is to say no. I want to know. It feels important. My daughter is going to receive bone marrow from a total stranger. Who is this person?

I look at my daughter, noting the look of pure relief on her face. If I take a step back and try to think about this rationally, I guess it shouldn't matter. I mean, if you need a blood transfusion you don't ask to speak to the person that donated blood before receiving it. That'd be ridiculous. I don't have a clue whose blood Damien received that night he died on the ice. None. And up until this point, it's not something that's ever crossed my mind.

Not to mention, we've been waiting over a month already, and it's hard enough to find a match that meets the criteria as it is. What am I going to do? Reject this one just because they want to do a good thing without praise. If anything, that makes whoever this is even more remarkable. Right?

"Um, sure. Right? Astria? Damien?" I ask, needing their validation.

"We've waited long enough. I think we move forward." Damien says through the phone, his voice coming through stronger than it did before. I wish I could see him. I wish he was here for this.

"Me too. I'm just ready to get it over with." Astria says and with that, it's decided.

I guess we're moving forward with an anonymous donor.

CHAPTER TWENTY-EIGHT
GIA
One month later

"Freedom!" Astria waves her arms in the air as we finally return home.

This is the first time she's been back here since she was admitted to the hospital for the transplant over a month ago.

She'll have another thirty days of monitoring that we will do from home with weekly visits to the doctor's office. The doctor has assured us that everything appears to be going according to plan. Every step of the way Astria has met and exceeded the benchmarks in the clinical trial.

In the beginning, she was very weak. She had some nausea and fatigue. It was nothing that we didn't expect going into this, though. If anything, the procedure went smoother than I'd anticipated. I'd read all of the potential risks, and I was preparing myself for some of the worst.

Not Damien though, he was confident that our girl was going to pull through a fighter, and he was right.

Every day she continues to grow stronger. She's still experiencing some of the same symptoms from the autoimmune disease that she had before, but we've been assured that we should start seeing improvements soon, now that the transfer has been deemed successful and her body has accepted the donated marrow. We're all holding onto that hope.

"Not so fast Wonder Woman, you have thirty more days until you're officially free," I call out after her through the entryway as she rushes ahead of me.

Freedom, it's kind of a relative word in her world, I guess. She'll always deal with this disease, even after having gone through the trial program. Even at a one-hundred-perfect success rate, she will still never be free. I can't choose to focus on that though. We will take our wins daily and celebrate those together.

I roll our suitcases inside and begin dropping things on the kitchen counter to put away later. I didn't realize how much we accumulated at the hospital over the last month, Astria especially.

Her friends brought her books and stuffed animals. Her classmates and teammates from her hockey team showered her with gifts and cards. And don't get me started on the things that Damien's teammates sent. We're going to need to rent a storage unit.

"But my bed! I can sleep in my bed tonight! I missed the couch, and this lamp, and the refrigerator." Astria runs her hands along the back of the couch and twirls in place. God, I hope she doesn't get dizzy.

"You're ridiculous, you know that." I smile at her basking in the brief moment of euphoria.

We made it. I hope we've gone through the worst of it.

"I mean, don't get me wrong," Astria pauses in the hallway outside of her bedroom door, where the door is closed, "the digs at the hospital were pretty sweet, but it feels so good to be home. It smells like home. Ahhhhh, do you smell it, Mom?" She lifts her nose into the air and sniffs.

I do the same, humoring her. "Yes, baby, I smell it. I'm happy to be home too. Maybe you should go check out your room and see if everything is still where you left it."

I look at the door to her bedroom with tight-leashed excitement. Damien's waiting for her just behind that door. He wasn't supposed to be home until tomorrow, but when he found out we were being discharged a day early, he made it his mission to get here.

Astria grabs the doorknob and pauses as if just thinking of something. "Why wouldn't everything be where I left it? Wait, did Camden come over while I was gone? If he touched my signed puck collection, I swear I will…"

This girl, I swear she's too smart for her own good.

"Astria, honey, Camden was not in your room." I roll my eyes and motion for her to move along with my hand. I can hardly contain my anticipation.

Slowly, she turns the doorknob and pushes the door open.

"Surprise!" Damien says as he steps into the doorway,

and her face lights up.

"But your daddy is!" I shout, and bounce up and down on my toes, matching her excitement. I watch Astria jump into his arms and am overwhelmed with pure joy.

"Dad! I thought you weren't flying in until tomorrow! Mom said you guys had a layover because of the weather!"

I might have told a tiny white lie. I didn't want her to get her hopes up in case he didn't make it. I should have known better, though.

"A raging volcano couldn't keep me from being here. I didn't get to fly back with the team and had to make a few transfers, but I made it. I would have rented a car if I had to." Damien's eyes fill with tears as he peeks over her shoulder at me and holds her tightly in his arms.

"I'm totally worth it." She says as he finally places her down on her feet.

"You are, I'm so happy you're home."

God, I'm happy we're all home. Finally.

"Knock, knock." A familiar voice comes from where I left the front door ajar, bringing in our things. We've barely been home for five minutes. No way.

There is no way…

I round the corner, and my eyes widen with surprise, "Mom? What are you doing here?"

"I couldn't let my favorite grandbaby come home from a month-long stay at the hospital and not be here to welcome her back. What kind of grandma would that make me?"

She follows me back into the kitchen and clasps her

hands in front of her body. She looks at me as if she walked across the street to get here, and not across the entire country.

I stand there in shock, my mouth slightly open, unsure of what to say to her.

"There's my girl." She says as she looks over my shoulder, completely ignoring me.

"Grandma Patterson!" Astria squeals, wiggling out of Damien's arms.

She loves my mom, but she doesn't get to see her as much as I think either of them would like. Our schedules just don't allow for it. They spend a lot of time talking on the phone and video chatting. My mom's been teaching her to crochet via video chat while we've been living in the hospital. She's almost completed her first blanket.

"Thank God, we're about to eat so fucking good." Damien places his hand on his stomach and rubs circles over his rock-hard abs.

It's truly unfair that he looks like that and eats like he does. I don't think he ever even allows himself to get hungry. He better watch it, or I'll cut off his supply of turkey sandwiches.

"Watch your mouth, Damien Henderson. I can still put you over my knee." Mama smiles at Damien, as she threatens him.

Like she ever put any of us over her knee, please.

I give Damien a side-eye for the language and then bring my attention back to my mama.

"How did you get here?" I stare at her in confusion. She never flies out to see us. We always go to her.

I don't miss the way she glances over her shoulder

briefly. Her jet-black hair is salted with silver and white strands, all braided together and tied up in a knot on top of her head. She's wearing a matching two-piece set. A light purple top, with flowy pants that hit at her ankle, just above her brown leather sandals. Time stands still, she's ageless.

"I flew." She unclasps and reclasps her hands together again, straightening her shoulders to her full height, which isn't much taller than Astria.

She's hiding something.

I narrow my eyes. "By yourself? Is Jeff here? You hate flying, Mom." I peek around her shoulder just in time to see movement coming from the front entry.

A brief moment of panic flares somewhere in the back of my mind, just in time for my stomach to tumble to the floor.

"I brought her."

Three words from one man knock me straight on my ass. I'm taken by complete surprise. It feels like I've just plummeted from a roller coaster with broken tracks.

The excitement of today curls up and dies in my throat.

What is *he* doing here?

The last time I saw Tyler was the night I thought I lost Damien. And before that? The night I swore he would never be a part of this family again.

My stomach rolls.

I'm stunned into silence. I stand and stare at him in shock, unable to respond to his presence. It's so strange, seeing him standing in my kitchen after all these years.

It annoys me that age has been so good to him. He

looks older, but not in a bad way. The fact that he and Damien are the same age still baffles me. My brain can't reconcile it. Tyler will always look *older* to me. I don't want to give him authority, but I still feel like he holds that over me.

He's wearing a pair of pressed slacks and a navy polo shirt. The most shocking part of his appearance though just might be his hair or lack thereof. It seems the hair on his head has relocated to his jawline, and dammit if that doesn't make him only look more distinguished. He's still fit, towering over me and everyone else in the room with the exception of Damien. He must have continued his gym regimen after losing his hockey scholarship. I really wish he hadn't. I'd feel a little better if he was old and overweight. Unfortunately, he's none of those things.

He's a big-name sports attorney now, or so I've heard. Apparently, he finally got that law degree.

Leave it to Tyler to follow the backup plan to a T when plan A doesn't work out. No surprise there. Anger bubbles up inside of me, replacing the initial punch to the gut from being blindsided in my own home.

I roll my shoulders and prepare for war. We're on my turf this time, brother.

"Really, T? You think you can just waltz into my house, unannounced? After everything we've been through?" I say, unable to keep my voice from sounding defensive. Hell, I am defensive.

Damien walks up beside me, looping his arm around my waist. I can't tell if he's holding me to support me or holding me to contain me. Truthfully, I probably need him for both.

"No, I don't. But I knew if I asked, you'd turn me away. I tried calling. You didn't answer." He doesn't walk further into the kitchen, he stays in the doorway, bringing his hands up in front of his body, almost as if to say he means no harm.

I don't believe it.

"I've been a little busy. We've been in the hospital for over a month." I snap, and Damien squeezes my hip as if to tell me to reel it in. I don't plan on it. Thanks anyway, bud.

"I know, and I'm so sorry for everything you've gone through."

It irks me how reasonable he sounds right now.

"You sure? You don't think this is karma coming back to haunt us for all of our childish indiscretions?" Maybe I'm the one being immature here, but who does he think he is? He may have forgotten, but I haven't. I promised myself I wouldn't forget.

"No, that's not what I think at all," he says calmly.

My mom shuffles around the kitchen until she's standing in the hallway in front of Astria's bedroom. I'd forgotten they were both here.

"Astria, baby, why don't you show me your crochet in your room while the other children speak to one another." She suggests softly, with a hint of exasperation in her voice, that I don't miss.

She's not wrong to take Astria out of the room for this though. We don't need an audience. I'd rather my daughter not see me completely lose my shit.

Why did she bring him here with her in the first place? She knows exactly how I feel about him.

Tyler interrupts before I can say anything. "It's okay, Mama. Gia has every right to be angry with me. I deserve it." That's right asshole. You do fucking deserve it, but I get to say that – not you.

Who is this man?

"Wait, you're my mom's brother?" All of our eyes turn to Astria, who remains standing in the doorway of her bedroom staring at Tyler with wide eyes.

"I am, and I'd like to meet you, if she says it's okay." If I say it's, okay?

What's his endgame here?

"I'm not the only one that makes decisions in this house. I feel like you pounced on us without so much as a warning. We just got home. We walked in the door less than thirty minutes ago." I ignore his claims that he called in advance. Maybe he did, maybe he didn't. I have his number blocked, so, there's no way I can be sure.

I hear the door to Astria's room close behind us.

"Gia, let him speak," Damien's voice commands the room.

I glare at him over my shoulder. He's always backed me up. Why is he on T's side all of a sudden? I search his green eyes but come up short.

"I need to apologize." Tyler starts.

"You don't get to do that." I interrupt him.

Damien stares down at me, and that's when I see it in his eyes. I see the forgiveness. He's already there, two steps ahead of me. How can he forgive someone who's put us through so much? Something in the way Damien looks at me throws sand on the flame that's been burning inside of me for so long.

Tyler starts again, and this time, for some reason, I don't try to stop him. "I hear your anger, and I'm so sorry that I did this to our family. I'm sorry I hurt you. I should have been there for you, and I wasn't. I let my anger and my emotions overrule my ability to make sound decisions. I was young, and you hurt me. That's no excuse for the things I said to you or my actions. I don't expect immediate forgiveness. I'm just asking for you to open the door to consider it."

This time when I speak, emotion colors my words. The hate that I've worn as a band-aid for the last decade is ripped off, and all that's left is an open, bleeding wound. "You weren't there when I needed you the most, T." Tears fall from my cheeks.

We're standing in my mama's living room all over again.

Tyler runs his hand over his neck. "Let me ask you something, Gia. Do you believe in redemption?" He asks hesitantly.

"What do you mean?" My voice wobbles.

"It was me." He says in an exhale, looking more nervous than he did when he walked in unannounced.

"What…what was you? What are you talking about?" I stutter over my words in confusion.

"I saw you guys on the news. I got tested and…and I came back as a potential match. I made the donation anonymously because I wanted to tell you myself. I didn't want you to turn me away because of our past. I wanted to do this for you, for all of you."

I drop my hands to my side and stare at the man in front of me. I try to make sense of what he's telling me but can't reconcile the two people.

Selfish versus selfless. They can't be one and the same.

He lied to me. He lied to me, but he saved my daughter. I'm hurt and deceived, but also…grateful. And I don't know what to do with those feelings.

"It was you?" I ask in utter astonishment and disbelief.

"I didn't know any other way to do it. I'm sorry if you feel like I've betrayed you again. That wasn't my intention."

"No, I. God, I need a minute."

I step out of Damien's hold and walk to our bedroom. Astria is in her room with my mom. Damien doesn't try to follow me, and for that I'm thankful. I need to be alone for a minute to process.

I'm filled with so many mixed emotions. I walk into my closet and grab an old photo album from the top shelf. Opening it, I pull out a photo from years ago. I didn't take this picture, Damien did. It's from the day Astria was born.

The woman staring back at me isn't the same person I am today. I run my fingers over the film.

I wonder if that's how Tyler feels. Has life changed him? It sure as hell has changed me. I'd be foolish to think that circumstances of life haven't had an effect on him. Right?

I press the picture to my chest and drop to my knees.

I cry for the young girl in that photo. I cry for what she went through. I cry for all the hard days. Here we are though, and today is not the same day. We are not the same people. I can't continue living like this.

I think of my daughter, and her bravery in the face of

uncertainty. I think of her life, and how she'll be able to live it without restriction. I think of the clinical trial, and all of the lives it could affect in the future. It's selfish of me to think that this is only about me. It's not about me at all anymore.

It's my turn to make a decision.

When I walk back into the room Damien is embracing Tyler, tears in both of their eyes. Two grown men, holding each other. It's almost more than my fragile heart can take.

As I get closer, I hear Damien say, "You might have taken my life, but you gave my baby girl hers back. I forgive you, brother." My throat grows tight.

They release each other and I stand there, feeling like a young college-age kid again. I clutch the photo in my hand. This was one of many important days in my life, and he missed it.

I remember all the reasons I fought against him. I try to will myself to feel that hate in my heart again, but I can't. I can't find it in me to keep this up. I'm exhausted.

We've been fighting this war for so long. I have to accept that the battle has changed.

Damien steps out of the way as I approach Tyler. I take a deep breath and try to steady my racing heart before speaking. "I made myself a promise years ago. I think I've come to realize some promises are meant to be broken. I've already cheated the game of life too many times, and you know what? Life is too short. I can't live with the hate. I don't want this anymore, T. I don't want this hate inside of me. I owe it to Astria to offer you forgiveness. I owe it to myself. But it's not going to be easy for me. I won't heal overnight. The hurt that you caused our family was deep. I understand that you sacrificed for us, and I'm willing to set aside my anger and try. Is that okay? Is that enough?"

It's all I have to offer. I hand him the photo and he looks down at it with tears in his eyes before looking back up at me.

"You've grown up so much. You're a whole-ass woman, Gia. I'm so proud of you. Thank you. Thank you for giving me this chance. I'd have done it either way, you know? Once I knew I was a match. I needed to do this for her, and for you. I knew there was a risk coming here, like this. I'm so sorry about everything, Gia. I know sorry isn't enough, but…I'm sorry." His voice is full of remorse and compassion. I can feel his sincerity, and it continues to ease the hurt, bit by bit.

Never in a million years did I think we'd be here, speaking like this again, but one thing I've learned over the years is that life is anything but predictable.

"That's why you brought, Mama? You scared, T?" I crinkle my nose and try to clear the snot from my airway so that I can breathe again.

This feels weird, us standing here, talking to each other without someone hurting or screaming.

"No, I brought Mama because she wanted to come and was afraid to fly." He answers honestly.

I don't have time to respond before another person I don't recognize appears out of thin air in my kitchen.

Where are they all coming from?

"He brought me because he was scared. Hi, I'm Casey."

A stunning blonde woman with tattoos covering both arms and bright-red lipstick steps between Tyler and me and offers me her hand. She's wearing a pair of black pencil pants, paired with black wedges and a gold-trimmed blazer with the sleeves rolled up to her elbows.

"Um, hi. Who are you and why are you in my house? When did this become a rave?" I stick out my hand tentatively, and she shakes it with the grip of a man.

"Actually, I'm this guy's legal representation. I hate all men though, so I totally get the whole hate in your heart thing." She pulls back long enough to give me a once-over. "Damn girl, you are smokin' hot. You have great hair, has anyone ever told you that?" Her smile is beaming.

Tyler physically picks up the tiny blonde and sets her back down again behind him.

She doesn't so much as wobble in her high heels. Even with them on, Tyler is easily a full head taller than she is.

"Don't mind her, she's driving the Uber." He cuts his eyes at her over his shoulder. "Isn't it against your policy to get out of the vehicle?" He says through clenched teeth. His annoyance with her is kind of comical.

She swats at his arm with more force than I was expecting, and he flinches.

"Eugene. Don't set me off." She reels back and he fully covers her face with his large hand, which only appears to anger her more.

No way is this woman his Uber driver.

"Oh my God, dude, she knows your middle name?" Damien chuckles from beside me, clearly not connecting the dots fast enough.

"Are the two of you together?" I ask, needing to know if the chemistry firing off between them is coincidence.

"No!" She shouts.

"We're engaged," Tyler answers at the exact same time.

"Wow." It's all I can manage to say. My mind explodes, all of my preconceived thoughts obliterated. I tilt my head to the side, and study the two of them together, happy to give my brain something else to focus on.

They're complete and total opposites. She's feisty, I'll give him that. He's just always seemed so, I don't know, strait-laced to me, and she looks so…I don't know what the right word is. She looks like a baddie.

Tyler grabs her left hand and holds it up in front of where he wrestles her to remain still at his side. "I submit the following proof into evidence."

I take a step closer because I recognize that ring.

I study the sparkling diamond on her finger. She stops trying to fight his hold on her. "It's Dad's ring, isn't it? The ring he gave Mom?"

My mom would only have given that ring to him if she was sure this woman was the one for him. She was saving it.

"It is." He says, and I can instantly feel how serious he is about this woman. She's his Damien. She's the chicken to his waffles.

She huffs as if to say the charade is up. Tyler drops her hand, and she smiles up at him adoringly. That's when I see the truth of the duo in front of us.

She steps forward, and this time Tyler lets her. "I'm Casey Stafford, and yes, I'm entering into a legally binding contract with your older brother. Don't let it get out though, I like to keep my options open, just in case." She winks as if that's a totally normal statement, anyone else would say in the same position and then keeps talking. "He's pretty sweet, and he's hella cute, am I right?"

She covers the side of her mouth and leans into my space to whisper. "If I tell him, it goes straight to his head, and we can't have him walking around with an ego the size of Texas, now, can we?"

She pulls back again and speaks to the room. "The bit about me hating men was true though. Disgusting creatures, the lot of them." She sneers, and I turn to watch Damien's reaction to the scene unfolding in front of us.

I really hate to admit this to myself, but I kind of like her.

"Wow, I'm so glad to know that you think so highly of me." Damien places his hand over his chest as if to say he's wounded by her words, even though I know he's teasing. "Damien Henderson, by the way, nice to meet you."

It feels good, to be able to stand in the same room all together, and not feel the suffocating pain and hate that's hovered over us like a dark black cloud for nearly ten years.

I feel lighter than I have since, well, I can't even remember. How long has this been weighing on me without my knowledge? Even when I thought I'd put it to rest, I hadn't. It was still there, sucking life and joy out of me.

I don't want to give hate that much of a hold over my life anymore.

Casey's cheeks flush ever so slightly under Damien's gaze.

"Oh, she thinks highly of you, all right." Tyler laughs from behind her, and she shrugs unashamedly.

"The towel cover. You took that photo, right? You freaking nailed it." Her lips tilt up into a grin, that says she would eat a lesser man for lunch and not think twice.

Oh, the infamous towel cover. I can't help but smile to myself. Half of the country has seen my husband in a towel, and I have to agree that it was a glorious sight. I don't know which was more fun, Damien's initial reaction to it, or the reaction he has every single time someone brings it up. It's the gift that keeps on giving, honestly.

A few months back I was contacted by Sports National. They needed a portfolio of photos of Damien for a story they were doing on him. With the potential for a Cup win this year, they were highlighting some of the starting players on the Renegades. I *might* have not so accidentally slipped in a photo of him wearing nothing but a towel. That photo *might* have ended up on the cover of the magazine.

It was from my personal collection; I took liberties.

"Thanks, it was some of my best work." I smile, and finally feel myself start to loosen up. This feels right. This is how it was always supposed to be. "Listen, um…why don't you guys come in and have a seat? I know a little girl that you need to meet."

EPILOGUE
DAMIEN

"It's cute that you think you're in charge." She says slyly as she takes the room key from my hand and slides it over the scanner on the door.

I don't say anything when the light turns green. She turns the handle and pushes the door open, revealing our suite for the night. I spared no expense in booking this room. She deserves nothing but the best, and I intend to give it to her.

"Wow, Damien, this is stunning," she slips out of her persona, stepping fully into the room and marveling at the floor-to-ceiling windows that overlook the city down below.

I flip the lock on the door as it closes behind us. My body vibrates with post-game adrenaline that has nowhere to go.

We fucking won.

I wouldn't be here without the woman standing in

front of me.

I waste no time eating up the space between us. I hook my finger through the loop of her painted-on jeans and yank her backward until her back is pressed flush against my chest.

I run my hands over her body, starting at her thighs and moving up, up…only pausing long enough to pop the button on her jeans and shove them down her thighs. I splay my hands over her soft stomach, inching my way up until I reach the white lace of her top.

This damn top has been teasing me from the moment she walked into the bar tonight. She lifts her arms, reaching over her head seductively, and wraps her hands behind my neck. She arches her back into me, and the movement sets my blood on fire.

I run the palm of my hand over the lace material covering her breasts until I feel her nipples harden beneath my touch, only then do I reach inside and pull them out, putting them on full display.

We're close enough to the window that there's a chance we could be caught, but far enough away that it's unlikely. The risk, albeit slight, only hitches my desire for her higher.

I massage her perfect tits in my hands, rolling her hardened nipples between my fingers and pinching until she hisses my name.

"Damien," she tosses her head back into my neck. Her fingers tangle in my long hair.

"I know what you want, baby." My voice is raw as I drag my hand up to her throat, wrapping my fingers around her neck.

My other hand snakes down her belly. I slide two fingers over her clit, noting just how wet she is for me already. I tease the hardened nub briefly but don't stop until I'm sliding into her warm, wet opening.

Her hips buck into my hand, and I tighten my hold on her neck. I feel the ripple of her throat as she moans, and the vibrations rattle the palm of my hand.

"You want me to fuck you with my fingers, Click?" I use her nickname knowing it will light a fire under her ass. I'm too damn wound up to play nice.

She growls and my hand tightens. The way she trusts me with her body is so fucking enticing.

I nip at her ear and neck, pulling her skin between my teeth and leaving my mark on her as I pump my fingers in and out of her perfect pussy.

I watch our reflection in the window and feel my cock harden at the sight playing out before me. I'm still in my suit. I wasted no time. She is so fucking beautiful. Every inch of her. *Mine*.

She moves her ass along the seam of my slacks, putting pressure on my throbbing erection.

"Harder, more." Her words are a whispered rasp, barely audible, but I see it in her eyes. I know what she needs. Slow is for later. Right now, I need to fuck my wife.

I squeeze her neck, knowing full well she'll need to cover my fingerprints in the morning. I fuck her hard and fast with my hand, curling my fingers, until I feel her pussy clamp down around me. Her body convulses in my arms, her movements overtaken by her orgasm. I watch as she comes undone in front of me. So damn gorgeous.

I release her neck, and she drops her hands, heaving for air. She spins in my arms and looks up at me, her eyes shrouded in the haze of her orgasm. Her chest rises and falls, still catching her breath.

"It was always you, Damien." She says as she pushes my jacket from my shoulders and begins unbuttoning my shirt. I unbuckle my belt and unbutton my pants, working with her to rid myself of the barriers between us. We don't stop until we're both standing stark naked in front of each other.

I can't keep my hands off of her. I want to touch and explore her. We've overcome so much. Tonight is a rarity. It takes me back to that first night in Chambliss. The night that I knew in my heart, I would spend the rest of my life worshiping this woman.

"It's always been you, Click." I smirk.

I walk her backward toward the large king-size bed that sits in the center of the room.

"You know the rules." She presses her palm to my chest and pushes me away playfully, a flirty smile teasing her lips.

I grab her hand before she can pull away and wrap my fingers around her wrist, tugging her into me.

My hardened cock presses into her belly. She looks up at me in surprise, her mouth popping open ever so slightly.

"You think I'll get in trouble for fucking my best friend's little sister?"

"I don't know, why don't you do it and find out? I dare you."

Four Score

-o-

I stretch my arms out over my head. The sun streams brightly through the windows of the hotel room.

Clothes are littered all over the floor. A champagne bottle sits empty on the nightstand.

I look over to Gia, who appears to be sleeping peacefully in the bed next to me, a white sheet barely covering the luscious curves of her delicious body. Her skin glistens in the sunlight, dark and creamy.

Bite marks cover her breasts, and an outline of my fingerprints darkens the skin on her neck. I look at the way I've marked her with pride. She's going to play hell covering that up when we see Tyler today, and that thought alone gives me immense joy.

I ravaged her body last night until we both, finally, collapsed into the bed.

Talk about taking date night to the next level. How long has it been since we've been alone like this?

"Stop looking at me, Damien. It's creepy." Gia says, her eyes completely closed. Her voice is hoarse with sleep. My heart is so fucking full. Last night was *everything*. It was a culmination of everything we never thought we could do. We beat the odds.

I'm alive.

Tyler and Gia are working through a process of reconciliation. Our family is healing.

Astria is showing improvements daily. The clinical trial is still ongoing, but it's showing promise.

And last night…we won the fucking Cup. Best of all? Flirty-doc'flirterson was sitting in that damn box to see it.

Take that motherfucker.

Life might have beaten us the fuck down, but we won.

Gia slowly opens her eyes, taking her time stretching, and allowing the sheet to fall from her body. I lick my lips with anticipation as more skin comes into view. We might need a late check-out.

"What do you think they're doing this morning?" I ask, trying to distract my thoughts from eating the woman in front of me alive before she's even good and awake.

I can't wait to see Astria today after our win last night. I can't wait to celebrate with her.

"If I had to guess, Tyler probably went to pick up donuts. Casey and Astria are most likely in matching pajamas watching movies. *If* they even went to sleep last night."

"Tyler text me a picture of the two of them in matching unicorn onesies last night celebrating the win."

I reach over and grab my phone. I open it up, flashing the photo at Gia so that she can see them. Astria and Casey are smiling ear-to-ear, hoods up, or I guess I should say, horns up. They each have a sparkling unicorn horn shooting from the top of their heads. They look ridiculous, but happy.

"I'm still kind of offended she chose to stay at their lake house for the weekend over coming to the game," I say as I sit the phone back down again and lean back against the headboard of the bed.

"I'm not." Gia's eyes travel up the length of my chest, not stopping until she reaches my eyes. "I thoroughly enjoyed our evening."

"You know, now that we have access to a private jet, and babysitters, I'm thinking we should do this more often than once every decade…" I motion for Gia to come closer with my finger, and she leans over my body, placing her chin on my chest.

"Is it weird that I like her?" Gia asks.

"Like who? Casey? No, honestly, I'm not surprised. She gives that man hell." And that's the truth. Casey Stafford is something else. She's a damn spitfire. Tyler's got his hands full with that one.

"She's good for him." She sighs lazily.

I look down at my wife, running my fingertips slowly over her bare shoulders. I brush softly against the marks that are still very evident on her skin from last night.

"Are you worried about Astria? Staying with them. I know we talked about it extensively, but it's a big step, right?"

Letting Astria stay the weekend with Casey and Tyler was probably the biggest step we've taken yet. It was Astria's idea, and we just didn't have the heart to tell her no. She's still getting to know them, and this felt like a pivotal moment in their relationship. Casey and Tyler were over the moon when we called.

"You know, I thought I would be. But, not really. I don't know, I guess it feels like we're healing."

"I agree, I feel that way too."

"Tyler asked me that day if I believe in redemption, and at the time I wasn't sure what he meant by that. I think I get it now."

"Yeah?"

"Forgiving doesn't mean that I have to forget. Our

past is what shapes us. It molds us and prepares us for our future. We grow and change, but at the heart of it, we're still family. I don't have to forget. But I can make the decision in my heart to forgive him. I think I have. I think I've forgiven him, and that's something I'm okay with. Because I'm not just healing my heart. We're all healing together, shaping our future. Because of Tyler, Astria will have a future. I can live with that."

-o-
GIA

Four score and seven years ago, or so it seems, a teenage boy warned me never to grow up. Life had other plans for me - for us. The game of life has a way of changing, especially when you don't play by the rules.

In the end, you can cheat the game, but the game always wins. That doesn't have to mean you lose. And sometimes, growing up just becomes part of the adventure of getting there.

Forgive. Don't forget. Heal.

And when the day is done…let your light shine.

This little light of mine,
I'm gonna let it shine,
This little light of mine,
I'm gonna let it shine, all the time, let it shine.

Don't miss Nicole Dixon's

Three Wishes

Keep reading for a preview…

CHAPTER FIVE
CASEY
Chambliss School of Law – Year Two

"Casey's milkshake brings all the boys to the yard, and she's like, it's better than yours." Soph sings to her own tune from where she sits on the sofa with her laptop open. Her dark hair is pulled up into a sleek ponytail and her face is completely devoid of makeup. Sophie is naturally beautiful. It's completely unfair.

Sophie is from Tennessee, and girl-next-door is written all over her distinct features. There must be something in that Smoky Mountain water. I mean, look at Dolly.

"What are you singing about, Sophie? Marlie, what she is talking about?" I pause just inside the doorway to our apartment, leaving the door slightly ajar at my back.

Marlie proceeds to stare at her tablet and completely ignore me. Lovely.

"Your beau, obviously. We saw him drop you off last night." Sophie explains like she knows what she's talking about. She doesn't. I swear, she wants so badly for one of us to find love. Why does it have to be me? Why can't it be her? Damn.

"Shove it, Sophie. I do not have a…whatever it was that you called it." I drop my backpack down on the counter in our shared kitchen and prop my tired bones up on the tile countertop. Whoever thought tile countertops were a good idea should be strung up by their shoelaces over a lagoon of crocodiles.

Okay, maybe that's a little extreme. Falling asleep watching Nat Geo last night was probably a poor choice. This is why I stick to Hallmark movies.

I'm fully aware of my anger issues. I repeat. I am fully aware of my anger issues.

Whew, my therapist was right, that totally helps.

"Beau. I believe it's Tennessee for man. Also, survey says, you're lying. We both saw him. He's a stud." Marlie finally acknowledges me. She stretches out with a yawn on the couch across from Sophie. Her chocolate brown curls bounce over her shoulders with her movement.

That poor couch, it's so hideous that it's almost comical. I left Mr. Woo all of the furniture in my old apartment. I didn't have the heart to take anything with me when I had a feeling he might need it. It was just the two of us there at the end, and although neither one of us ever admitted it out loud, we had become a family. I miss the old man. I even kind of miss that damn cat, Hissy.

So, instead, I picked these up from the side of the road

about a week after we moved in – my contribution to our communal living space. I told the girls a little white lie about them being vintage - my great aunt's. If I have a great aunt, I don't want to meet her. Nope. My mama is dead, and I have no other family. Period. I'm not searching out a single relative that may or may not be living for the rest of my life. Been there, done that. Almost got abducted by the mafia or some shit. No, thank you.

I didn't want to tell them I went dumpster diving for our furniture. We'd just met! That's definitely not ice-breaker conversation material. I did at least disinfect them. I'm not a total barbarian.

"I am not lying. What is wrong with the two of you?" It's the truth. Steve is my supervisor down at the bar where I flip bottles for extra cash most weekends and a handful of weeknights. Okay, fine, most weeknights. He's good-looking, but he isn't my type. Please, who am I kidding? I don't have a type. There is not a single man on the face of this earth I want anywhere near me. Not a single one.

The truth is, Steve followed me home after my last few shifts. Some creeper's been hanging around, and it's just a precaution for my safety, blah blah blah. It's not the first time, and I'm sure it won't be the last. I can take care of myself, of course, but safety in numbers and all that. I top five feet on a good day. Maybe an extra inch or two in heels. It doesn't matter how well I know how to defend myself when a man twice my size shoves a loaded gun into my hip bone. We're not all trained martial artists, like Soph.

"Seriously?" Sophie looks up from her laptop. She pushes her glasses up her nose with her fingertip and stares at me like I've just grown a second head. What is it with them and this boyfriend thing?

"Yes, seriously. I'm a lawyer, and everyone knows lawyers never lie." I roll my eyes at the ridiculous assumption and try to keep a straight face. Really though, they should know me well enough by now to know this. Ask a stupid question, get a stupid response.

"Ha. Ha. Ha. *You're a law student…not a lawyer.* You think you're so funny. Everyone knows I'm the funny one. You're such a buzz kill. Romance in this apartment is dead." Sophie's head drops back on the couch with a dramatic sigh.

"You've been reading the historical romance novels again haven't you, Soph? Those men aren't real. They don't exist. Period. Move on. Besides, his name is Steve. He is my supervisor. Nothing more." Sweet, Sophie. She just doesn't get it. Romance isn't butterflies and roses, and those men in her books don't exist. They just don't. To even consider that they do is dangerous.

"Speaking of men. We've got a match on the vacant room." Marlie interrupts us.

My ears perk up. My eyes dart to Marlie. We never discussed bringing a man in. I just always assumed we'd select a woman. I thought that went without saying.

Sophie jerks back up so quickly that she nearly gets whiplash from her ponytail. "They're hired! Whoever they are. I'm done looking, and I can't afford this place split three ways much longer."

I keep my mouth shut about the money. I'm not using

that man's dirty money unless I have to. That's why I work for tips. That, and I just need to get out sometimes. If I sit still too long, I start to overthink and overthinking usually takes me to a place I don't need nor do I want to go.

I do use my trust fund to pay for what tuition my grants don't cover. Not because it's necessity, but because there's something satisfying in knowing it's that assholes hush money that's paying for my law degree. The degree that I'm going to use to defend women against self-righteous dickwads just like him.

"Says the woman that's got a shipment sitting on the kitchen counter." Marlie points to where a small brown package sits next to the coffee pot.

"Jalapenos on a tortilla! My glasses are here?" Sophie tosses her laptop off of her lap with lightning speed and hops to her feet, racing to the kitchen counter near where I still stand.

"Marlie, please translate the Tennessee food language." I look to Marlie for help.

Sophie and I come from two totally different worlds. She's country, and I'm, well, anything but country. Marlie is our balance. She's city, but she's also small town. Plus, she seems to have a weird annual obsession with cowboys. I've found it's easier not to ask.

"I think Soph's excited about the frames that probably cost more than her part of the rent," Marlie answers factually.

Sophie rips open the box and pulls out a pair of glasses with hot pink frames. The color is blinding. Pink is not in my color wheel. Actually, I think my entire color wheel is black. Just like my heart. It contrasts well against my white-blonde hair.

Sophie slides her old frames off and promptly replaces them with the pink pair. "Priorities, ladies. Priorities. I will have you know these glasses have been on my wish list for six months! I promised myself that if I nailed my midterms, I would buy them as a celebration gift to myself. Obviously."

Like she wouldn't nail her damn midterms. Soph is arguably the smartest of the three of us, and that's saying a hell of a lot.

"I bet that list was laminated." I can't help but chuckle to myself.

It's funny how the three of us ended up together. We're not a likely trio by any stretch of the imagination. I'll never forget the night I met the two of them. I was working at the bar, per usual. It was karaoke night. I don't typically pay attention to the drunk college kids embarrassing themselves via microphone. It's half torture, half hilarity. I serve the drinks and keep moving.

But that night was different. The moment the beat dropped I paused. Reba blasted from the sound system. *Fancy*. It sounds silly, but it was Mama's favorite song. I might not be country, but my mama…well, she was raised during a different time. And when that chorus hit, I couldn't help but sing along with the brunette with wild curls on stage that had very obviously had too much to drink.

She wasn't doing half bad either, but then the strangest thing happened. She started to cry. Out of nowhere. Tears. Big ugly ones. It was Marlie. The date was August thirteenth. That's when I saw Sophie. She hopped onto the stage with her out-of-place pencil skirt and glasses and hauled Marlie up onto her shoulder in one swift move.

I don't know what made me do it. I never get involved with customers, but I left the bar and walked over to where Sophie was comforting an inebriated and still crying Marlie. Hell if I know what drew me to them. But there I was, telling a total stranger to get her shit together while simultaneously pulling her hair back out of her face to keep the snot out of it.

At that moment I made my very first friends. *Ever*.

Sure, I might give them a hard time, but they're all I have. We're a trio. The very best trio. They are quite possibly the only humans restoring my faith in humanity. Other than Mr. Woo, obviously.

This place has four bedrooms. We've had a few roommates fill that extra room, but not a single one has stuck it out for longer than a month or two. The last girl was the longest. She made it an entire three months. But then she graduated over the summer and just as quickly moved out. We just can't seem to find the right fit.

We've trashed more applications than I can count. I sure as hell don't see how these two think a man is going to fit in with the three of us. Gross.

"That was snarky, Casey. Apologize." Marlie gives me the look, the one that says I'm being the asshole and need to check myself. Marlie's right. Sophie is sensitive to emotions, she's an empath. I – am – not.

"I'm sorry, Soph. It was a long day, okay?" We're barely into the first semester of our second year, and I'm already overwhelmed. The work's not difficult, it's just a lot. Throw in the hours I put in at the bar just to get out of my own head and I'm exhausted. But, what's new?

"You're forgiven, cupcake. Besides, the list really was laminated. How cute am I in these glasses?" Sophie props her hands up under her chin and bats her eyelashes up at me in exaggeration. I love these women; which is exactly why we don't need a man coming in here and messing it all up.

"You're fucking adorable. Makes me want to barf, but in a good way. You know, like rainbows." I smile at her because I know she gets me. She understands my dry humor, and for that I am grateful. Most people just assume I'm a bitch. If we're being honest, I like it that way, it keeps people away. Peopling is hard. Well, it keeps everyone away except the creeps. A fucking grenade wouldn't keep the damn creeps away. They're relentless. Which, I guess, is why they're creeps.

"Better, girls." Marlie draws our attention back to where she scrolls slowly with her finger on her tablet. "Back to the application. What do you think? He's a hockey player. Or, I guess, he was."

"Absolutely not," I answer immediately.

"Why not?" Marlie raises her eyebrows but doesn't look up from where she's reading on her screen.

"He's a man. He's an athlete. Need I say more? Hell no." I can't understand why this is so difficult to understand. We're three very educated women. We're independent. We do not need to bring a penis into this. Our dynamic works. End of story.

"You're not wrong about the man thing. He is

definitely all man. He *was* an athlete. Was being the operative word here." Marlie chews on her lip, very clearly debating something that is not up for debate.

"What? Did he submit pictures with the damn application? Tell me he didn't send you a dick pic. This is too much. Even for me." I drop my face into my hands. What is it that compels men to send pics of their genitals? Like, why? Just say no.

"Shut up, he did not send you a dick pic. Did he?" My eyes bore into Sophie as she speaks. I need someone on my side here, and she's not helping the situation. I'm so disappointed in these two right now.

A muscle in my face moves involuntarily. I think I'm getting an eye twitch.

"Is he cute?" Sophie asks and decides now is the moment she wants to test our friendship.

I'm done. Is this a joke? There's got to be a camera hidden in here somewhere.

"Are the two of you insane? That's all we need. Some testosterone-driven frat boy to bring his stinky man pants-wearing, hair gel-using, muscles in here and ruin everything. He'll manipulate our relationships and destroy our friendships. May as well go ahead and flush our law degrees right on down the toilet too while we're at it."

I'm being dramatic. I know I'm being dramatic, but I can't stop it. If we're being honest, I'm scared, okay. I'm fucking terrified. Who is this man? What do we know about him?

"Well, someone needs to schedule an appointment with their therapist. Do you feel better now that you've released that, Casey?" Sophie walks over to where I'm still propped against the counter and throws her arm around me. Always the touchy one.

"No. Maybe. Yes. Whatever. You're seriously considering this, aren't you?" I look from Sophie to Marlie in disbelief. This can't be happening.

"I've already drafted a lease." Marlie barely speaks above a whisper.

She's nervous. Why is she so nervous? Her nervous is making me nervous.

Pieces of the puzzle in front of me begin to click together slowly. Oh, God.

"Tell me you didn't send it to him. Tell me the truth, Marlie Quinn. Do not perjure yourself in this apartment while sitting on the sacred furniture." I shrug out from beneath Sophie's arm. I can't handle the touching at a time like this. This is a no-touch situation.

"I..." Marlie starts to speak but is interrupted when the door to the apartment begins to move. What idiot left the door standing wide open? Me. It was me. I'm the idiot.

Marlie sits straight up on the couch. Sophie pulls her hands up like she's preparing to throw down with our intruder while wearing her brand-new hot pink glasses.

And I freeze.

I'm frozen in the moment, unsure of what to do next. Great, I'm getting murdered first.

"Knock, knock. I'm looking for a Marlie ummm...Quinn? I think that's what the email said." I hear his voice before I see him. It's rough and masculine. It sounds nothing at all like it should. He should sound like a frat boy, or like some surfer kid. But he doesn't, not at all. He sounds like a *man*.

The door swings open wider, and I choke on my own saliva.

"Fuck." The word squeaks out from the depths of my throat at a level ten awkward on the Richter scale.

"Uh huh, on a biscuit." Sophie drops her hands down to her sides and straightens to her full height next to me, effectively dwarfing me next to her long legs.

"Don't make this about food, Soph. It's weird." I try to recover, but I can't divert my eyes from the man that stands in front of us. It's embarrassing. I'm an embarrassment to myself, but I can't look away.

He's tall, and hard in all the right places. And broad. He looks sturdy. Jesus, it's like I'm describing a fucking oak tree.

The t-shirt he wears is doing nothing at all to contain the muscles I can see from where I stand. Why do I care about man muscles all of a sudden? I've never cared about man muscles before.

He carries a stack of boxes like they weigh nothing. Maybe they don't. Maybe they're empty, but I doubt it. I wouldn't be that lucky. Nah, this man is ripped. But not in that obnoxious *I take steroids and have a tiny dick* way. His hands span the entire bottom of the stack of boxes. And the veins in his arms, they're his own personal interstate of sin. His skin is a warm toasty brown. Like hot chocolate when it's snowing outside. He looks cozy. If a man can look cozy. Can men look cozy? A cozy tree. Why am I thinking about cuddling a total stranger? I'm a tree hugger. What in the living hell is happening?

Caught. He sees me staring and smiles. Or is he laughing at me? Am I drooling? I'm drooling, aren't I? No, I can't be drooling, I choked on my saliva, it went the opposite direction.

He wears a worn baseball cap, but it doesn't hide the caramel color of his eyes. Eyes that are smiling. His eyes are fucking smiling at me. He's beautiful.

I've never seen a beautiful man. This is not good. Not good at all. I loathe myself right now. Is this like some delayed phase of puberty? There has to be an explanation.

"He's yummy. I mean, um. Hi, I'm Marlie. I believe you were looking for me." Marlie drops her tablet down on the couch without a second thought and stands to greet this total stranger.

Reality begins to settle in. In the midst of the beauty that is the man that juggles boxes in front of me in an attempt to shake Marlie's hand like a gentleman, I realize something. I was right. He's going to ruin everything.

"We need a contract. I'll be in my room. He doesn't unpack a single item into this apartment until we all sign. Understood?" I snatch my backpack up off of the counter and hurry toward my room.

"Uh-huh. Sure. Whatever you say." Marlie brushes me off as she helps the new guy in with his things.

They don't get it. Neither one of them get it. They're not listening to me. I grumble to myself as I slam my door behind me and pray to God that he doesn't start unpacking his tidy whities in the room that shares a wall with mine.

We need something in writing that will protect us.

I need something that will protect me.

CHAPTER SIX
TYLER

What in the sea of estrogen have I gotten myself into?

I deserve this. This is my punishment. I need to buck up and take it like a man.

But hot damn.

Academic probation wasn't enough.

Being banned from the league I've devoted my life to? Not enough.

Completely obliterating any chance I might have ever had of reconciling my relationship with my sister and best friend. Apparently, still not fucking enough.

I was kicked out of the on-campus housing within twenty-four hours of being discharged from the hospital. Twenty-four fucking hours.

Gia refused to see me. But what was worse? She wouldn't let me fucking near Damien. She had the entire floor locked down.

I didn't do it on purpose. It was an accident. The

whole thing was an accident. That's exactly what I tried to tell the panel when I appealed their decision, but no.

I moved first. I lost control. My fault. No excuses.

According to Coach, I was lucky they didn't press charges. The thought that pressing charges was even a consideration makes me sick to my stomach.

My memory of what happened that night is fragmented into small sections at best. A therapist might say I'm repressing the trauma. I still haven't been able to bring myself to watch the tape. I'm not sure I ever will. I know how serious Damien's injuries that night were…and the blood. There was so much blood, and it was my fucking fault.

I was essentially homeless for two weeks. I was surfing couches, but I couldn't keep bumming off of my former teammates. I couldn't watch them dress for practices and games that I will never be a part of. I had to move on from that life.

I can't dwell on what did or didn't happen.

This is the hand I've been dealt, and that's something only I can come to terms with.

I haven't. I haven't come to terms with a damn thing. I just keep making the next best decision and compartmentalizing everything else. It's a survival technique at best, but it's working.

I found a place to live. But the hits just keep coming because my new roommates are none other than three strong-willed, highly opinionated *females*.

Marlie, the brunette with wild curly hair. I can already tell she thinks she's in charge of the entire apartment and everyone that lives in it. She talks when she's nervous, like, a whole hell of a lot. She's glued to her Kindle when she's not studying. I've learned that her dad is a cop, and her mom is also an attorney in the small town she grew up in.

Oddly enough, I'm pretty sure she has her own personal PI firm following her around. I don't know what kind of witness protection deal her mom has her wrapped up in. All I know is that a couple of investigators reached out to me within minutes of submitting the interest form for the apartment. I had to sign a shit ton of paperwork and complete a background check. I was even required to go to some clinic and piss in a cup. The evaluation was more extensive than the testing they did for the hockey team for the University. If I wasn't so damn desperate, I would have walked, but it's the middle of the first semester. There's nothing available. Trust me, I've looked.

Then, there's Sophie. She's the eccentric one. She spends most of her time in the library. I think she must have some sort of work-study position. She always has a book in her hands. She themes her outfits to match her eyewear, which is…odd. She's so Southern I'm certain sweet tea runs through her veins. The woman makes me put a quarter in a swear jar every time I cuss in the common area, which is a lot. She's the mother of the group, passive-aggressively reminding us to clean up after ourselves daily. And she's always staring at me because she's trying to sort out my aura. Whatever the hell an aura is.

Last but most definitely not least, is my nemesis. The absolute thorn in my side and the reason I now stand in the hallway of our apartment at one in the morning with a roll of fucking toilet paper because who really buys fancy tissues in the box besides teachers?

Is every other person in this apartment oblivious to the crying?

To be so damn mean, her sniffles are fucking adorable, and I just…I need it to stop. I can't take it anymore.

I moved into this apartment three weeks ago tomorrow to be exact, and I haven't had one decent night's sleep yet. I'm on academic probation for the remainder of the year. I need sleep to function. I can't afford to slip up. My degree is the only thing I have left.

This woman. She's infuriating. She's a stick of dynamite with long, shiny blonde hair that I have an odd fascination with daydreaming about running my fingers through. I haven't touched though, I do have some dignity left.

She needs a step stool to reach the top cabinet in our shared bathroom. Oh, I didn't mention we share a bathroom? Yeah, that's fun. My dick gets hard now every time I hear running water, which is extremely inconvenient.

But the shower isn't what is keeping me up at night. The way she blasts Taylor Swift at five in the fucking morning isn't what is keeping me up at night. I mean, when does the woman sleep?

Nope. It's the crying. On the nights she works down at the local bar, which I do not condone for any woman, let alone a woman that looks so…whatever it is she looks like, she comes in and showers – cue uncomfortable dick, and instead of going to sleep like a normal human being she heads back out into the common area. She thinks she's the only one awake, but she's not.

I am wide ass awake, staring at the ceiling with a hard dick and my newly developed supersonic hearing listening to her watch whatever chick stuff I know she's watching in the middle of the night and then the crying begins.

And that is how I have ended up in the predicament that I currently find myself in. Last night I made it to my bedroom door to confront her before I chickened out like a pansy. I've never been scared of a woman before. Let alone a woman half my size, but this woman is different. She isn't just any woman. She's a hard ass, and maybe I know her routines and her schedules by now, but her moods are completely unpredictable. There's something about not knowing what she's going to say next. It makes me want to stick around for more and run for cover all at the same time.

So, I stand here, shrouded in the darkness of the hallway, and debate the merits of going back to bed or actually walking over and offering her the roll of toilet paper I stole from the bathroom to dry her tears. It's the good stuff, so, her nose won't turn pink. Then maybe the sniffles will stop and we can all get some sleep. Or maybe she'll shank me with the remote. Damn the unpredictability.

"Leave now and we never have to mention this." She speaks.

I freeze. My hand tightens around the roll of toilet paper.

"Casey?" I take a couple of steps into our living space, but I still can't see her where I know she's hiding on the couch closest to where I stand.

"I said leave. Go back to your room and pretend like you never saw me." She tries to keep her voice even, but I hear the strain in the way she whispers. She's trying to act tough. She's oblivious to the fact that I've already figured out her little secret. Interesting.

"That's the problem, I can't." I walk the rest of the way in and stop in front of the only light in the room, the television.

"And why the hell not?" She sits up on the couch and I try to hide my smile. Now isn't the time for smiles, but she's so fucking cute I can't help it.

"You're crying." I lift my hand toward her to point out the obvious.

"That's none of your fucking business." She crosses her arms over her chest. She holds the remote in one hand. Her eyes are red and puffy, but it's nearly impossible to take her seriously right now.

"It became my business when it interrupted my sleep pattern." I step toward her.

Her eyes dart to my hand. The hand that I've forgotten holds a roll of toilet paper.

"Why are you holding *Charmin*, Tyler? This just got really awkward." She giggles and a single snort escapes from her nose. It's a welcomed sound after knowing that she's been out here upset by herself.

"Says the woman wearing...what exactly are you wearing?" I take a second to really look her over now that I can see her. All four-feet-something of her. She might claim five feet, but it's a lie.

We surpassed awkward a long time ago.

She's covered from head to toe in a black contraption that zips up the front. Her blonde hair is tied up inside a hood that has…ears. Just when I think I've seen it all, an actual fluffy black tail falls over the side of the couch next to her.

Her face pales when she realizes what she's wearing, but she recovers quickly. "It's a onesie, thank you very much. They're all the rage right now."

A onesie? Like, a one-piece unit for sleeping?

"With what? The five and under crowd? It has feet. Did you buy it in the children's section?" I glance to where her feet are also covered by the same black fabric. There are hints of white scattered across the material, and a little pink up around the ears.

"For your information, this is one size fits all, and I don't even have to wear socks." She shrugs.

There is no way that getup is one size fits all.

"And a tail?"

She shifts on the couch and that's when it hits me.

"Are you wearing a skunk onesie, Casey?" I double over placing my hands on my knees. I try to keep my laughter quiet, but I can't believe what I'm seeing.

"It was the only black one they had on Amazon, and it's soft. I don't have to use a blanket, and it has pockets for snacks. Leave. It. Alone." I swear steam billows from her cute little skunk ears.

I stifle my laughter and straighten back to my full height. I walk over to where she sits. My shins touch the old, worn-looking brown couch. This thing has seen its better days, but the afternoon naps on these busted springs are surprisingly enjoyable.

"You're mighty feisty for a woman crying on the couch in a skunk costume." I bend down and touch the tip of her nose with my finger. She scrunches her nose in distaste. Her bright blue eyes sparkle even in the darkness.

"It is sleepwear, Tyler, and I am not crying. I told you already, it's none of your business." She shakes her head to rid her nose of my finger and I pull back my hand. I won't touch without permission. Even if my finger is doing some weird tingly thing after touching her skin.

"What are you watching?" I look back to where the television is paused.

Despite the late hour, I'm wide awake now.

I'm nearly knocked off my feet when Casey twists my t-shirt in her small hand and pulls me back down to meet her at her level with a strength that is surprising. Nothing should surprise me with this woman at this point. I mean, she's wearing a skunk onesie.

"Don't try to change the subject. We will never speak of this. It goes against the contract." *The contract.*

Women, they think that just because a man has a dick someone is getting fucked. Literally and figuratively. The day I moved in Casey drew up a ridiculously in-depth contract and made every person living in the apartment sign it. In short, there is no fucking in the apartment. Fine by me. I don't need the drama or distractions.

Doesn't mean I can't bite back when I'm being snapped at. Casey likes to push. I don't like to budge, and I'm too petty to let it slide. We aren't in violation of anything right now. I call bullshit.

She clutches the thin fabric of my shirt in her fist. I lean into her hold until my face is just inches from hers. My chocolate eyes bore into her blue. So distinctly different. She sucks in a breath, and I relish the effect I'm having on her. One she will die before admitting to.

"My lips are sealed, Princess," I speak slowly, not daring to look away from her. I refuse to give her the satisfaction of dropping eye contact first. I feel her grip tighten against my abdominal muscles with every word that leaves my mouth. I smirk to myself, and it doesn't go unnoticed, judging by her quick intake of breath. The air in the room surrounding us is charged with a heightened electricity. One that I feel humming beneath my skin with her proximity. This is going to be fun.

"Don't call me that." The words come out in one swift breath. She's soaked. I'd bet money on it. And dammit if that doesn't make my dick hard again.

"As you wish." I smile, and she drops her hand like my shirt caught fire.

Gia always loved the *Princess Bride*. It was one of her favorite movies growing up. Sadness washes over me for a moment, but then it's gone just as quickly. I can't afford to think about things I no longer have control over.

"This isn't that kind of movie."

I straighten back up, but instead of looking at me as she speaks, Casey looks at the frozen screen of this television. She refuses to look at me. She feels the electricity too.

"Then what kind of movie are we watching?" I ask again.

I'm genuinely curious. Is it the movie that makes her cry, or is she crying and the movie is comforting her?

"Hallmark Christmas." She answers.

Christmas? Christmas is still months away.

"Never heard of it. It's a little too early for Christmas, don't you think?" I run my hand up behind my neck. I can't figure her out. She seems like the Halloween type. I didn't peg her for tinsel and mistletoe.

"It's a thing, okay? Sit down and shut up if you want to stay." She presses play and goes back to watching her movie as if I'm not still standing in the room right next to her like a fifteen-year-old that was just invited to seven minutes in heaven in the basement closet of a dance party. She told me to sit. She invited me into her private space.

Something about this moment feels important. I need to make the next best decision. But what is it? Do I go back to bed with my hard dick and toss and turn until daylight? Or do I stay and see what it is about these movies that captivate this woman? A woman I'm not allowed to touch. A woman that hates my guts but breathes harder when she's close to me.

She tucks her fabric-covered feet into the cushion of the couch. The action is so normal, and yet something about it makes me feel warm inside. I don't remember the last time I felt warm.

I flex my hands by my side. I want to stay. I shouldn't, but she's not crying now that I'm here. Maybe, if I stay, we can both get some sleep on the couch without the crying. Decision made.

I eye the spot next to where Casey is snuggled up on

the couch. Her eyes dart up at me, and then over to the couch on the opposite side of the common area.

"Over there. This couch is mine."

Fine. Looks like it's Christmas in October, and I have a very distinct feeling my thoughts about this woman are going to land me directly on the naughty list.

Carlton Harbor

Book 1 – Mirror Image

Book 2 – Surprise Reflections

Book 3 – For Always

Book 4 – Starting Over

Silent Hero

Book 1 – Devil You Know

Book 2 – Until Death

Paint by Numbers

Book 1 – One Night

Book 2 – Two Strangers

Book 3 – Three Wishes

Book 4 – Four Score

Book 5 – *Coming soon…*

ABOUT THE AUTHOR

Nicole Dixon is a forensic accountant with an affinity for writing sexy novels. She loves data, coffee, travel, and making sure all the voices in her head get the happily ever after they deserve. She made the decision to begin publishing her work in an effort to teach her children to never give up on their dreams, nothing is impossible.

Made in the USA
Columbia, SC
10 January 2025